Advance Praise for
Bottled Lightning

Bottled Lighting is a blistering high stakes story revolving around a cutting-edge energy invention designed to dramatically reduce the earth's carbon footprint, those working to bring it to the world, and those determined to not let it see the light of day. Savvy tech lawyer, Torn Sagara, who heads the Tokyo office of his international law firm, is forced to take matters into his own hands to protect magnetic super-scientist, Saya Brooks, and her world-changing creation. Who is behind the desperate attempts to stop Brooks, and ally Sagara, dead in their tracks— literally? Is it industry or government forces or some combination of the two that wants to bury Saya's technology? Author L. M. Weeks has written a highly entertaining, engaging, and provocative thriller that will keep you on your toes and guessing the answers until the final page.

— **Ronald S. Barak, author of the bestselling Brooks/Lotello thriller series**

L. M. Weeks takes us on a journey of underworld violence, boardroom intrigue, and high-tech advances with geo-political implications. Weeks's combination of nerdish attention to detail and sweeping cinematic plot takes us on a breathless ride akin to his hero's daring motorcycle escapades. Torn, the lawyer-turned-action hero, as well as other biracial characters in the novel, provide a unique and revealing perspective of life and social interaction in Japan. *Bottled Lightning* is a page turner!

—**Roy Tomizawa, author of the highly acclaimed** *1964 The Greatest Year in the History of Japan: How the Tokyo Olympics Symbolized Japan's Miraculous Rise from the Ashes*

This action-packed saga follows Torn Sagara—biracial lawyer, motorcycle maniac, and flawed ladies' man—on a quest to stop a series of mysterious attacks on his inventor client. As the story escalates into murder and international intrigue, the reader is in for a wild ride from Tokyo to Alaska to the Russian Far East. Fans of Barry Eisler and Barry Lancet will want to jump right in! An impressive and intelligent debut.

—Leza Lowitz, author of *Jet Black and the Ninja Wind*

The heart of this fast-paced and enjoyable novel is its protagonist, Tornait Masao Sagara. Also known as Torn. He's a high-powered lawyer based in Tokyo. Half American-half Japanese, a passionate motorcyclist, a man with a complicated family and romantic background, Torn's life is turned upside down when he and his beautiful client are almost killed by a motorcycle gang during a high-speed chase through the streets of Tokyo. The twists and turns of this novel are engaging and cinematic. The behind-the-scenes details about life in upper-class corporate Japan are fascinating. Well done! I can highly recommend L.M. Weeks's *Bottled Lightning*.

—Susan Breen, author of *The Fiction Class* and the Maggie Dove mystery series

Bottled Lightning reveals both the author's deep experience and expertise on the book's many topics and his keen ability to craft and deliver a thrilling, fascinating, and sexy tale of international intrigue.

As a fellow American with a long history of living in Japan, I was impressed not only by Weeks's thoughtful and accurate depictions and explanations of Japanese traditions and society, but also of international business transactions, motorcycle culture in Japan, and the inner workings of Japan's notoriously opaque justice system.

Weaving together sophistication, detail, and knowledge into a high-energy story that consistently keeps up the pace set in its opening scenes, *Bottled Lightning* is tightly written with a wide scope of topics all expertly conveyed. Really a joy to read.

—Jeff Wexler, producer, Studio Ghibli and Studio Ponoc, and cross-border entertainment and intellectual property lawyer

Never in my wildest dreams would I have thought that writing a captivating and page-turning novel about a corporate lawyer in Japan would be possible. *Bottled Lightning* proved me wrong! Pulls you in from the first page and leaves you wanting more. The best part is that *Bottled Lightning* accomplishes this without using the poetic license that other authors so often utilize to make lawyering seem like something it's not. The author's bona fides as an attorney who knows Japan are clear. The book manages to draw you in without once straying from the path of authenticity. Reads like a James Bond novel, if (and no disrespect meant) Ian Fleming actually knew something about Japan. Brilliant!

—Tony Andriotis, Partner and Head of International Arbitration, DLA Piper, Tokyo

Not your father's legal thriller. L. M. Weeks's debut novel, *Bottled Lightning*, hurtles the reader from one chapter to the next. The combination of his cinematic writing style and command of details, such as the book's futuristic technology, motorcycle racing, legal ins and outs of international business, and cultural touchstones of Japan, have enabled Weeks to craft an exhilarating and thought-provoking thriller like none I've ever read. Truly a winner!

—Larry Bates, General Counsel at Panasonic; former Chief Legal Officer of LIXIL Global; former General Counsel, Japan at GE; former president of The American Chamber of Commerce in Japan

An intriguing client.
A passionate attorney.
A deadly game.

BOTTLED LIGHTNING

L. M. WEEKS

SOUTH
FORK
Publishers

Nampa, Idaho

BOTTLED LIGHTNING
L. M. WEEKS

Printed and published in the United States of America by:

SOUTH FORK *Publishers*

Nampa, Idaho
info@southforkpublishers.com
www.LMWeeks.com

FIRST EDITION

Project Management: Marla Markman, *www.marlamarkman.com*
Book Design: TLC Book Design, *TLCBookDesign.com*
Cover: Tamara Dever; *Interior:* Erin Stark
Author Photograph: Tobias Everke

Tokyo skyline: 2022 Greens87. Image from Bigstock.com. | Lightning burst: 2022 Rogatnev. Image from Bigstock.com. | Japanese sword: 2022 joker3753. Image from Bigstock.com

Publisher's Cataloging-in-Publication Data

Names: Weeks, L. M., author.
Title: Bottled lightning / L.M. Weeks.
Description: Nampa, ID: South Fork Publishers LLC 2022.
Identifiers: LCCN: 2022900486 | ISBN: 979-8-9855880-0-2 (hardcover) | 979-8-9855880-1-9 (paperback) | 979-8-9855880-2-6 (ebook) | 979-8-9855880-3-3 (audio)
Subjects: LCSH Attorneys--Fiction. | Technology--Fiction. | Information technology--Fiction. | Energy development--Technological innovations. | Japan--Fiction. | Thriller fiction.| BISAC FICTION / Thrillers / Suspense | FICTION / Thrillers / Legal | FICTION / Thrillers / Crime | FICTION / Thrillers / Technological
Classification: LCC PS3623.E42238 B68 2022 | DDC 813.6--dc23

To Brendan, who represents the best of both worlds.

Table of Contents

Dramatis Personae

Agency for Natural Resources and Energy
Japanese agency considering financing Raijin Clean's development of lightning generation and energy storage technology

Alexei Chomkov
Lawyer in the Russian Far East

Asahi Susono
Executive Assistant to Tamayo Watanabe

ChinaPetrol Co., Ltd.
A Chinese state-owned enterprise (SOE), parent company of CPV

China PV, Inc. (CPV)
Renewable energy subsidiary of ChinaPetrol

Harden Industries, Inc.
A company founded and owned by Vince Harden

Hilsberry & Carter
Law firm in which Torn Sagara is Managing Partner of its Tokyo office

Hiroki Okaguchi
Head of the Yamakawa Gumi

Kenji Ishikawa
Yukie Sagara's older brother

Kiwako Meyers
Torn Sagara's long-distance girlfriend and former flame from college

Larisa Anismova
Managing Partner of Hilsberry & Carter's Moscow Office

Magadan Oil & Mining
Russian company doing business with Harden Industries and Wakkanai Drilling

Makoto ("Mak") Karahashi
Torn Sagara's private investigator and best friend

Mayumi Ino
Torn Sagara's borderline personality girlfriend

Miki Watanabe
Daughter of Tamayo Watanabe; Member, Board of Directors, Wakkanai Drilling

Raijin Clean, Inc.
Technology company founded by Saya Brooks

Saki Katayama
Attorney for Torn Sagara

Saya Laura Brooks
Inventor of lightning generation and energy storage technology

Sean Reiji Sagara
Son of Torn Sagara

Sergey Bogrov
Owner of Magadan Oil & Mining

Shinsuke Taniguchi
Police Detective

Sophia Haruka Sagara
Daughter of Torn Sagara

Tamayo Watanabe
President and Chairwoman of Wakkanai Drilling

Tomohiro ("Tom") Saito
General Manager, Strategic Planning, at Wakkanai Drilling

Tornait ("Torn") Masao Sagara
Managing Partner of Hilsberry & Carter's Tokyo Office

Vincent ("Vince") K. Harden
Founder of Harden Industries, investor in Raijin Clean, Vice Chairman of Wakkanai Drilling

Wakkanai Drilling Co., Ltd.
Japanese company run by Tamayo Watanabe

Yamakawa Gumi
One of Japan's largest organized crime yakuza syndicates

Yasuo Tsujikawa
Prosecuting attorney

Yoji Watanabe
Husband of Miki Watanabe; Member, Board of Directors, Wakkanai Drilling

Yukie Sagara
Estranged wife of Torn Sagara

Zephyrus Oil & Drilling, GmbH
German company Wakkanai Drilling is purchasing in Project Ibis deal

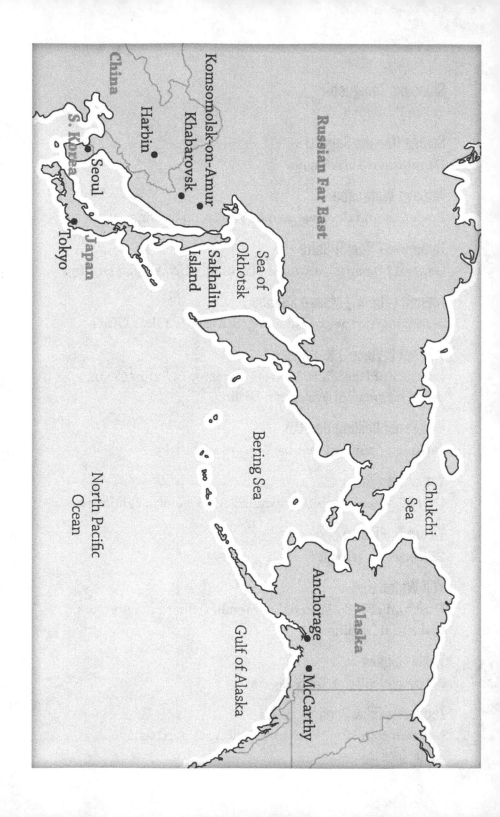

CHAPTER 1

Savior

救世主

"Go faster!" Saya yelled as Torn hit the expressway, merging into the Tokyo-bound traffic.

Giving in to the fun, he laughed. "No need to yell. I can hear you just fine!" Torn said through the mic in his helmet. He throttled up to 120 kilometers per hour and seamlessly moved the motorcycle from the left lane through the middle lane to the outside passing lane.

Saya released the passenger side handles she'd been holding and wrapped her arms around Torn's chest. He felt warm all over but tried to suppress the feeling. Saya was a client, after all. And not just any client, but the most intriguing client he'd ever had.

He'd been surprised when she'd asked for a ride, but it was obvious she was serious. She'd let her dark hair down and swapped her business clothes for jeans and a navy-blue leather jacket.

When he had half-heartedly suggested she'd be better off schmoozing with her investors, she'd cocked her head and smiled. "The technology does all the schmoozing necessary, don't you think? It's like showing someone lightning in a bottle."

Torn agreed. He'd been impressed by her demonstration, even though he'd seen it before. "I like the imagery of selling little bottles of lightning at convenience stores," he'd said enthusiastically.

Saya had smiled. "I'm glad to hear that. Anyway, I told them I needed a few minutes to discuss an IP matter with my lawyer before I met them at the hotel. So..." She'd paused playfully, her piercing green eyes meeting his. "Do I get a ride or not?"

He'd had to pull himself away from those eyes, which he never tired of looking at. Sometimes he wondered whether they were real or contacts, but he'd never seen them any other color. He'd handed her a full-face helmet.

Only a few minutes had passed since she'd hopped on his BMW K 1200 LT, but that conversation already seemed like yesterday.

Now, he accelerated to 140, taking advantage of any openings in the three lanes to pass slower traffic.

Saya hugged him tighter, as if she found the frequent weaving in and out of traffic exhilarating.

"It's like the motorcycle in the movie *Tron*," she said. "Can't you go faster?"

Torn grinned. "I guess it's now or never. Traffic will slow as we get closer to downtown. And we gotta exit at Hatsudai because tandem riding's illegal on the inner city Circuit."

"Why's that?"

"Back in the seventies, Japan banned it on expressways because *bosozoku* used to attack cars with chains."

"What're *bosozoku*?"

"Car and motorcycle gangs. You've really lived a sheltered life, haven't you?"

He couldn't see her blushing.

"Anyway, the ban was lifted for most expressways but kept in central Tokyo. The older, narrower winding expressways were considered too dangerous for tandem riding."

"It's not as if the narrow local streets are any safer," Saya replied.

"Preaching to the choir."

He raised the adjustable windshield to its maximum height and accelerated to 180. The aerodynamically shaped fairing and the bike's weight kept the rubber side down. Even this speed didn't feel too fast because of the bike's stability and the protection against buffeting provided by the windshield. But the louder engine and much faster rate at which they passed the guardrail posts were proof of their speed.

"Oh my God!" Saya put her helmeted head on his shoulder.

Torn smiled. It was intoxicating when the bike had the desired effect of lowering a woman's inhibitions.

Traffic reappeared as they got closer to Hachioji.

"Please don't slow down!"

"Sorry. Got to." He throttled down, knowing there were tollbooths ahead. He weaved in and out of the cars, using all three lanes to keep progressing faster than the flow of traffic until they had reached the toll plaza.

Just enough traffic remained after the tollbooths to make things fun. He pulled into the left-hand lane and toggled to Imagine Dragons. "Demon" poured from the bike's speakers.

"This is more fun than I ever dreamed!"

Despite himself, Torn agreed. He sensed her interest in him was more than as just her lawyer. For the first time in his career, his resolve never to become romantically involved with a client began to waver, but he knew it was a bad idea. He already had enough problems.

A few minutes later, a big black Mercedes pulled up behind them, its front bumper almost touching the bike's license plate. Torn sped up, but the car continued to tailgate.

Saya, eyes closed and lost in the music, didn't notice.

The car sped up, forcing its way past them on the left between the bike and the shoulder. Torn swerved into the middle lane to avoid a collision. He turned off the music, causing Saya to open her eyes. The Mercedes pulled in front of them and slowed down, forcing Torn to decelerate and swerve back into the left lane. It had no rear license plate, rare and illegal in Japan.

"What's that guy doing?" Saya asked, alarmed.

"I don't know."

The big Mercedes changed lanes, slowing down in the middle lane until it was parallel with them. The tinted rear window opened. Before Torn could react, a man stuck a gun out of the window and fired. The bullet passed through the soft padding under Saya, exiting the other side of her seat.

With well-practiced fluidity, Torn squeezed the left handlebar lever to open the clutch and shifted down to fourth gear with his left foot, then throttled up with his right hand while releasing the clutch lever with his left. The Beemer raced away from the Mercedes. He shifted back up to fifth gear as the RPMs shot up.

"Holy shit!" Saya exclaimed, tightening her hold even more.

"Are you hit?" Torn asked as calmly as he could. He'd broken into a cold sweat.

"I don't think so."

"Thank God!" he replied, wondering what the hell just happened.

Things moved in slow motion. Torn thought, *No one has a gun in Japan except yaks.* He was relieved neither of them had been hit, scared shitless about being chased by yakuza types, and pissed off at the damage to his motorcycle.

The big car again appeared next to them in the center lane.

Torn slammed on the brakes with his right hand and foot, letting the Mercedes fly by. He shifted down two gears to third and throttled up, accelerating to 120 so fast he almost popped a wheelie. He flew by the driver's side of the car, the high RPMs making the bike's engine scream. Shifting up to fourth gear, he rocketed to 160.

The powerful car caught him quickly. He sped up to 180 but the big Mercedes stayed on them. They approached more traffic, forcing both vehicles to slow down. As they reached the Mitaka Highway Bus Turnout, the three lanes of traffic became two, creating a traffic jam.

Salvation.

Torn threaded between the two lanes of stalled traffic. Their pursuer briefly flanked them on the left shoulder until being thwarted by a wall built to protect surrounding homes from expressway noise.

They were safe, but only for a moment. He heard a motorcycle engine being revved to the ugly, deafening sound of a bike with its muffler removed. At the same time, he saw the blinding light of a single high beam behind him and heard loud death metal music. His heart sank.

"Motherfucking Yankee," he muttered, forgetting his mic was still on.

"Yankee?" Saya repeated.

"Over-the-hill punk ex-*bosozoku*," he explained, doubting this was a coincidence. He wasn't even sure if it was a real Yankee. He had encountered them many times, and while always obnoxiously loud, they'd never hassled him.

"Great," Saya replied wryly.

The bike veered left onto the narrow shoulder and flanked them, barely squeaking by between cars in the left lane and the five-meter-high soundproofing wall.

Torn saw that the hot-pink bike had the Yankee trademark Norton Commando-like fairing with the headlight recessed into a bubble in the fairing's front and a heavily padded extra-long sissy bar attached to the back of the empty passenger seat. The rider wore a silver Nazi helmet and black mask. What looked like a long PVC pipe was attached to the bike's side.

Another screamingly loud bike with its high beam on appeared immediately behind them, revving its engine. It pulled into the right lane and flanked him on the narrow shoulder between the cars and the center guardrail.

Torn accelerated to get ahead, then swerved slightly to the right and left in front of cars in each lane. As expected, the cars moved toward the outside of their lanes, leaving no room for the pursuing bikes to proceed between the cars in the left lane and the wall on the left and the cars in the right lane and the central guardrail on the right. Still, this slowed the Yankees down for only a moment and they soon caught up to Torn and Saya again.

With the Yankees continuing to flank them on both sides, they approached the Eifukucho Exit, which was both an exit and a connector between the Chuo Expressway coming into the city center from the west and the inner city Metropolitan Expressway.

"Why didn't you get off?" Saya screamed.

The fear in her voice made Torn's heart beat even faster. He took a deep breath and responded calmly, "They'd catch us at the first light. They're smaller and more maneuverable."

The matter-of-fact nature of his response worked. She lowered her voice. "We could find a cop."

"Not before those guys would be on us. Hey, try to squeeze the bike with your knees and move with the bike. Don't fight it."

"Okay." Saya loosened her death hug.

On the other side of the Eifukucho Tollbooth, traffic thinned for a moment as more cars exited. It would soon increase again, and it would be difficult for the big BMW to lane split because the lanes were narrower on the much older inner city expressways.

The Yankee bikes pulled up next to them. The driver on the left drew a long metal pipe with a chain and spiked ball from a sheath.

"Is that a mace on the end? He has a mace!" Saya shouted.

"It's a flail," he corrected her.

"Right," she said, then closed her mouth.

Torn decided to go on the offensive with his much larger bike, which was surprisingly nimble for its size. He swerved toward the biker wielding the homemade weapon.

His move had the desired effect. The smaller bike swerved away. Torn accelerated like a rocket, pulling away from both bikes, but he soon heard them gaining. He could not outrun them in the afternoon traffic. They again pulled up on either side of him with their ridiculous—but lethal—weapons in hand. Torn slammed on both the hand and foot brakes so hard he thought he might pop a reverse wheelie, but the Beemer only skidded slightly before the antilock brakes did their job. The Yankee bikes flew by, then quickly slowed down.

Now Torn needed to pass them. He aimed for the left side of the bike on his left. He calculated that, because the biker held the threatening pipe in his right hand, placing himself and Saya on the left would make it difficult for the assailant to swing at them across his own chest.

Torn forced his way between the Yankee and the wall. Despite the maneuver, Torn had underestimated the biker's resolve and dexterity; he was able to swing at them across his body and shatter the BMW's windshield, spraying safety glass on Torn and grazing his right arm. Torn grimaced when the flail's spikes tore through his jacket and into his right triceps, while his body shielded Saya from harm.

He couldn't avoid them much longer. The Yankees would get them sooner than later.

"I'm going to crash into them. Watch your legs," he warned.

The other biker approached on their left, swinging his flail with his right hand. Torn shifted down and countersteered the left handlebar hard, instantly flicking the BMW left into the other bike. The Yankee tried to avoid the big bike but it was too late. The motorcycles collided with a hard fiberglass-on-metal crunching sound. The smaller bike, already headed toward the wall as the driver tried to avoid Torn's bike, slammed into it with a loud crash followed by the clanging of metal on asphalt. The rider bounced off the wall and cartwheeled across the expressway at an angle before hitting the center guardrail. The BMW's fairing and front left fin had protected Torn and Saya as it hit the other bike, leaving them unhurt.

One to go.

Traffic increased as rush-hour cars merged onto the expressway from the local roads.

"Look at that sign. Aren't we supposed to get off?!"

Torn saw the sign showing a bright red circle-backslash symbol over two figures on a motorcycle. He saw another sign directing tandem riders to exit at Hatsudai.

"Yes, but driving tandem may save us if we stay on."

"Oh, I feel so much better now," she said, totally deadpan.

"I thought you would," he replied. They passed Hatsudai on the right. Torn could see the remaining Yankee gaining on them in his side-view mirrors. When they reached the Shinjuku on-ramp, traffic slowed to a crawl as more cars merged onto the two narrow curved expressway lanes. The moment of truth.

He maneuvered the bike to the centerline.

"Torn! There's not enough room!"

"Who needs mirrors? Keep your legs in tight."

He sped up. The right mirror was the first to go, then the left, followed by angry honking from the cars his mirrors hit as he threaded the needle between the narrow lanes. The bike remained upright because the big mirrors were designed to pop off on impact.

Torn saw the Yankee's high beam in the side-view mirrors of the cars he drove between and heard the bike's screaming engine.

"He's right behind us!"

"I know. We're almost there."

Traffic thinned out right before the Yoyogi Rest Area. Torn accelerated. *Please be there.*

As he passed the on-ramp from the Yoyogi Rest Area, he heard a siren.

Yes! And there's our savior.

The patrol car pulled up next to them.

"What's he doing?" Torn asked, his eyes trained on the road.

"He's waving you over!"

The loudspeaker command rang out. "You there, on the blue motorcycle. Safely pull over at the next exit."

Torn exited at Gaienmae. He stopped at the bottom of the off-ramp and held the bike as Saya got off.

The police car pulled up behind them, lights flashing.

Torn stood while straddling the bike as he pressed a button to lower the electric center stand. The bike lifted slightly as the small electric motor whined and then dropped back down when the stand locked into place. He dismounted and removed his helmet.

The Yankee bike followed them off the expressway a moment later. The helmet and mask obscured the driver's face. There was no license plate.

Torn wished he had a gun. He made eye contact and flipped the guy off.

He turned to Saya. "Are you all right?"

She already had her helmet off and was shooting the Yankee with her phone as he drove by.

She stopped filming. "Yes. At least I think so."

"Good," he said, not even bothering to hide the relief in his voice. "Great idea. Please AirDrop those to me."

Saya hugged Torn as hard as she could, burying her head into his chest for what felt like an eternity. She was shaking.

He wondered if he was shaking too.

Saya looked up, green eyes flashing, and kissed him on the

cheek. "You're amazing, and here I thought you were just a lawyer." She kissed him again, this time on the lips.

Before he could reply, two uniformed police officers, one visibly much younger than his partner, approached.

Releasing Saya, Torn turned and said, "That guy on the Yankee bike tried to kill us!"

The young officer, eyes wide, hesitated before saying, a bit shakily, "You're under arrest."

How Did I Get Here?

俺は誰、ここはどこ?

Hungry and thirsty, his right arm aching and head throbbing, Torn sat alone on a hard metal chair in a small gray windowless interrogation room, his mind racing. He needed to talk to Mak.

He tried to focus on the positives: they were alive and his client was unhurt. And the cops had arranged for a doctor to sew up his arm. But being almost killed, and then arrested, and now stuck in this gloomy room with no food or water made it difficult to look on the bright side.

Being a lawyer, he dwelled on issues and risks. Who attacked them and why? Who were they after? Saya? Him? Both? Is Saya safe? Would the police hold him for as long as they legally could? He had no clue. Regardless, he assumed the worst: someone had hired the Mercedes goons and the Yankees, and whoever it was now had unfinished business. Did they know where he lived, where Saya lived? Probably. What would his firm and clients say when they found out? His reputation was everything. *But at least I'm alive.*

He didn't have high expectations of fair treatment by the Japanese police. The Japanese criminal justice system wasn't known for its due process or fair treatment of suspects. There was a reason for its high conviction rate: almost all suspects confessed. Holding people for weeks without charge and aggressively interrogating them facilitated confessions.

The door opened. Two young, skinny detectives wearing dark blue polyester suits and limp black neckties sauntered in. One of them dramatically dropped a file on the gray metal table with a smack.

"Tornait Masao Sagara, you're in a lot of trouble," one of them said in Japanese.

They both sat down across from him.

The detective's omission of the honorific *san* from his name was not lost on Torn. As the managing partner of an office of more than 100 lawyers and staff that was part of a prestigious international law firm, he wasn't accustomed to such rudeness. Stomach churning, bile in his mouth, he somehow managed to put his hands on the table, bow his head, and say in flawless Japanese, "Thank you very much for your help, officer. We owe you and your colleagues our lives. I apologize for causing the police any trouble and for wasting your time."

Surprised at Torn's sincere expression of gratitude and regret, which Torn knew went a long way in Japan, the two detectives paused and looked at each other, clearly unsure how to respond. They hadn't expected him to be so effusive; he hadn't said a word before that point, except when responding to questions about his identity. And they certainly didn't expect him to say thank you or apologize because they considered Torn a *gaijin*, a foreigner, genetically incapable of that kind of sincerity.

Quickly regaining his composure, one of the detectives said lamely, "You won't get off that easy."

Then, returning to the usual script, the other one explained, as assertively as he could muster, "Sagara-san, you're under investigation for excessive speeding—you could end up serving time for that alone—driving tandem illegally on the Metropolitan Expressway—you have a large bike license and should know better—endangering a passenger, public mayhem, vehicular homicide, and reckless driving."

Torn coughed. *Public mayhem?* He smiled through his head-ache. *That's a funny name for a crime.* He noted that the detective had added *san* to his name. A small victory. He figured this was the "good cop" in their "good cop, bad cop" routine.

"It was self-defense. The Mercedes and those Yankees tried to kill us. There's a bullet hole in my bike and one of the Yankees smashed my windshield and cut my arm." He wanted to scream at them, "There's a fucking bullet hole in the seat of my bike! We almost died, you stupid piece of shit!" But he didn't. Raising his voice or cursing would only be counterproductive.

The other detective leaned forward. "We don't know what caused that hole or when it happened. The broken windshield and that scratch on your arm could've been caused by your crash into the other rider, and there's no proof that a car or any bikes were chasing you. We only know about the one bike you intentionally crashed into. You killed that rider."

Ah, the bad cop. Torn could feel his face getting hot with rage. "Your forensics people can tell you a bullet made the hole. What else could it possibly be? And crashing into that bike wouldn't have caused the broken windshield or my shredded arm. The flail hit the windshield and my arm on the right side. I crashed into the bike on the left side. Talk to Brooks-san. She'll tell you. The bullet missed her by only centimeters." He held his thumb and forefinger close together as he said this. "She's got photos of the other Yankee. And I know you have surveillance cameras all over the expressways. There must be some footage of our attackers. How many giant black Mercedes and souped-up Yankee bikes can there be?"

"We'll talk to Saya Brooks-san, but it doesn't look good for you," the bad cop said, ignoring Torn's assertions.

Torn's head ached. "This doesn't make any sense. I have no record. Why would I lie? Why would I intentionally crash into someone if he wasn't trying to kill us? And why would I do it with someone on the back of my bike?"

"Are you calling me stupid?" asked the bad cop.

Ah, deflection. An interrogation tool. Attack on the small issues to confuse and rile up the suspect. Torn looked the bad cop in the eye. "I can call an idea stupid without impugning the intelligence of the person expressing the idea." *But now that I think about it, you are kind of a dumbass*, he thought. Torn kept that part to himself, but his impudence came through in his tone of voice.

The bad cop started to stand, but the good cop grabbed his arm and pulled him back. Then he sighed. "Quite frankly, we don't understand how you could survive an attack from a car *and* two motorcycles."

"Look, I've ridden scooters, off-road bikes, and street bikes all my life. I've taken racing courses and defensive driving courses. I love to ride and know exactly what my bike can and can't do."

The bad cop scoffed. "No one's that good."

Torn rubbed his forehead. "I wanna talk to my lawyer, Saki Katayama. She's a former prosecutor and she knows me well. You have her contact information. I also want to talk to my family and the American embassy."

The bad cop frowned. "We'll contact your lawyer, and she can inform your family. But you're a Japanese citizen, so you have no right to contact the US embassy. They have no jurisdiction over you in Japan. And you don't need them since your Japanese is perfect."

It's so Japan, thought Torn. Japanese often treated him like a foreigner because of his name and the way he looked, and to a certain extent the way he acted: more "foreign" than Japanese. Unless, of course, it was more convenient for them to treat him like he was Japanese. So, he'd expected that response and only threw the US embassy idea out there because he wanted the cops to know he also had a US passport. Torn had spent years trying to "be Japanese" but eventually gave up when he realized he would always be pigeonholed as an outsider, which still caused him to feel rage from time to time. But the double standard did have its advantages. Japanese often treated Western *gaijin*, particularly Americans, with a certain deference.

The bad cop wasn't finished. He stood and put his hands on the table and his face just centimeters from Torn's. "Because you're Japanese, and in particular because you are a lawyer, you know that in Japan suspects are presumed guilty until proven innocent. Also, we can hold you for more than three weeks and interrogate you whenever we want. So best you drop the attitude."

It was hard for Torn, fit and strong, 190 centimeters tall, to be intimidated by someone weighing fifty-five kilograms soaking wet. He had to suppress the urge to laugh, but he knew the detective was right. They could even interrogate him without a lawyer present. He was screwed, at least for now.

"I'm happy to cooperate," Torn responded.

The bad cop lifted his hands off the desk with a flourish. "Good!"

The good cop continued. "So where were you born?"

"Anchorage, Alaska."

"Your mother's Japanese?"

Torn sighed. "My father." Always the same assumption, but it was true that in most cases where only one parent was Japanese it was the mother.

"I'm surprised. You're very tall and don't look Japanese."

He thought of the lyrics from a Stealers Wheel song:

"Clowns to the left of me, jokers to the right; here I am, stuck in the middle with you."

He'd heard so many Japanese say he looked Western and

so many Westerners say he looked Asian that this type of comment didn't really register much anymore. Thus, he was surprised that he was mildly surprised at this kind of stereotyping from the police.

"My father was one hundred and eighty-five centimeters."

"Where's he from?"

"Oma. In Aomori."

The good cop raised his eyebrows. "Ah, famous for giant tuna fishing."

Torn felt a tinge of pride and allowed himself a smile. "That's right."

"Why were you born in Alaska?"

"My father moved there to fish for crab. That's where he met my mother."

"Your mother is white?" asked the bad cop.

Torn failed to see the relevance of the question but didn't wish to sound uncooperative. "She's an American."

"She's a housewife?"

Torn resisted the impulse to roll his eyes. "No, she's a retired lawyer."

"Ah, so you became a lawyer like your mother. Why not a fisherman?" asked the bad cop.

"I'm a lousy fisherman," he lied.

The detectives laughed.

"So, you say you're a lawyer..."

"Yes."

"Admitted in Japan?" the good cop asked, quite obviously assuming that the answer was no.

"Yes, and New York."

The two detectives sat up straight. "You're a *bengoshi*?"

Torn nodded. "*Hai.*"

The detectives looked at each other. It was news to them that anyone not born in Japan had passed the notoriously difficult Japan bar to become a *bengoshi*, a Japanese lawyer.

"Well, whether you're a *bengoshi* or not, these are very serious charges," said the bad cop without conviction.

Torn leaned forward. "To be precise, you haven't charged me with anything yet." He leaned back. "But yes, I know the charges could be serious. However, I'm not worried... because I'm innocent."

The detectives looked at each other again. The bad cop said, "That remains to be seen. What's this law firm you work for?"

"Hilsberry & Carter. It's an international firm with around two thousand lawyers worldwide."

"What's your position there?"

"As my card says, I'm Managing Partner of the Tokyo office."

"So, who would want to harm you?" asked the good cop.

"Other than my ex-wife, no one that I know of."

The good cop laughed while the bad cop tried to suppress a smile.

"Seriously, though, I have no idea who attempted to kill us, or why."

The bad cop's sternness returned. "So, you're divorced?"

"Technically no. Separated for more than two years, but she won't agree to a divorce."

The two officers looked at each other again.

"So how do you know Brooks-san?"

Torn rubbed his eyes and yawned, a shot of pain running through his arm as he tried to extend it. "She's a client."

"Nothing more?"

"I don't follow you." Torn understood the question but wished to force the detective to say it out loud.

The bad cop pointed his pen at Torn. "Don't play dumb with me. No personal relationship?"

Torn's head felt like it was going to split open, and he could barely move his throbbing arm without it barking at him. "No, it's unethical and against firm policy." His mouth tasted like cotton with dust on it. He was tiring of the theatrics.

"Then why is this beautiful woman riding on the back of your bike? Do you often take clients for motorcycle rides, or just the pretty ones?"

Torn had to admit that was a fair point. "No, I don't. First time, in fact. She asked me to drive her to a dinner with some investors we'd met earlier at her offices. Again, please ask her. She'll confirm."

"Well, you have a lot in common. She's *hafu* too."

Torn clenched his fists. He wasn't particularly chivalrous, but this was disrespectful to Saya. "That's irrelevant."

Also, he didn't like the word *hafu*, slang for half Japanese and half another nationality or race. He preferred to think of himself as Eurasian, biracial, or mixed race because he didn't like to be thought of as half of anything. He would sometimes tell people, "If it has to be a math reference, I prefer 'double' or, like Toguro from *Yuyu Hakusho*, I'm 100 percent of 100 percent." Some of his Japanese friends called him a banana because despite his northeast Asian features, his personality was more "white," or American, than Japanese. He found that both offensive *and* funny.

A Different Approach

異なるアプローチ

"Why were you riding on the back of your lawyer's motorcycle?" the female detective asked.

Saya Laura Brooks sat with two detectives in a clean room with a window. The detectives, one male and one female, couldn't have been more than twenty-five years old. They sported police department pins on their left lapels and name tags over the left breast pockets of their jackets. They had been courteous, even bringing her green tea and *senbei*, rice crackers. But Saya was tiring of the same questions and still wasn't sure if she was being treated as a suspect or just a witness.

"Well, as I said earlier, I'd always wanted to ride one. Sagara-sensei rode to our offices for a meeting, and I asked him to drive me to a dinner with investors." She was still wearing her leather jacket, jeans, and boots from the motorcycle ride. She had excused herself from the dinner, explaining that she was not feeling well.

"What does Sagara-san do for you?" asked the female cop, sitting across the table.

Saya bristled. She didn't like them using *san* when *sensei* was more appropriate for lawyers.

"Sagara-*sensei* is the lawyer for my company," she said matter-of-factly. Saya sat with her legs crossed and her hands wrapped around the front knee. She was making every effort to act nonchalant.

The male detective asked, "But what exactly does he do?" He was standing next to his colleague.

"He advises me how to protect my inventions using intellectual property laws and how to protect my rights when others invest."

"And what're your inventions?"

Saya took a sip of tea. "It's a new form of energy production and storage technology."

"Like solar or wind power?"

"Much better. It generates electricity without any pollution and stores it for long periods of time, but it's not weather dependent and takes up less space."

The cops looked at each other. Saya could almost hear them shrugging.

The young woman looked back at Saya. "Why did you hire Sagara-san?"

Saya smiled. "He has an excellent reputation as one of the best technology lawyers in the world. And as a start-up, that's what we need. He has a physics degree from Keio University, master's and PhD degrees in electrical engineering, and a master's in chemical engineering from Drexel University, which gave him a full scholarship. So, he has the necessary science background to understand my technology. He graduated second in his class at the University of Virginia Law School. And he's admitted as a lawyer in both New York and Japan."

"Is the University of Virginia a good law school?"

"Yes, excellent." *It was founded by Thomas Jefferson, for Christ's sake*, Saya thought to herself. But she knew most Japanese had heard of only Harvard and Stanford, and sometimes Princeton and Yale.

The man leaned forward. "Do you have any enemies?"

"Not that I know of," Saya responded honestly. "I'm just someone who likes to tinker with electricity." She added somewhat dramatically, "That may change once the industry finds out they're doomed."

"What do you mean, 'doomed?'" the female detective asked.

Saya smiled. "My technology will replace all current forms of energy generation." She was quite proud of herself, like a kid who'd built the biggest tree fort in the neighborhood.

The detectives looked at each other again and then back at Saya with blank stares.

The woman detective asked, "Does Sagara-san have any enemies?"

Saya sighed. "I don't know why anyone would want to harm him. He's one of the best technology lawyers on the planet and helps companies commercialize their cutting-edge technology. He works with nerds like me and venture investors, most of whom are also nerds."

The woman detective crossed her legs and leaned back in her chair. "You know he's married with children, right?"

Saya's eyes opened wide. "No, I didn't know that. He doesn't wear a wedding ring, and we don't discuss personal matters. Why do you ask?"

"So, there's nothing going on between you two? After all, it's odd that you'd ride on a motorcycle with someone who's just your lawyer," the female cop said in an accusatory tone.

Saya tossed her head back and laughed a full-throated laugh, without covering her mouth as many Japanese women do. "I don't think it's odd at all. I just wanted to ride on a motorcycle. Nothing else."

"Are you married?" asked the man.

Saya frowned, sat up, and put her hands on the table. "I don't understand the relevancy of that question, but no."

The female cop looked down her nose. "Do you have a boyfriend?"

"No. I work too much. Why do you ask?" Saya did like

men but since her father had left her mother for another woman, she found it difficult to trust them. Her relationships never lasted long, and she compensated by burying herself in her work.

"A significant other would be jealous if he knew about your affair with Sagara-san."

Saya looked at the young woman for a moment and then laughed so hard her eyes teared up. "My life should be so interesting!" She composed herself. "We're certainly not having an affair. It's strictly business. I don't think Sagara-sensei wanted to give me a ride. I used my prerogative as his client to convince him."

The two detectives looked at each other and then the man asked, "What's your company called?"

Saya's face lit up despite her fatigue. "Raijin Clean, Inc. It's named after the Japanese god of thunder, *Raijin*."

"Why?"

Saya smiled broadly. "Because the company's technology generates lightning, which is then harnessed and transmitted or stored for later use."

The two cops looked at her like she was crazy.

They didn't know that a lightning strike generates plasma six times hotter than the sun and generates ten million to one hundred million volts of electricity. Or that until Saya came along, no one knew exactly how thunderclouds generated or released electricity. It was common knowledge that when water droplets and ice crystals in a cloud rub or bump against each other, static electricity can build up until it's eventually released in the form of lightning. But Saya had figured out not only exactly how clouds create the static electricity and release it as lightning but how to replicate that process on demand, generate lightning bolts of the same strength every time, and store the energy generated.

The man said, "Let's get back to your ride. Do you really expect us to believe that a man in a Mercedes shot at you and then two flail-wielding motorcyclists attacked you?"

Saya, now wanting to scream, clenched her fists, looked up as if she were seeking deliverance by a higher power, and rolled her eyes. "Why would I make that up? I'm sure you saw the hole in the bike's seat, right? The bullet went right under my legs!" She wanted to tell them she had the feeling she was being followed around town even before the attacks on the expressway but thought they would think she was making things up just to support her story.

"To cover up a crime," the female cop said, her face an emotionless mask.

Saya could tell they were grasping at straws. She leaned in, held her hands out with the palms up, and shrugged her shoulders. "That's just ridiculous. What crime? Sagara-sensei will corroborate my story."

The cops looked at each other again. Then the female cop asked, "Isn't it true Sagara-san was driving recklessly? Or perhaps he killed the other biker on purpose?"

Now she knew they had nothing. "No, absolutely not. Why would he want to do that? That's even more ridiculous. He drove brilliantly," Saya said, almost gushing. "If he hadn't driven like he did we'd be dead."

The man asked, "What do you mean?"

"What do I mean? Haven't you been listening?" She was becoming impertinent, but she didn't care. "First, he shook off the car that shot at us, then he saved us from one of the bikers by crashing into him. Haven't you seen his arm and the shattered bike windshield? The biker cut it up with a flail!" She stood up and put her hands on the table. "Then, to get away from the other bike, he drove between the lanes where he knew it was too narrow. That's how we lost the mirrors.

And he drove to where he knew a patrol car hangs out. Sure enough, there it was, and they pulled us over." She paused. "Yes, he most definitely saved our lives." She stood back with her arms folded, glaring at them.

And he kept calm, even though I was freaking out, she thought to herself.

The female detective said, "Well, that's just your story and..."

But Saya had stopped listening. She was thinking about Torn. She had never trusted a man more.

I've Got That Going for Me

思ったよりいいかも

"We've got video footage from the expressway and the patrol car. You can't deny what happened."

Torn sat in another interrogation room, this time with a window. He'd initially seen the move as a good sign, because cops weren't nice to suspects unless they provided the desired information or the cops started to believe them. But the interrogation wasn't going so well for him.

Torn had for the third time gone through his ride with Saya from start to finish, walking them through moment by moment what had happened, starting with when the black Mercedes first appeared in his mirrors. The cops seemed genuinely concerned that such brazen attacks might have occurred in broad daylight on a public expressway, although they wouldn't acknowledge the veracity of Torn's account. It was obvious they'd never heard of anything like it during their careers. Just when he thought he'd convinced them, the bad cop had become antagonistic again.

Bleary-eyed, he replied, "I'm not denying what happened. I'm saying I did it to save ourselves from those assholes trying to kill us." He knew he shouldn't be cursing, but he was too tired to care anymore. "The video footage will show exactly what I've been telling you all along. And at the risk of repeating myself, Brooks-san has a photo of the other Yankee and will corroborate my story if she hasn't already."

The bad cop, who had been standing with his back against the wall, stepped forward and shouted, "Don't be stupid! The video footage shows you intentionally driving your motorcycle into the other bike. It doesn't show any car or bikes chasing you! The footage from the patrol car shows you riding tandem where you shouldn't be. And Brooks-san's photo is of some random guy driving by."

Torn almost stood up but managed to remain seated. He said slowly, "You need to get more footage. And show me the existing footage. The footage should show the two bikers with their flails. If we weren't attacked, why is my windshield broken, and what happened to my right arm? And as I told you, I *intentionally* lane split where it's too narrow for my mirrors to escape the second biker and *intentionally* rode tandem in the single-rider-only area because I was praying a cop would pull us over."

"Well, the footage doesn't show anyone chasing you, let alone with a flail," said the bad cop.

"I don't believe you. Let me see it."

The bad cop charged the table, grabbed Torn's shirt with both hands by the collar, and put his face so close to Torn's that Torn felt spray when the detective asked through gritted teeth, "Are you calling me a liar?"

Torn wiped his face with the back of his hand. "Look, Detective, I didn't do anything wrong. If you're going to charge me, then do it. But stop spitting on me."

Outraged, the bad cop lifted a pointed finger to Torn's face and started to say something when the good cop grabbed the bad cop's arm. "Take it easy. Let's take a break. Sagara-san, please wait here."

While waiting, someone brought him a bowl of stale rice, a raw egg, pickled cucumbers, miso soup, soy sauce, chopsticks, and a pot of green tea. He quickly mixed the egg with the rice and soy sauce and ate it with the soup and pickles. He was so hungry he didn't mind that the rice was a little dry or that the soup lacked any seasoning.

Two hours later, a senior detective in his forties by the name of Shinsuke Taniguchi entered the interrogation room with a prosecutor in his thirties named Yasuo Tsujikawa. Detective Taniguchi was stocky with a thick bulging neck and the cauliflower ear of someone who wrestled or practiced judo. He had a crew cut, with thick eyebrows over large dark-brown eyes. There was a detective's pin on the left lapel of his cheap suit. Prosecutor Tsujikawa, skinny and pale, with thinning longer hair, wore an expensive three-piece suit with a prosecutor's pin on the left lapel. His glasses had ivory-colored frames and thick lenses that made his large eyes look like Nobita's from *Doraemon*.

Torn stood to meet them. They introduced themselves and presented their business cards.

After sitting down, Detective Taniguchi looked at Tsujikawa and back at Torn. "Sagara-san, we apologize for the overnight interrogations, but please understand that this is a very serious matter and we're just following standard procedure. My colleague, Tsujikawa-sensei, and I have reviewed the matter and we believe you're telling the truth. Moreover, Brooks-san corroborated your story."

Stunned, Torn thought, *So why the Spanish Inquisition routine?* But he wasn't about to look a gift horse in the mouth.

Taniguchi looked down, took a deep breath, and continued. "Nevertheless, given that a man has died and there was a shooting on the expressway, we'll need to investigate until we determine who's behind the attacks and whether you acted reasonably under the circumstances. But since you have no prior record, you are a well-respected attorney, and your lawyer is Katayama-sensei, a former colleague of ours, we're going to release you on your own recognizance. She's agreed to act as your guarantor. We'll need to hold your passport and ask that you not leave the country without permission."

Torn couldn't believe his good fortune. He knew it was extremely rare for anyone to be released on bail, particularly on their own recognizance. What's more, Torn had dual nationality and in a pinch could travel on his US passport.

Taniguchi seemed to be reading his mind. "We'll need both passports. You should've chosen one nationality by the age of twenty-two, as required by the Japanese Nationality Act, but we'll leave that issue to the immigration authorities."

Taniguchi, despite his bulldog appearance, was so smooth that Torn thought he would sound like a detective from Scotland Yard had he been speaking in English. Still, there was something "fidgety" about him that Torn couldn't put his finger on.

"We won't disclose your names to the press for now; however, we won't be able to keep it secret for long."

Torn smiled. "It's gratifying to know you understand we were attacked without provocation and that I acted only to protect my client and myself. I am grateful for your trust in me. Please allow me two questions. First, when will my passports be returned? I'm scheduled to fly to New York the week after next."

Taniguchi smiled. "We'll need to discuss internally. Please check with us early next week. What's the other question?"

"When will my bike be returned so I can have it repaired?"

"It's important evidence and will take time to process. Incidentally, we found a tracking device on your bike. That might explain how the perpetrators found you on the expressway. You should assume they know where you work and live. And if you have other vehicles, you should check those as well."

Maybe they're just after me, Torn thought. He shuddered, thinking again that Saya could have been killed because he was stupid enough to give her a ride. Still, he wondered who would want to kill him, and why.

⁓

Eyes still adjusting to the morning sun, Torn stood outside of the police station checking his phone and saw numerous work-related emails and texts from clients and colleagues. He desperately needed to get back to the office. Work was piling up. But that was nothing new; the reward for doing great legal work was more work.

He also saw many texts and attempted calls from Mayumi and Kiwako, two women he was dating. He spoke to them both almost every day and they'd be worried.

But he had other calls he needed to make before he could deal with work or any personal matters. He called the Hotel Okura to reserve one of their executive suites.

Then he called his lawyer, Saki Katayama. He had met Saki many years before when one of his partners recommended her to represent the son of a client who'd been busted for drug possession while teaching English in Japan. Torn thanked her for helping him get out of jail, and they discussed the best way to handle his case. "And get one of my passports back as soon as you can," he implored her.

"I'll do my best, Torn, but I can't make any promises."

Spoken like a true lawyer, he thought.

Then he dialed Mak's number. Makoto Karahashi was an American computer programmer and partner at Longstreth, an international private investigations and security firm that often collaborated with Torn's firm to investigate embezzlement, fraud, bribery, cartel, and other claims against corporations and individuals. He was also one of Torn's few friends.

"What's goin' on, Torn? You sound stressed, or at least more stressed than usual."

"Well, the good news is I'm outta jail."

Mak paused. "Ooh, so the bad news is that you were in jail."

"Exactly. I need your help again. As usual, this is all confidential. And I need you to work with Saki on this. To protect the attorney-client privilege, she'll hire you directly to assist with my legal matters."

"I know the drill. Shoot."

Torn briefed him about Saya, her start-up, Raijin Clean, the attempts to kill them, and his arrest.

After Torn's explanation, Mak said, "That's very interesting. I can do some preliminary digging into Saya, Raijin Clean, and its investors, but without any suspects, there's not much more to investigate."

"I know it's a fishing expedition, but give it some thought. I gotta find out who's behind this. Soon everyone, including the firm, will know about the attacks and that I'm being investigated for murder. I need to get out in front of this thing."

Torn could hear Mak scratching his beard. "I'll touch base with Saki to put the contract in place."

Torn responded, "And please check my other bike and car for tracking devices. They found one on the 1200."

"Roger that. Anything else?"

"Do you know a Detective Taniguchi?"

"Big guy? Looks like a bull? Bad ear?"

"That's him."

"Yeah, he's a judo guy. I've met him but don't know him well."

"What about a prosecutor named Yasuo Tsujikawa?"

"Sickly looking guy?"

"That's the guy."

"Not much other than he has a reputation for being a hothead."

"Try to find out whether he or Taniguchi is calling the shots."

"I'll ask around." And before Torn could say anything, Mak added, "Don't worry. I'll be discreet."

From the Mouths of Babes

赤子の口から

"Dad, I can't believe you still haven't filed for divorce. How long are you going to drag this out?" Sophia, Torn's daughter, was visibly upset.

Torn, Sophia, and her brother, Sean, were dining in a private room at Kyubey, a sushi restaurant in the Hotel Okura, where Torn had been staying since the attacks. Afraid someone might be watching his apartment building, he'd been back to his apartment only once to pick up some things. Sophia and Sean knew nothing about the attacks. So, when they had suggested a meeting at his apartment, Torn had invited them out to dinner because he didn't want them to know he'd moved out.

He slowly placed the wide ends of his chopsticks on the table with the tips on the chopstick holder and looked at his daughter. "Honey, I was hoping your mother would come around so we could do this amicably." He didn't say that he hadn't been pushing very hard for a divorce because being separated—but still married to someone who refused to grant him a divorce—enabled him to date other women *and* gave him a convenient excuse not to commit to anyone else. It also allowed him to maintain control of the marital assets. He hadn't planned things to go this way, and he wasn't proud of the gray world in which he lived, but he took the good with the bad.

"It's been more than two years since you moved out. She's not going to do anything unless she has to," said Sophia. She wore clean yoga clothes and had her long dark hair tied in a ponytail. She had large eyes and a nose that was prominent for someone with a Japanese mother. Tall, slender, and athletic, she was only a few centimeters shorter than Sean, two years her senior. Having just come from kendo practice, her kendo bag and *shinai*—bamboo sword—sat in a corner of the room. She was staying with her mother during a holiday break from college in Seattle, yet she always practiced wherever she went.

Torn clasped his hands together on the table. "It's not really any of your business. This is between your mom and me."

Sophia clenched her fists and glowered at him. "None of our business? We're collateral damage but it's none of our freakin' business?"

Wishing he could disappear, Torn fidgeted in his seat.

"The barrel bombs you guys throw around are not exactly surgical," Sean added dryly. He wore a T-shirt and jeans and held a glass of cold green tea. He was stocky and almost as tall as Torn. Handsome, but with more Japanese features than Torn or Sophia, his eyes were more elongated with sharper corners and not as deep-set, his nose not quite as prominent.

Torn took his hands off the table and looked down. "I don't deny that. And I'm sorry."

Sophia put her hands on her hips. "We're tired of hearing you two say you're sorry. If you're so sorry, get along better or at least keep us out of it. As it is, you keep dragging us back in."

"Wait a minute. I don't consult or talk with you about any of this."

"Yeah, but Mom does," Sophia replied. "She tells us everything. So we know all about what you've done and what you say to her."

"I know our relationship issues have been very hard on both of you. I don't know what your mom has told you, but please take it all with a grain of salt. I've been trying to do the right thing."

Sean looked his father in the eyes. "Dad, you have no idea. We understand that in many ways you and Mom have been wonderful parents. We don't want for anything, and despite your crazy work and travel you always find time to spend with us."

"Thank you, Son. That means a lot to me," Torn said, somewhat relieved but leery of the further dressing down he suspected was coming.

"Don't thank me yet. Sophia and I never expected you to be perfect. But to be honest, there's a lot you did, and I still think you do, that we can't understand, much less accept. So, although you may think you've been trying to do the right thing, you obviously haven't been trying hard enough."

Torn shrugged his shoulders and held up his hands. "I don't understand. I've been nothing but straight with you guys."

Raising her voice, Sophia said, "Really, Dad? Have you? Anyway, you're missing the point. I for one have felt very resentful toward you about your relationship with Mom. I feel resentment toward her too, but I can't stand the way you've treated her."

Torn pursed his lips and crossed his arms. "What are you talking about, Sophia? I've barely spoken to your mom since I moved out."

Sophia looked down. "It started long before that. You know what I'm talking about. Just because you move out doesn't mean the memories go away."

Sean took a sip of his cold green tea. "Don't get me wrong. I'm also tired of Mom's backward, masochistic, and unquestioning love and affection for you. I have wished for a long time that you'd get divorced."

Despite Torn's anger at Yukie for her intransigence, he sighed at Sean's stinging criticism of his mother, and yet was encouraged by his support for a divorce.

Sean put his glass down. "But I got over your marital issues a long time ago. What Sophia is saying is that before you moved out there was this constant uncomfortable air in the house, crying, and disgusting harsh words from both of you, driven by what I can only assume was temporary insanity. That experience has stayed with us."

Sophia was shaking slightly. "We may have gotten over it, but we have eyes and ears and know what went on. We know about your continuing affairs, even before you moved out, your harsh and sarcastic comments to Mom about her drinking and smoking, and you're trying to buy us off with your money." She almost spat out the word "money."

Obviously, they're not over it. But I can't blame them, Torn thought to himself. Nervous sweat began to soak his armpits. His mouth was dry.

Sean leaned forward. "We understand no one's perfect and we know all about Mom's issues. Her drinking, her smoking, her constant mood swings, and her sometimes incoherent banter. We've been dealing with them for years. But she's also been excessively indulgent of you and your petty problems... and you took advantage of that."

Sophia wiped her eyes with the back of her hand. "Sean's right. It's not all your fault. But you left us with Mom when you moved out despite knowing all about her problems. Did you ever stop to think that we might want to be with you? Do you know how clingy she's become and how much she relies on us? I love her, but it's like we're the adults and she's the child. Why didn't you ask us who we wanted to be with?"

Torn looked down, speechless. It had never crossed his mind that they might want to be with him instead of their mother.

He sat staring at his hands, wondering how things had gone so wrong with Yukie, his estranged wife, when they'd started out so right. He thought about her carefree nature when they first met.

On their first date, a bicycle trip to an *otera*, a Buddhist temple, Yukie rode a folding bike with small wheels and an impossibly long seat post. Her long black hair, which contrasted beautifully with her porcelain skin, fell straight down her back. She wore, untucked and loose, a sheer strapless black-and-white-striped blouse perfectly framing her breasts. Every so often he glimpsed her flat tummy when the breeze lifted the bottom of her blouse.

They met at a major intersection before heading to the temple grounds. When he saw her riding down a hill, he was surprised by how tall she looked and by how much she stood out in a crowd. Cars slowed to a crawl as drivers rubber-necked to watch her ride by. She was a glamorous hazard to traffic safety.

He remembered marveling at how smooth, fearless, and independent she was. One example was the way she kept him at bay, refusing to even kiss him for several weeks but seemingly unconcerned that he might lose interest and start seeing someone else. At the time, he had wondered why he went on seeing her when she refused every advance. But he knew the reason. He was mesmerized.

"Did you hear me?" Sophia asked.

Torn responded slowly, "Sorry, honey. I thought it would be better for both of you if you remained with your mom. I also thought she'd sue and you'd get dragged into court if I tried to take you with me. I didn't want that."

Sean gave his dad a sideways glance. "And you thought it would be easier for you because you wouldn't have to take care of us, and you could date."

Before Torn could respond, Sophia said, "Are you still dating Kiwako-san? I like her. She's nice."

Torn regretted having carelessly introduced them to Kiwako at a time when he hadn't even filed for divorce and was still dating Mayumi. At the time, he thought Kiwako might be a great fit for him. She was mature and emotionally stable, close in age, bilingual and bicultural like him. She also understood what it was like to raise a family but wasn't interested in having more children and was ambitious and career minded. He hadn't introduced the kids to Mayumi because he had an inkling they wouldn't approve, and besides, Mayumi had told him point blank she had no interest in meeting his children.

He decided to ignore Sophia's question and respond to Sean. "I had no idea you wanted to come with me. Had I known..."

"Look, the purpose of this meeting is not to beat you up, although we did want to get some things off our chest. Sophia and I talked and what we want is what you want—closure. I understand it could take years but, if you leave it to Mom, she'll never agree, and she'll wallow in booze and self-pity forever. So, if you're serious about getting divorced, then you should show her how serious you are by starting the process."

Torn stared at them and was about to say something when Sophia said quietly, "Dad, we know it's your decision, but we thought you should know where we stand."

He filed for divorce the next day.

Hypocrite

偽善者

Vincent K. Harden never answered the phone himself. So Torn sat with his associate, Hiroshi Yoshida, in a conference room with floor-to-ceiling windows in Hilsberry & Carter's Tokyo offices listening to Wakkanai Drilling Co., Ltd.'s classical hold music while waiting for Vince to come on the line. They knew he was going to rip them a new one.

Torn remembered meeting Vince for the first time at a pitch meeting for Project Ibis, an M&A deal for Wakkanai Drilling. Wakkanai was trying to buy Zephyrus Oil & Drilling, GmbH, a German company and long-time supplier to Wakkanai. Based on Saya's strong recommendation, Vince asked Torn to participate in a "beauty contest," the bidding process for the legal work. He had beaten two other law firms to get the deal.

Vince, a ruggedly handsome man in his mid-fifties with olive skin, neatly cut light-brown hair, and light-blue eyes, recently had been appointed Vice Chairman of the Board of Directors of Wakkanai Drilling. He was a proudly born-again Christian and self-made billionaire from Milwaukee who loved to ramble on about his many accomplishments, possessions, and children.

It was also the first time Torn met Tamayo Watanabe, the diminutive *shacho*—the President—and Chairwoman of Wakkanai Drilling. She had been very gracious to him when they'd exchanged business cards. Tamayo was an eighty-four-year-old Japanese woman with thinning white hair, jaundice-like yellow-stained skin, gray teeth, and age spots on her hands. Her smile turned her rheumy eyes into half circles above flat cheeks. Torn recalled the contrasting youthfulness of her striking dress: half white with black polka dots on one side and half black with white polka dots on the other.

At the meeting, Tamayo sat at the middle of the large dark maple conference room table with Vince—wearing an open-collared dress shirt, khakis, and loafers—on her left, and Asahi Susono, her executive assistant, on her right. They were flanked by several Japanese colleagues, all men clad in suits. Vince refused to visit law offices, which is why they'd met at Wakkanai's tired corporate headquarters. Torn had the feeling Tamayo didn't visit "the help" either. He remembered Vince doing all the talking, much of it about himself, with the Japanese sitting erect and stone-faced like Easter Island statues.

"I started my first company when I was eighteen. At the time, I had nothing. Now I own twenty-six companies doing business in thirty-one countries. I retired at the age of thirty-four to play polo and practice taekwondo. I found the Lord when I was thirty-six."

Oh Jesus, Torn remembered thinking.

"I've done business all over the world. I once met Muammar Qaddafi. He sent a cavalcade of late-model S-Class Mercedes to transport me from Tripoli airport to his compound. On the way there, two SUVs, escorting us and brandishing machine guns, forced a truck coming in the opposite direction off the road. I'm sure that poor guy must've been stuck in the sand for days. Praise be to the Lord, I got out safe and with my money." Vince laughed at the recollection.

"I have several homes, including a beautiful house in Milwaukee in an exclusive community on the lake, a house in Florida in a gated community on the ocean, a house in Brera in Milan, and an apartment in Paris right off the Champs-

Élysées. I have a private jet, a Bombardier Global 7500, that I use to fly all over the world for business, and I love to collect rare sports cars.

"God has blessed me with six wonderful children, including my older daughter, Mallory, who's traveling in Europe as we speak." Vince's eyes lit up when he mentioned his daughter. "She texted me early this morning about her dinner at the home of Richard Branson. Can you believe it? Mallory's really something." Vince laughed again.

Torn remembered smiling politely and thinking it would've been appropriate for him to say something at that juncture. But he'd been rendered temporarily speechless by Vince's self-aggrandizing ramblings.

Thankfully, Vince continued. "Mallory texted that Richard Branson's daughter was a brat and asked if she was as big a spoiled brat. I had to assure her she wasn't."

Torn used all of his willpower not to roll his eyes.

Vince looked up at an angle as if intently examining something on the ceiling and wistfully explained, "Ya know, God made both girls and boys but they're not the same."

Hold the presses, Torn thought.

"A daughter holds a special place in a father's heart, making it difficult not to indulge them. They deserve special treatment, particularly if they're not very attractive or good in school, because life's harder for them than for boys, and the good Lord expects fathers to take care of them. That's why I set up trust funds for my daughters. My only expectation is that they be good Christians.

"A son, on the other hand, you can't coddle. You can put a boy on an oil rig and they'll figure out how to survive. They need tough love. But it's not fair to expect the same of daughters."

Without thinking, Torn said, "It must be great to be your daughter."

He was leaning back in his chair recalling the surprised look on Vince's face when a booming voice snapped him out of his reverie.

"Yoshida-san, I want to talk about this Twain letter agreement. Why's it taking so fucking long?"

Torn thought it odd for a born-again Christian to use such language, but it was par for the course with Vince.

Torn stood, put his hands on the table, and leaned into the speakerphone. "Hi Vince. It's Torn. I'm here with Hiroshi and we'd be happy to discuss the Twain Advisory Agreement."

Vince paused before replying, "Torn, I didn't know you'd be on this call, but thank sweet Jesus you are, because most Japanese, including your colleague there, don't speak English well. My Japanese colleagues tell me *bengoshi* are the smartest lawyers in the world, but you certainly wouldn't know it from talking to 'em."

Although there was some truth to Vince's comments about the English skills of some *bengoshi*, Torn wasn't about to agree with Vince in front of Hiroshi, a longtime associate and wonderful lawyer. Torn often thought it odd that the Japanese were so insecure about their relatively low level of English skill, while the Brits and Americans often wore their lack of knowledge of any foreign language as a badge of honor. Vince was a prime example. Torn thought to himself, *How many languages do you speak, you barely monolingual prick?*

Instead, he responded, "I'm familiar with the Twain engagement letter for Project Ibis, which as you know was drafted and is being negotiated in Japanese. When I heard about this call, I thought my participation might be helpful."

"Why'd you let me agree to Japanese instead of English?"

Torn said, "That was agreed upon by the parties before you got us involved."

"Next time I'm about to jump off a cliff, stop me."

"Will do." Torn thought, *But in this case, you'd already taken the leap.*

"Have these comments been sent to Twain?"

Torn looked at Hiroshi, who said, "Yes."

They heard Vince sigh. "I've read the English translation and you've deleted lots of Twain's language and added new language. I've worked with these guys for years, and unlike Sakurajima, Twain can handle both the accounting due diligence and financial advisory work. Their draft looks fine to me. Can't we just accept it as is?"

Torn looked out the window at the giant crane being used to build the sleek new glass-covered green skyscraper on the other side of the elevated expressway, and then back at the phone. "Vince, I understand you have a long-term relationship with Twain. But Twain is asking for a one percent success fee, which is high, particularly since they didn't even originate the deal. We suggest point five percent, at most. The letter also provides they'll charge by the hour at their standard global rates, with no cap, for accounting due diligence and IT and other consulting work. That's going to be a lot of work. Their fees on Project Ibis for those services could turn out to be astronomical with no way of knowing beforehand how much they'll be. That's why we suggested Wakkanai ask for (a) a discount of fifteen percent off their standard rates and (b) caps for their work."

Vince replied, "Fifteen percent? Why would I ask for that much of a discount? You guys haven't offered any discount."

Torn was thankful his middle finger couldn't be seen through the phone. "Actually, we agreed to a fifteen percent discount *and* a cap of seven million dollars, assuming the deal closes this year."

"Oh right. I forgot. But I want this letter signed soon."

Torn thought, *How could you possibly forget? You dictated the terms!* "Understood. Our comments are pretty standard and in Wakkanai's interest."

"OK, well, perhaps you should talk directly with Twain and leave me out of it. I want to preserve my relationship with them."

Torn took a deep breath. "We would be delighted to discuss the terms of their engagement letter directly with Twain."

"Great. Keep it civilized."

Torn looked at the phone. "Twain's an internationally recognized accounting and advisory firm. I'm sure they know what's market for global deals like Project Ibis. We'll be professional while at the same time protecting Wakkanai."

"Good. I want it done tomorrow so they can start their work."

"We'll do our best, Vince."

The first thing Vince had done after being appointed Vice Chairman of Wakkanai was hold a beauty contest with three law firms bidding for the project. Torn suspected Vince would've brought in his usual American law firm if they'd had a Tokyo office. Luckily for Torn, Saya had suggested that Vince consider Hilsberry when he'd asked her for a recommendation for an international law firm with an office in Japan.

Later, Vince fired Wakkanai's financial advisor, Sakurajima Financial Advisors, and hired Twain Advisory, his own longtime deal advisor, the stated reason being that Twain could handle the IT and accounting due diligence as well as the number crunching, and Sakurajima couldn't. But Torn had always wondered why Vince hadn't put Twain through the same bidding process as the law firms. He'd initially dismissed the idea that Vince might be getting a kickback from Twain. Now, he wasn't so sure.

But he had no evidence. Besides, he had a more personal concern. He guessed Vince would be the first to fire him once he discovered Torn was suspected of committing several crimes, including murder. And he wanted this deal. It was perfect for a global law firm like Hilsberry, and the legal fees would be huge. He also wanted it on his deal list. Closing Project Ibis, a global M&A deal involving assets and employees all over the world, would be quite a feather in his cap.

"Good. And one more thing. Wakkanai wants to invest in Raijin Clean. A few people at Wakkanai have already seen the technology. I've sold Tamayo on it, and she wants to see the demonstration next Tuesday with China PV. As you know, Wakkanai, which is trying to diversify into renewables, owns twenty percent of CPV. I told her you'd be there, and you know more about Raijin's technology than anyone other than Saya."

Torn, who had remained standing thus far, sat down and leaned back in his chair.

"I look forward to seeing her there. Will you be joining?"

"No. I know all I need to know about Raijin, but Tamayo is very interested in their technology. She's concerned about the future of fossil fuels and wants to hedge her bets. She likes you and wants you to represent Wakkanai."

Torn shook his head and looked at Hiroshi again. "Unfortunately, Hilsberry can't represent Wakkanai against Raijin. I'm sure you understand there's a conflict of interest because we already represent Raijin." He knew Vince's next question.

"Can't you get a waiver?"

"Unfortunately, no. Saya's adamant that Hilsberry represent Raijin in all financings. In fact, we'll need a waiver from Wakkanai."

Vince raised his voice. "Tamayo's not going to want to give you a waiver to be adverse to her when she's got her mind set on you representing Wakkanai."

"You know Saya. Once she makes a decision, it's next to impossible to change her mind. I assume Saya knows Wakkanai is interested in investing?"

"Yes, she knows all about it and is very excited."

Torn mustered as much enthusiasm as he could. "Understood. We'll take good care of your chairwoman."

"Thank you, Torn, and God bless you both."

———

Torn's mobile phone rang as he returned to his office. It was Vince.

"Hey, I didn't want to say anything in front of Yoshida, but as you can tell from my ten-million-dollar investment, I think Raijin is a unicorn in the making."

Torn closed his office door and walked to the window to look out at Tokyo Bay. "I'm not surprised. It's great technology."

Vince laughed. "It's not just great. It's revolutionary! If it takes off, it could put me out of business."

Torn thought that was an odd thing to say. "I'm sure Saya would be happy to hear you still believe in her technology. We'll continue to provide the best legal support we can to Raijin Clean."

"Don't give me that party-line crap. You need to watch out for my interests. You owe me since I got you involved in Project Ibis. And I know you lawyers like to complicate things since you charge by the hour, but I want you to handle the remaining patent work and the China PV transaction as efficiently as possible. That's my money you're burning. By the way, I assume you're attending the license negotiations next week before the demonstration?"

Torn ignored everything but the question. "Yes, definitely."

"Good. You need to protect Saya from the Chinese. You can't trust 'em as far as you can throw 'em. As you know, CPV is just an extension of ChinaPetrol. In fact, you need to protect her from the Japanese too. I don't trust those bastards either."

Torn massaged his temples with his thumb and forefinger. "You mean Wakkanai, the company on whose board you serve?" Earlier in their relationship, Torn had been stunned at Vince's lack of boundaries, but then realized that, as the sole founder, owner, and operator of numerous successful businesses, Vince probably wasn't used to hearing the word "no" or the words "you can't do that."

Predictably not picking up on Torn's sarcasm, Vince replied, "Yeah, and the government. Someone senior from the Agency for Natural Resources and Energy is planning to attend the demonstration. They've already seen it but things are getting serious. Tamayo thinks the Japanese government's involvement would make Raijin Clean even more valuable." He paused, then added conspiratorially, "Also, there's a faction within Wakkanai that doesn't support me. The Japanese always want to get rid of the foreigner. Look at what happened to Carlos Ghosn!"

Torn continued massaging his temples, closed his eyes tightly, and took a deep breath. "You do realize that we represent Wakkanai and not you individually, right?"

"Yeah, I know but you should understand what's going on."

Against his better judgment, Torn asked, "Why would they want you out?"

"They're suspicious of my recommendation that they invest in Raijin." Vince paused. "And they think I want to take over their company."

Before Torn could stop himself, he asked, "What gave them that idea?"

"Because Wakkanai isn't doing nearly as well as its competitors, and they know I'm always looking for opportunities. They're a paranoid lot."

Torn opened his eyes and looked down at the terraced Swedish embassy with plants dangling from each level, invoking an image of the fabled Hanging Gardens of Babylon. "If you're interested in taking them over, you're going to need separate counsel. We can't help you."

"I'm not saying I am, but a struggling company I know I can turn around is clearly an opportunity. Anyway, take care of Tamayo. She's been good to Harden Industries, and I want to make sure she understands Raijin's technology before Wakkanai invests. Gotta go."

Borderline

境界

"I'm really horny."

Torn winced slightly whenever Mayumi said "horny." Her English was excellent, but he didn't like the word and assumed it was something she'd picked up in Texas. He'd suggested to her that it was uncouth, and she should use another word like "amorous" or "excited," but she ignored him. Once she'd said she was "aroused," which was almost worse, forcing him to suppress a chuckle.

Sitting at a corner table in an Italian restaurant on the forty-second floor of Six Trees High-Rise, they had a panoramic view of Tokyo Tower, an illuminated red-and-white, Eiffel Tower-inspired landmark; the Rainbow Bridge, lit up like an elegant prone Christmas tree; and Tokyo Bay, with its endless boat traffic.

"I want you to touch me."

"Shall we order a drink first?"

She cocked her head, smiled, and arched an eyebrow. "Are they mutually exclusive?"

Always the troublemaker. He shifted in his chair and looked around the crowded restaurant.

"Oh, relax, Sagara-sensei," she said, emphasizing the *sensei* and laughing. "I'm dying for a glass of champagne."

He signaled a waiter. Mayumi ordered champagne and Torn ordered an oolong tea. He never drank before sex.

Sitting up straight with her chest close to the table and

the long tablecloth draped over her thighs, she put his hand between her legs, spreading them slightly. He moved his hand up and soon realized she wore no panties.

As the waiter approached with their drinks, Torn brought his hand up and licked his fingers. Mayumi slapped his hand away from his mouth.

"You started it," he said.

"Yeah, but I haven't taken a shower since this morning."

"I like the smell of your day."

She laughed her infectious laugh. After the waiter left, she leaned over, kissed him, and put his hand between her legs again.

They never finished their drinks. Torn dropped some cash on the table and they headed toward the elevator. Holding hands, they kissed deeply when the elevator doors closed, Torn's hand inside the top of her dark blue-black cocktail dress.

When they reached her place, which was closer than his, Mayumi got on all fours and pulled her dress up on her back. She glistened. He blew on her softly and then touched her with his tongue. She was surprised at where he directed his attention. He sucked on one of his thumbs and started rubbing a more traditional area lightly. He paused his oral stimulation to suck briefly on the index finger of his other hand. Soon he was stimulating her both inside and out, simultaneously. Mayumi loved this, but demanded he enter her.

Thank God for vasectomies, he thought.

She lay on her back, letting her long hair spill around her head. He slowly inserted himself while she watched, using a hand mirror so she could see her favorite part next to actual orgasm. He started slowly and then moved faster, pushing up slightly to keep his weight off her. Soon, she pulled him in close. He kissed her, put an arm under her neck, and buried his face in her cheek, just as she had instructed early in their relationship. She was very clear about what she wanted in sex, from kissing to how he held her during the afterglow.

He slowed to a deliberate rhythm not quite fast enough for his liking. He knew, however, that Mayumi liked it very slow, until right before the end. She was breathing heavily now. She started to whimper. He picked up the pace. She opened her mouth, grunted, and began screaming at an almost painful decibel level loud enough to alarm the neighbors.

Then he pushed his chest up and increased his speed while his hands found their favorite playthings. She was more voluptuous than other, often anorexic-looking, Japanese girls. He loved looking down at her beautiful face and body while feeling her tight wet warmth and kneading her breasts. He reached a point of no return and it was over before he wanted it to be.

Mayumi used to like him to slap her sometimes during sex. At first Torn had refused. But she kept insisting, and once he'd crossed that line, he grew to like it. He only did it when she demanded it, which generally was when she was depressed or feeling guilty after having screamed at Torn about something. It excited her to an unbelievable level and snapped her out of her funk.

Per her instructions, he used an open hand. Never a fist. And Mayumi controlled the strength of his slap. He would start with almost a tap, and she would demand that he hit her harder and harder until red marks appeared on her face. She would pull him to her and demand he say he loved her. Then she demanded that he hit her again. Committing this violence against her— that she controlled—became a huge turn-on for Torn for a time, causing orgasms so intense they were almost painful.

After a while, however, as her trust in and love for Torn grew, she requested it less and less. And as his love for her grew, he found himself not wanting to do it anymore.

They snuggled and she ran her finger over a scar on his right hand from where it had hit the corner of a guardrail on a mountain road when his bike slid on an oil patch in the middle of a sharp turn. She wasn't there at the time because she didn't like motorcycles, owing to a bad scooter accident her sister had had. She often told him not to ride, but she knew it was one of two things he didn't listen to her about.

Torn couldn't believe how happy he felt. *It must have something to do with getting out of jail*, he thought. He couldn't imagine what it must feel like to have sex after being incarcerated for several years.

Mayumi jumped up and started to pull on some jeans. "Let's get some ramen."

They went to a place nearby with four bar stools in a back alley barely wide enough for a bicycle to pass. Mayumi ordered for them both: two *tonkotsu*, pork bone, ramen; a plate of *gyoza*, dumplings; a bowl of *chahan*, fried rice; a draft beer for her; and a water for Torn.

Both famished, for several minutes the only sounds they made were slurping noises.

Mayumi put down the porcelain spoon she was using to drink soup from the ramen bowl. "Why did you never ask me out when I was at Hilsberry?"

Torn was chewing on *chahan*. "You know I wanted to, but I don't date colleagues."

Mayumi grew up in Niigata Prefecture, north of Tokyo on the Sea of Japan, the younger of two sisters. Her father ran a lumber mill and her mother managed a pet shop. They doted over their older daughter, who had delicate Japanese features: average height, lithe, perfectly white skin, a delicate nose, and a diminutive mouth. She also rarely talked and spoke softly when she did. By contrast, Mayumi was taller, curvier, and darker in complexion with a more prominent nose and a larger mouth with very full lips. Her radiant smile lit up a room like a sunlamp. And she loved to talk and laugh. There was nothing delicate about her.

Her sister was a vision in a kimono, whereas Mayumi's voluptuous figure looked awkward in the traditional Japanese clothing. It wasn't until later when Mayumi, and everyone who saw her, realized how well she filled out a dress. Her parents, believing Mayumi's sister could marry into a prominent family, hired tutors to teach her tea ceremony, calligraphy, and *ikebana*—flower arranging. The more tomboyish Mayumi, who enjoyed sports and spending time in the woods fishing and chasing giant helmet beetles with the boys, was left to find her own way.

Always desperate for her parents' attention, Mayumi excelled at everything she tried. In high school she was first in her class, first chair violin in the orchestra, and captain of the ski team. She was also the first in her family to go to college. She graduated from International Christian University in Tokyo with a degree in economics, followed by a master's degree in business administration from the University of Texas at Austin. She always had a job after moving away from home and paid her way through both ICU and UT. Although fiercely independent, Mayumi was starved for affection and didn't spend much time alone between relationships.

After returning to Japan from Texas, she worked in the Finance Group at Hilsberry & Carter's Tokyo office as a paralegal before being poached by Germanic Bank, where she became head of compliance.

She grabbed the last *gyoza* with her chopsticks. "Why did it take you a year to ask me out after I left?"

Torn's brain started screaming, "DIVE, DIVE, DIVE!" The truth was that he hadn't really thought about asking her out.

"I was married and trying to stay out of trouble. But when I saw you at our Tokyo office twentieth anniversary party, I couldn't resist."

He remembered spying her across the room looking ravishing in her long red dress, lighting up the room with her smile. Fortified with a martini, he had sauntered over and said, "Now that you're not at Hilsberry, I'm free to sexually harass you."

Mayumi had grinned. "Yes, you are, and that would be great."

He had struck gold.

"But even after you talked to me you didn't call me like you said you would. I had to text you."

"Guilty as charged. I apologize but I got buried in a deal."

In fact, at the time Torn still had feelings for his wife, Yukie. She'd given him two beautiful children, taken care of their home, and built her own business. But intimacy hadn't been part of their relationship for some time. He later learned that sexless marriages were not rare in Japan. Something he hadn't signed up for.

A Japanese *bengoshi* friend of Torn's once said *uwaki*, extramarital affairs—the *kanji* literally meant "that floating feeling"—were part of Japanese culture. But he didn't know if he was ready to try the Japanese custom of having a concubine. Mayumi had taken the initiative, however, and texted Torn.

He finished his water. "Frankly, I'm surprised you texted me since you'd just broken up with that other married guy."

"Yeah, I didn't want to date another married man, but I couldn't help myself once I knew you were available. I wanted at least a taste, although I was sure it wouldn't last. To be honest, I thought you were a little out of my league."

Torn paused.

Never shy about what she wanted, Mayumi directed, "This is when you say you're not out of my league, and I couldn't help myself either because you're so beautiful."

Torn laughed.

Her face, slightly red from the beer, tightened. "I'm not joking. Say it."

Torn remembered once early in the relationship when Mayumi had asked, "Are you still sleeping in the same bed with your wife?"

Stupidly, he'd answered, "Yes." Rookie mistake.

Her eyes had bored into him. "Since we started going out?"

He had replied weakly, "Yes, but we don't have sex."

"I don't believe you!" she had screamed. "If you're sleeping in the same bed, you're fucking. I can't believe you would do that!"

"Why? You know I'm married. I don't want to lie to you," he had responded, burying himself deeper.

"All married guys tell me they're not having sex with their wives, and they're not sleeping in the same bed!" she had screamed again.

"Jesus, how many have there been? Anyway, they're lying, probably on both counts, whereas I'm telling you the truth."

"Shut up! I don't give a fuck about the truth. Tell me what I want to hear! Lie to me if you have to."

Still not getting it, he had said, "I don't like to lie."

"You lie to your wife every time you see me! Figure it out. I'll be happier if you lie to me!" She had paused, lowered her voice, and added, "But you must be convincing."

After that, he learned to lie to her when necessary, and over time it became almost second nature. He told himself when he finally made a commitment to one person he would stop lying again, while at the same time getting used to the convenience of being a good liar. He also became better at avoiding situations requiring him to lie. He didn't consider an omission, regardless how material, a lie, even though he counseled clients regularly that the law did.

He smiled. "You're the one who's out of my league. And clearly, I can't resist you. Or leave you. Because you're so beautiful and sexy."

It was her turn to smile. "Very good! You have learned well."

Torn's mind wandered. He thought about how tumultuous their four-year relationship had been.

They broke up many times, only to get back together each time a few weeks later. At one point after breaking up, Torn had wooed Mayumi back by promising to divorce Yukie, but had backed out at the last minute. He told Yukie he was moving out and then moved in with Mayumi for a couple of weeks while finalizing the lease for a new apartment. He would never forget seeing Yukie sitting on her bed in a white-and-black nightgown, her calves pulled up next to her thighs, looking up at him plaintively and waving goodbye.

But Torn started having doubts about the wisdom of jumping into living with someone else. He was unable to sleep when he stayed with Mayumi. So, like a groom leaving the bride at the altar, he told Mayumi the day before they were to move into a new apartment together that he was moving back home because he wanted to try and make it work with Yukie. Like a crazy person trying to do the same thing over and over again but expecting a different result, he thought her excessive drinking and smoking must be his fault and that, if he tried just once more, Yukie would be able to get sober. He was delusional. He had tried many times to help Yukie before he'd met Mayumi, but nothing had worked. Not rehab, not drugs, not counseling. Nothing.

Mayumi was beside herself with sadness and rage. She held Torn in her apartment at knifepoint for several hours. She finally let him go when she realized there was no changing his mind.

Torn's betrayal initially sent Mayumi into a tailspin, but she couldn't stand to be alone. So, she got back on the horse immediately and that very night invited out to dinner another lawyer who'd been pursuing her. She stayed over at his place that night.

Torn moved back home, but Yukie wasn't ready to take him back. Understandably upset, she insisted that he stay in the guest room. She continued sleeping in the master bedroom. But at least he could sleep.

He had naïvely and selfishly assumed Yukie would welcome him back with open arms. He could sleep, but he was lonely, and remained estranged from Yukie emotionally. She did not welcome him back as he had hoped. Instead, she routinely worked late at her company, drank heavily, and sometimes stayed overnight at a hotel. Torn called Mayumi.

Fear of intimacy was one of his core issues, with the reasons for it buried in his subconscious. He was driven by something he didn't understand and therefore couldn't control. He had deeply respected and dearly loved his father. Like many children, he believed his father to be immortal. His sudden death when Torn was sixteen left Torn afraid that those he loved would leave him without warning. His subconscious defense mechanism was to remain emotionally detached, to always assume those close to him would someday leave, to have a backup in case they did, and to be ready to leave first at any hint that he might be abandoned. But it was not a foolproof plan because he empathized with people. He found himself falling in love when he put time and effort into a relationship. He liked to think he could walk away at any time because he had not committed with all of his heart, but he was lying to himself on top of lying to the women he loved.

Mayumi was very happy to hear from Torn despite his devastating betrayal, and she returned to him. At first, she said she was going to continue to date other men. But she was a one-man woman. When he asked if she'd been dating, she had told him everything in great detail about her most recent encounter. Torn wanted to hear details initially because he thought it might help him get over her. But being jealous excited him. She got very turned on, too, so much so that she told him to come over "right now and fuck me." The combination of feeling betrayed, jealous, and titillated excited them like never before.

She lifted the ramen bowl, finished the soup, and wiped her mouth with a small napkin. As if reading his thoughts, she said, "Whenever we break up, I try to think only of your bad points: married with children, arrogant, flaky, and not always available when I want to be with you. And I try to focus on the good points of breaking up: I'm doing the right thing for you and your family, I'm free to do when and what I want, I can focus on my career and finding someone unattached, and I don't have to worry about what you're doing with your wife or, worse, someone else."

All of these things, however, were but like methadone to a heroin addict. They only masked the withdrawal pains without satisfying the addiction. So even as they tried truly to break up many times, they always found their way back to each other.

"That's a lot of ammo. I'm surprised you ever came back."

She frowned. "Me too. But when I date someone new, I remember the feeling of your muscular body on top of me, and the way you treat me like I'm the most important person in the world when we're together. And you're a great listener, have a great face, and most important," she paused dramatically, "you tell me what I want to hear!"

Torn was betwixt and between, but eventually realized the arrangement suited him quite well. He had the security of his long-term relationship with Yukie and the romance with Mayumi. Unfortunately, it took two women for him to get what he wanted from one.

Mayumi finished her beer. "Ya know, I'm doing your wife a service by keeping you happy, which enables you to stay with her, which makes her happy."

"That's a positive spin on what we're doing. But it would be nice to be able to talk to you about my children. They're an important part of me."

"You can't have everything, and you talking about them hurts me because it's a reminder that I can't have all of you."

He wondered how such a dysfunctional relationship had lasted so long.

They returned to her apartment for round two.

After they satisfied each other completely, and as he started to put his shoes on in the foyer, Mayumi, now barefoot and wearing panties and a sheer T-shirt, the outline of her perky nipples clearly visible, asked, "So when're you going to leave your wife?" She had that look again—taut jaw, pursed lips, and angry eyes—the look her face assumed when her border-line personality had crossed the border.

Oh shit, here we go. It was at times like this when his love for her evaporated. The Mayumi of a few minutes ago was gone.

"Mayumi, we've been through this a million times." What he didn't say, and what made him feel like a heel, was that he'd actually moved out two years ago. By the time he finally mustered the courage to move out, he and Mayumi were again on hiatus. They got back together after she'd texted him again. He couldn't bring himself to tell her he was separated because he was worried she would harangue him to death about get-ting married, or at least moving in together. Also, he liked his newfound freedom.

Mayumi looked up at him, cocked her head to one side, and smiled. "OK, just asking."

He knew she was doing everything she could to control her-self, but he needed to leave quickly before she erupted.

He said in the sweetest and most soothing voice he could muster, "Sweetheart, I told you I have a client call with New York tonight. I can't stand leaving you, but the client's a real stickler for punctuality." He knew work was the one excuse Mayumi understood. "I love you. Talk soon," he said, and kissed her on the forehead.

It was like dealing with a different person, and he sometimes literally feared for his life. The only thing to do when she got like this was to leave before things escalated to a bunny boiler level. But he knew if he didn't have a good excuse for going, she'd berate him relentlessly for "leaving so soon" or "after he got what he wanted," resulting in an endless discussion about when it was reasonable for him to leave.

"When?" she asked.

He sighed. "When what?"

"When will we talk?"

"I'll call you tomorrow." He knew that was the only acceptable answer.

He always enjoyed his time with her, but he inevitably felt relieved after leaving. Too much time with Mayumi and he started to suffocate, in part because he knew it was only a matter of time before Evil Mayumi would put in an appearance.

On his way home, Torn fretted about what Mayumi would do if she discovered Saya had been riding on the back of his motorcycle. He'd been able to explain away his stitches as an injury incurred on the rock climbing wall at the gym, but he knew eventually she would learn the truth. He was less concerned about what she'd think when she heard he was being investigated for murder. She actually might find that exciting, even though it was keeping Torn up at night.

Saya

桜彩

"I thought they'd never let you out."

Saya wore just enough makeup to subtly highlight her cheekbones, her small mouth with full lips, and those startling green eyes.

"How do you think I felt? They could've held me for twenty-three days. But whatever you told them helped me get out of there."

Saya and Torn walked in the inner garden at Meiji Jingu, a palatial Shinto shrine in the middle of Tokyo dedicated to the deified spirits of Emperor Meiji and his wife, Empress Shoken. The spaciousness of the grounds and the lush forest belied the fact you were in the middle of a metropolitan area of thirty-five million people. He had expected that they'd meet at his offices as usual, but she'd insisted they meet somewhere outside with lots of green, "because I spend too much time in the lab and the office."

"I just told them what happened. But they didn't seem to want to believe such scary mob-like attacks could take place in Japan. It's evidently easier for them to imagine a foreigner going crazy and killing someone."

He smiled slightly. "It's funny how they view us as foreigners, even though we're both Japanese citizens."

They stopped at a wooden platform overlooking a large pond and surrounded by trees. Small islands of lily pads dotted the pond.

"Yeah, I used to feel schizophrenic in Japan because I was always trying so hard to be 'Japanese,'" she said. "I can be completely American in the US, but I'll never be completely Japanese here. Japanese don't see me that way, for better or worse. But I'm used to it now, and it does have its advantages. Japanese cut me slack sometimes when I'm assertive or aggressive because they think I'm a foreign woman who doesn't know any better."

"I know exactly what you mean, and I play the *gaijin* card from time to time too. In fact, Japanese clients often hire me because I can hook and jab on their behalf with the barbarians in their native English but still consult with them in Japanese. But it can be infuriating to be discriminated against based on something you have no control over, even if it does sometimes work in your favor."

The sun appeared from behind a cloud, and Saya put on her sunglasses. "So what's the next step? Have you heard from the police?"

"No. It's only been three days since I got out, and Saki, my attorney, says it'll take the police a while to complete their investigation and then coordinate with the prosecutor's office to decide next steps. By the way, I should apologize for getting you involved in these crazy attacks. I truly don't know who'd want me dead."

Saya looked at him. He wore a charcoal-gray suit but no tie. He looked both rugged and erudite. The word "swarthy" came to mind because he looked like he spent a lot of time outdoors. She'd never met such a fit lawyer. He had large dark-brown, almost black, eyes and thick, dark-brown, almost black, hair. She could tell that he used to be a pretty boy, but age and more than one mishap had taken their toll. He had a prominent scar across his chin, and although Saya couldn't see it, he had another one on his chest, both from the same skiing accident.

An avalanche had pushed him over a cliff. Landing in a very large Ponderosa pine tree first instead of directly on the ground had saved his life. Otherwise, he would've been buried in snow. There was a price, however. The pointy end of a previously broken branch sticking up at an odd angle pierced his chest. The impact broke the branch and he fell several meters before landing face first on a larger limb, smashing his chin into what at the time resembled hamburger.

Noticing the scar on his hand, which she had seen many times before, Saya smirked. *Must be a klutz.*

At last, she responded, "How do you know it wasn't me they're after? Maybe someone doesn't want my technology commercialized."

Torn looked at a turtle sunning itself on a rock. "Perhaps, but I don't think you're the issue. There was a tracking device on my motorcycle, and they were chasing *me*. They had no way of knowing you'd be on the back."

She turned to look out at the pond. "I'm not so sure. You know how disruptive my technology is."

She was right. Fully recyclable electricity generation and storage far more reliable than wind power and solar power would make all fossil fuels, nuclear power, *and* mainstream renewable energy technology obsolete.

"I can think of many countries, including the US, Russia, Saudi Arabia, and Iran, and energy companies like BP, Shell, China Nuclear, and Canadian Solar, that would be none too pleased to have this technology hit the market."

"Fair point. Remind me again, who knows about the technology?" He knew the answer but wanted to confirm.

"You, my employees, Vince Harden, Eagle Technology Capital, and some other potential investors. But as you well know, I haven't disclosed everything to anyone, even you."

Torn tensed slightly when he heard Vince's name. Vince

kept Torn on edge; he criticized mercilessly one moment and heaped praise the next. Vince was a founding partner in one of the Silicon Valley venture capital firms Saya had visited early on when trying to raise funds. They turned her down. Vince, however, said he wanted to invest in Raijin Clean directly, but only if Saya agreed to transfer all rights to her inventions to Raijin. She had negotiated hard and persuaded him to contribute ten million dollars for a two-and-a-half-percent ownership interest.

Vince was convinced immediately when he saw a demonstration of her lightning technology. He also liked Saya's track record as a serial entrepreneur. She had founded a start-up that developed artificial intelligence to ensure the solar panels used in central receiver solar power plants always pointed at the optimal angle for maximizing the amount of electricity generated. A large Israeli solar company later purchased her company. She used the proceeds from that sale to start Raijin Clean and build the first working lightning generation prototype, the one Vince saw in action.

After Vince invested, Eagle Technology Capital, LLC (ETC) also invested in Raijin, but at a higher valuation, paying fifteen million for the same size equity stake as Vince's. Saya used the proceeds from these two investments to build a larger prototype in the foothills of western Tokyo.

Torn helped her negotiate the higher valuation for the ETC deal. One of the founders of an offshore floating wind farm company had referred Saya to Torn. He hadn't been involved in the negotiations with Vince because Raijin Clean couldn't afford Hilsberry's higher fees at the time. So, she used a smaller local firm in California. Consequently, Torn had never dealt with Vince before the pitch meeting at Wakkanai.

As for the remaining ninety-five percent of the company, ten percent had been put in a stock option plan for management and the employees, leaving company control and eighty-five percent with Saya. Torn knew Saya wouldn't have been able to hold on to eighty-five percent—and more importantly control—of Raijin if her investors didn't believe her technology was transformational.

The other potential investors included Wakkanai Drilling, which Vince recently had introduced to Saya. Wakkanai made oil and gas drilling equipment, including components for oil platforms and derricks, piping, and drill bits. Vince's company, Harden Industries, Inc., had been Wakkanai's exclusive global distributor for thirty years, during which Vince helped Wakkanai significantly expand its business internationally. Because Wakkanai needed help closing Project Ibis—an M&A deal with a value equivalent to Wakkanai's market cap—its Chairwoman, Tamayo Watanabe, had recently appointed Vince as Vice Chairman of the Board solely for the purpose of getting Project Ibis done.

Two other potential investors were Japan's Agency for Natural Resources and Energy and China PV, Inc., the latter controlled by ChinaPetrol Co., Ltd., a Chinese state-owned enterprise (SOE) engaged in the oil and gas business. The "PV" stood for photovoltaic, and CPV was ChinaPetrol's wholly owned subsidiary for investing in renewable energy projects.

She walked closer to Torn. "Still, as I sat there in the police station, I started thinking I need to do something to ensure that my inventions can be developed without me. You never know when something might happen."

A dark cloud shrouded the sun and Torn removed his sunglasses, letting them hang around his neck by the strap. "First, let's focus on your security so you don't have to worry about having someone else commercialize your technology. I suggest you stay away from home until the police find the bad guys."

"As you advised, I'm already in a serviced apartment. I'll stay there until this is over."

"Good. As for the succession issue, the specifications for the machinery are kept in an encrypted memory stick in a safe at your office, right?"

She smiled. "Yes. And, as you know, the only thing I haven't disclosed to you is the formulation of the chemical mixture of active ingredients, the recipe, used to generate lightning, which you recommended I maintain as a trade secret. That information is stored on another encrypted memory stick also in the safe in my office. Only I have the decryption keys, one for each stick. Each person working with me has access to just the component they're working on. I am the only person who knows how to put it all together."

Torn scratched the back of his head. "We've already got patents on the basic technology, and we're working on patenting the various components of the machinery and the patentable aspects of the artificial intelligence technology. If you want to ensure someone can commercialize your technology without your help, you could patent everything and not keep anything as a trade secret, even the chemical mixture of active ingredients or the formulation process."

"How would that help?"

"Patenting an invention means you must disclose it to the public for all to see. In exchange, the patent owner receives a twenty-year exclusive right to exclude others from practicing— which basically means using—the invention. The quid pro quo of patent protection is revealing the invention to the public for the benefit of society. But no public disclosure is necessary for trade secret protection. To the contrary, once the invention has been publicly disclosed, trade secret protection is lost."

She smiled at his being so pedantic and lawyerly. "I know. Like the Coca-Cola recipe. And you recommended I keep the chemical mixture of active ingredients and the formulation process, the most important parts of my lightning generation invention, as a trade secret because trade secrets can last forever as long as they're kept confidential instead of just the twenty years I'd get with patent rights."

"Yes, that was my recommendation. If you patent the chemical mixture and its formulation process, they also will be disclosed to the public for anyone to take advantage of once the patents expire."

"Let me think about it. What about while we're in the process of patenting the inventions? That could take months." She sounded worried.

Torn raised his eyebrows. "Under any other circumstances I'd say you were being paranoid. But given the attempts on our lives, your concerns are well founded, although I continue to think they were after me, not you."

"Why would anyone be after you?"

He laughed. "Well, you've got me there. I've been asking myself the same question and have yet to come up with a good answer."

She folded her arms. "That's what I thought. Anyway, what's your suggestion?"

Torn paused for a long moment as he admired the thick forest on the other side of the pond. He looked back at Saya and walked over to the railing. "First, put an encrypted memory stick containing all of the mechanical inventions you are thinking of patenting into a safe deposit box at a bank. Put another encrypted memory stick containing the active ingredients and the chemical mixture and formulation technology you plan to protect as trade secrets in a second safe deposit box at another bank. Then, put a memory stick containing the decryption keys for those two memory sticks in a safe deposit box at a third bank. That way you can protect all of your inventions *and* compartmentalize the technology you intend to patent separately from what you intend to keep as a trade secret until you decide whether to patent it as well."

Saya asked, "Then what?"

He continued. "There are a couple of options, neither of which is perfect.

"The first option is to give copies of the keys for all three safe deposit boxes to your lawyer with instructions to send the keys to an heir upon your death. You should have a backup heir too, in case the first one dies or becomes incapacitated.

"Or if you think that's not secure enough, the second option is to select three people you trust and give each of them a safe deposit box key, instructing two of them to send the key they hold to the third person upon your death or incapacity. You should also tell the person who will end up with all the keys they'll be the one receiving the other two keys. You'll need backups for each of these three people too, which makes it much more complicated, but more secure, than the first option."

Saya stared into space while rubbing a finger on her lips.

Torn's phone buzzed and Yukie's name appeared on the screen. He ignored it. Even after being separated for more than two years, she still wanted him back and tried to call him regularly. The divorce he wanted couldn't be further from her mind. Yukie's approach to their conversations ran the gamut from indifferent, to polite, to cold, to friendly, to angry. Sometimes she would yell at him, often slurring her words, saying things like he'd ruined her life, he was inconsiderate, he thought only of himself, he was a loathsome human being, she had made him who he was today, he didn't appreciate what she'd done for him, and he treated her like *mono*, goods, instead of like a human being. She often would call back later to apologize profusely. Even if he hadn't been in a meeting, he wouldn't have picked up the phone. They could talk at the dinner she'd invited him to before their children had read him the riot act.

Torn continued. "The problem with the first option is that it relies on one person. The problem with the second option is that at least one of the three people could lose a key."

"Which is better?"

"I prefer the first option because a trusts and estates lawyer will have experience handling such sensitive matters, will owe you a fiduciary duty, and will keep the safe deposit box keys in a safe place. And if he or she is at a law firm, you are ensured that they will have a successor in the event your lawyer dies, retires, or otherwise becomes unavailable."

"Hmmm. Thank you for these ideas. Let me think about this a little more."

He walked Saya to the subway station. On the way, they discussed the upcoming negotiations with CPV. He glanced down at her long legs but checked himself. He couldn't believe he was even thinking about hitting on someone, particularly a client, when he was in such deep shit.

After dropping Saya off at the station, Torn grabbed a cab. On his way back to the office, he texted Mak. "Circuit loop tomorrow? I'll bring the other bike."

Mak responded immediately with a thumbs-up emoji.

Torn then sat back and looked at the lights of the city while marveling at how fortunate he was to be alive and out of jail. Little did he know how much his life was about to be turned upside down.

The Wheel

ルーレット

"Ride it like you stole it," Torn said, speaking into the helmet's mic.

"Don't worry about me, bud. Just keep your eyes on the road."

There was just enough traffic to make things interesting.

Focused on the task at hand, and oblivious to the stunning *Blade Runner*–like views of the illuminated city at night, Torn banked hard. Sparks flew when he scraped the bottom of his left foot peg on the asphalt. As the two lanes of the narrow elevated expressway snaked into a right curve, he countersteered into the right lane by pushing the right handlebar to tip the bike right. He didn't understand why people found the concept of countersteering so difficult to understand, even though they instinctively did it when riding a bicycle.

Mak fell behind on his Yamaha V-Max 1200, a beautiful red, black, and chrome muscular bike not known for being nimble in the curves.

Torn's bike straightened up as he accelerated out of the curve, and he found himself almost on top of a slow-moving truck. Braking hard, he pushed the left handlebar out to immediately countersteer into the left lane. Then he leaned right into another curve, scraping his right foot peg. Exiting the curve, he sped down a short straightaway, the reverberation from the expressway walls making his screaming engine sound like some giant metallic predator.

"Come on, son. Let's go!" Torn was laughing. It felt great being back on a bike. He'd been concerned he might be afraid of riding again, but if anything, he was more confident in his riding than before the attacks. He'd pushed the envelope, and he and Saya had survived.

"I'm comin', I'm comin'," Mak said.

As Torn sped up to 150 on a straightaway, the distinctive headlight of Mak's V-Max appeared in the mirrors of Torn's BMW K 1600 GTL. He then lost sight of Mak again as the road dropped into one of the many tunnels on the Circuit, a 14.8-kilometer circle at the center of the labyrinth known as the Tokyo Metropolitan Expressway system.

The narrow lanes, claustrophobically close walls, intermittent wet surfaces, numerous junctions connecting other expressways, constantly merging and exiting traffic, up-and-down winding shape and feel of the road surface, which at points rose above and at other points dipped below ground level, frequent merging of two lanes into one, numerous steep on- and off-ramps with poor visibility, and constant changes in lighting combined to make the Circuit a road not to be trifled with on a motorcycle or even in a car, particularly at speeds exceeding 100 kilometers an hour.

But it was precisely the complicated nature and roller-coaster feel of the Circuit that made it so popular with car and motorcycle enthusiasts wanting to test their driving skills. Called the *Ruretto-zoku*, the Roulette Tribe, because of their affinity for racing around the Circuit like a ball on a roulette wheel, they gathered at certain nearby parking areas to meet, compare rides, and prepare to race.

Heart pounding, Torn straightened up and accelerated again as he came out of the curve. Then he weaved in and out of traffic while listening to only the engine. No music. He could tell from the sound it was performing beautifully. No coughs or hesitations.

As the road straightened out briefly after exiting a tunnel, he spied Mak in his mirrors, closing in on him.

"Not so fast, brother," Torn teased as he increased speed.

"It's just a matter of time," Mak responded, laughing. He always enjoyed immensely his monthly rides, each different, with Torn.

Torn heard the loud sounds of modified car engines and saw the spoilers of two sports cars jockeying for position up ahead. He throttled up to catch them. They all ran into merging traffic at the next junction.

Mak pulled in behind Torn on the inside of the right lane. Torn, on the outside, heard the roar of Mak's bike.

"Jesus, dude, could those pipes be any louder?" Torn was laughing again.

"Loud pipes save lives," Mak responded, also laughing.

Torn was behind one of the sports cars now. The other one cruised in the left lane. They all dropped into a narrow and winding tunnel.

The sports car in the right lane raced ahead with Torn close on its bumper. He banked left into a curve, looking for an opening to pass.

Seeing that Torn was too far left, Mak yelled, "Don't forget there's water on..."

Too late. Torn's rear tire hit the perennial wet spot from a leak in the tunnel ceiling. Rookie mistake. When the back wheel hydroplaned on the wet surface, he felt the sickening feelings of sliding and weightlessness as he started to separate from the bike. With Mak close behind in the same lane and the second sports car slightly behind him in the left lane, this was no time to be sliding on asphalt. Not to mention that being stopped at high speed by a wall would not do a body good. Luckily, the heavy bike righted itself as the back tire caught the dry pavement on the water's edge.

Breaking into a cold sweat, he felt somewhat sick to his stomach.

"Whoa, keep the rubber side down, bro!" Mak exclaimed.

"Fuck me," was all Torn could muster in response.

"Let's get some coffee."

Torn let Mak lead as they drove over the Rainbow Bridge and headed south to the giant Daikoku Parking Area in Yokohama to check out the machines staging to run the Circuit. Torn noticed for the first time that evening the breathtaking views around him, including the bright lights of the bridge, the reflection of the moon on Tokyo Bay, and the lights of the massive Odaiba Ferris Wheel. He also noticed some soreness in his injured arm from moving his body around the bike like a spider as he repositioned his weight over and over to navigate the bike more effectively through each turn and slalom. But he was more concerned about his sloppy driving.

He blew into the parking area blasting Led Zeppelin's "Misty Mountain Hop." But his loud music had less shock value among the car and bike aficionados, all of whom were used to hearing blaring music and loud engines at rest stops late at night. He generally received more attention during the day when rest stops were populated with "civilians." Torn enjoyed the attention, positive or negative, as do all motorcyclists who blare loud music or have loud pipes or both.

He pulled into a car parking spot next to Mak's.

Mak dismounted and removed his helmet. "That was awesome, but I thought you were gonna eat it there for sure." He was a large, tanned, second-generation Japanese American from Hawaii with long dark hair, a thick salt-and-pepper beard, no neck, and bushy eyebrows. He wore a sleeveless black shirt and black unbuttoned leather vest. His gorilla-like arms were covered with tattoos a master Japanese tattoo artist had done the old-fashioned way, by hand. The tattoos didn't hide the veins in his arms; they only accentuated them. He wore weathered black leather chaps over faded and torn blue jeans, with a chain connecting his belt to the leather wallet in his back pocket. His belt buckle was a large skull and crossbones. He wore giant black riding boots and fingerless black leather gloves.

Mak had worked for the FBI in Washington, DC before the CIA recruited and stationed him in Russia and, later, Japan. After several years in the CIA, he joined Longstreth. Torn and Mak met through a mutual friend who played in Mak's band, the Big Mak Attack, which, despite the corny name, had a good following in Japan.

Growing up Asian in the US, Mak knew all about being a minority, and as an American he didn't completely fit into Japan either. Torn and Mak had hit it off immediately.

"You and me both. Serious pucker factor on that one."

They walked to a vending machine, bought hot coffees, and started walking around the parking area, eyeing the cars and other motorcycles. Mak took a sip and asked, "Hey man, you look even more stressed than usual. Shouldn't you take a break?"

"Can't. Too much going on. I gotta find out who's after me. And I still have that police investigation hanging over my head. It's creepy not knowing who's after you or whether the police are going to arrest you again." He paused, then: "I assume you found nothing?"

"Most of it you already know."

"Like what?"

"Well, Saya is clean. Normal parents but divorced. Brainiac. Successful entrepreneur. Founded Raijin Clean four years ago.

"Vince is the founder of Harden Industries, which represents several manufacturers of drilling, mining, and oil-related equipment. They seem very excited about a proposed new project off the coast of Russia's Sakhalin Island called the

Northern Okhotsk Project. The plan calls for at least three oil rigs in the Sea of Okhotsk. It would supply oil and natural gas to China, Korea, and Japan, and include a new pipeline for oil and natural gas to be piped from Aniva Bay on Sakhalin all the way to Tokyo. Estimated cost: twenty-five billion dollars. Harden Industries has been selling mining and oil and gas equipment in the Russian Far East, which is rich in natural resources, for some time. So, getting involved in this project would be a no-brainer for them.

"Eagle Technology Capital is a California venture capital firm, but other than Raijin Clean they have no investments in Japanese companies."

"So, what don't I know?"

Mak scratched his beard. "Well, Taniguchi's a straight shooter. Good family man. He's famous among the police for rebuilding his parents' home in Fukushima that the tsunami had destroyed. Taniguchi lives by the judo code of honesty, honor, respect, self-discipline, yada, yada, yada. He's a badass who follows the book, but he's hard to read. Dare I say inscrutable?" Mak leaned in and lifted an eyebrow when he said "inscrutable" and Torn laughed. "My Japanese informant's word, not mine. Because of Taniguchi's experience and track record, prosecutors defer to him a lot. My guess is he'll decide whether to bring charges against you."

Torn sipped his coffee. "That makes sense. Let's discuss next steps. First, look into Wakkanai Drilling and Tamayo Watanabe, the *shacho* and chair. Evidently, she inherited the business from her father, the founder. Are they involved in that Northern Okhotsk Project?

"Second, look into China PV. It's controlled by the Chinese government through ChinaPetrol. Why do they want to invest in Raijin Clean?

"Third, find out why Japan's Agency for Natural Resources and Energy is interested in Raijin Clean. Same reason or reasons as the Chinese government?"

He added, almost as an afterthought, "And finally, why would Vince be interested in acquiring Wakkanai? Is there some hidden value there?"

"You got it," Mak replied.

Torn stopped to look at a futuristic-looking Bimota Tesi 3D RaceCafe. "Enough about my problems. It must've been fun playing Budokan to a packed house. Did you get mobbed by groupies?"

Mak laughed. "Yes, but groupies aren't all they're cracked up to be. I should know, I'm dating one!"

"And a beautiful one at that. Tell Yuka hello for me."

"Will do. How about you? What's going on in your two-timing world?"

"Almost got busted the other day. Mayumi called when I was with Kiwako, and I had stupidly left my phone on. Mayumi's name pops up, so of course Kiwako asks who she is. Had to do some fast talking about how Mayumi was at the firm but now is at a bank we're pitching for work, which is true, but I could tell Kiwako was wondering why she was calling so late."

"Oh what a tangled web we weave. Nothing against Mayumi, but she's not right for you. Kiwako, on the other hand, now she is someone you could settle down with. Lots in common. Close in age. Two children. Divorced. Bilingual. An adult. Not some crazy psycho."

"Mayumi's not a psycho."

"Just crazy? Anyway, she's not exactly a model of stability. I like her, but your relationship has had more ups and downs than a yo-yo. And you don't want to end up like that banker whose wife killed him and then spent the day going round and round on the Yamanote Line holding a box with his head in her lap."

"But Kiwako is gone for long periods of time. Long-distance relationships are hard."

"Be careful what you wish for. You might change your tune if she's around all the time. Besides, you know the drill when it comes to 'international' relationships."

"Point taken. It does give me some freedom and makes it easier to juggle the two of them."

"Damned straight. And you're only getting away with this shit because we're in Japan."

"What do you mean?"

"Tokyo is a tiny dating market for accomplished bilingual women."

Mak was right. The pool of prospects for a relationship could be quite small for Japanese women straddling two cultures, because there weren't many men who understood or appreciated them. Domestic Japanese men often weren't interested—and vice versa—and there were relatively few non-Japanese and half-Japanese men in Japan. It was even harder if their job took them back and forth between two countries like Japan and the US, or they were working in a non-Japanese company while living in Japan.

"It's the same for guys like us," Torn said defensively.

"No, it's not. We're more open to being with a Japanese woman who knows little about the US because we're living in Japan. Mayumi and Kiwako would not put up with your shit if they had more options. And Kiwako's options are particularly limited because she spends half her time in Japan and half in the US, is older, and has two kids.

"On top of that, you're culture arbitraging. Like those white guys who come to Japan to teach English and stay forever because they're semi-celebrities in some small town in Japan and can get more women than they ever could in the US just because they're a rare commodity. They call it the

Japan Disease because, after staying in Japan where they can easily make enough money to live and getting girls is easy, they find themselves in their thirties and too soft to go back to the real world."

"I'm not white."

"Indeed. You're half and have dual citizenship. That makes you even more rare and exotic. Your stock is already high because you're a partner at a global law firm and have options as to where you could live and work. Being half in addition to that makes you a superhero in this market."

Torn smirked. "And here I thought it was because I was so attractive as a person. And I'm a good listener!"

"You keep telling yourself that, buddy, but you better hope they don't find out about each other. Mayumi may finally dump your ass this time if she doesn't kill you first. And Kiwako definitely won't put up with it."

They walked over to a blue and black Kawasaki Vulcan 2000.

Torn was talking about the one he used to own when Mak asked, "By the way, have you ever dated a non-Japanese woman?"

Torn smiled. "Western women have asked me that question too. Yeah, sure. It's not like I have yellow fever. It's just the market in which we operate. Most of the women in town are Japanese. So, most of the women I've dated are Japanese."

Mak said, "I've often thought it'd be harder for me to date an Asian from a country other than Japan than to date an American. I know American and Japanese culture, but the cultures in other Asian countries are just too foreign to me, and I'm too old to start learning all over again. But, of course, women can be persuasive and I try to keep an open mind."

Torn laughed. "That's big of you."

"Yup, that's me. Mr. Equal Opportunity."

They finished their coffees and started walking back to the vending machine where the only trash can in the immaculate parking area was located, next to recycling bins for cans, glass bottles, PET bottles, and paper products.

Torn asked, "Are you still doing judo at the Tokyo Metropolitan Police Department?"

"Yes indeed. I'm a fifth-degree black belt now. I've been doing judo with those guys for years, and they're a tough crowd. But they made me meaner than any of them."

"How'd they do that?"

"Well, for the first three months I went there, they kept calling me trash and screaming at me to quit. Maybe they didn't like the tats. And when I first did judo with them, they were much stronger and always dragged me off the mats and threw me down on the surrounding concrete floor or on the wooden veranda outside. I got so scared that I would actually be shaking before each practice. But I just kept going back until I became so mean no one wanted to practice with me. They became respectful. Over the years, some of them became friends. We've even worked together on some things."

Torn looked at Mak for a moment. "Why didn't you ever tell me that before?"

"You never asked. So, how're Sean and Sophia?"

"They're good. Still referring to you as 'Uncle Mak.'"

"They're good kids. Don't screw it up."

They walked back to their bikes.

Mak looked over at Torn's BMW. "Such a beautiful machine. Why don't you ride it more?"

"I like the look and feel of the 1200 better, even though it's an older model."

Mak had a slight smirk on his face. "By the way, didn't you tell me your seats are heated?"

Torn swelled with pride and walked right into Mak's trap. "Why, yes, they are. The grips are too. You turn on the heaters for each seat by pressing these buttons here." He touched two tiny levers under the seat. "The driver and passenger seats have separate buttons so they can control their own heat." He pointed to the right handlebar. "The button for the grip heaters is here. There're five levels."

"Very cool. So, with all those fancy accessories, gadgets, and functions on your bike, where do ya keep the microwave oven?"

"Fuck you, Mak."

They both laughed. It would be a long time before Torn felt this relaxed again.

Sino-Japanese Relations

日中関係

Saya smiled and held out her hands with the palms up. "I want to welcome you all to Japan. We look forward to working with you and China PV to structure a transaction that is a win for both parties and allows Raijin to develop its technology in a manner consistent with its goals and obligations to its shareholders. As you know, we are very confident Raijin's technology will revolutionize the energy market."

As Torn suggested, he and Saya sat facing the opposite wall of a conference room. Behind them a panoramic view of the vast Tokyo metropolitan area extended to the mountain range in the west. The hope was that the China PV team, which sat facing the windows, would be distracted during the negotiations by the spectacular view.

Janet Wang, China PV's outside counsel, spoke fluent English with a clipped Chinese-British hybrid sort of Singaporean accent. "My client agrees that the technology is very promising and has the potential to benefit people around the world. CPV also believes each party should strive to negotiate a win-win transaction."

"Great. You have our term sheet, but before we get into CPV's comments, I'll let Torn summarize our thinking." Saya looked at Torn and smiled.

Torn set the stage for the negotiations when he'd first entered the room. After exchanging pleasantries with Saya, he quickly and deliberately extended his hand to the very tanned

Ms. Wang. She seemed somewhat surprised he'd approached her first, because protocol called for Torn to first introduce himself to Mr. Li, the most senior person on the CPV team. Torn, however, deliberately avoided doing so because he wanted the negotiations to be handled efficiently in a direct American manner. To emphasize that he expected the discussions to be handled in that way, he handed his business card to her with one hand without formality and enthusiastically welcomed her to Japan. Quickly regaining her composure, she responded that she loved Japan and came often from Singapore to ski and visit Japan's ubiquitous *onsen*, hot springs.

To demonstrate to the two Chinese from CPV that he knew how to behave as was expected in Japan, his native American English and Western mannerisms notwithstanding, he was much more formal when exchanging business cards with them than he'd been with Janet. He went through the entire process of holding his card by the corners with both hands, looking them in the eye when exchanging the cards, feigning great interest in these small pieces of paper containing their professional information and asking pertinent questions about their titles and offices.

Torn was most interested in Mr. Li's decision-making authority, which he knew probably was limited because ChinaPetrol, CPV's majority shareholder, likely called the shots. Still, he assumed Mr. Li could approve an initial investment of ten million dollars. Also, he couldn't have cared less about where CPV's offices were, but protocol demanded he show a genuine interest in each person he met, and talking about their office location was an easy way to accomplish that. Thus, at one point, he had looked at Mr. Li's card intently, smiled, then looked Mr. Li in the eye and said, "Oh, Mr. Li, I see that your offices are in Shanghai. We have an office near the Bund."

Mr. Li smiled and responded slowly, almost painfully, slightly off point in stilted English. "Yes, we located only two... a half hours from Japan but this my first visit. I like view very much."

After the introductions, they sat down, with Mr. Li sitting across from Saya and Janet sitting across from Torn. CPV's in-house counsel, a woman in her late 20s, sat next to Janet and let her do all the talking.

Torn sat up straight with his hands on the conference room table. "I understand Raijin has conducted a demonstration of the technology for CPV and some of its shareholders. I also understand that, after another demonstration tomorrow, as the next step CPV wishes to test the technology in its laboratory using Raijin's mini-prototype."

Janet nodded. "Yes, that's correct."

"Our concern is that CPV's testing of the system could interfere with Raijin's ability to complete the patenting of its technology. Some of the technology is already patented, and we expect to file the remaining patent applications within the next six months.

"Therefore, as the term sheet provides, Raijin is willing to permit CPV to test the technology once the remaining patent applications have been filed, assuming Raijin hasn't granted exclusivity to another party. If, however, your client wishes to secure the exclusive right to test the technology and have a right of first negotiation for three months..." He paused for effect. "That will cost CPV ten million US dollars. Raijin believes this is fair consideration for an exclusive right to test the technology and a right of first negotiation for a license to such transformative technology."

Mr. Li said something in Chinese to Janet Wang before she had a chance to interpret what Torn had said. Clearly, Mr. Li understood much more English than his spoken English would have one believe.

Janet put a finger to her lips. The red fingernail extended above her upper lip almost to her septum. "Now I know why you suggested the right of first negotiation in the term sheet. But the risk is low because you've already got patents on the basic technology."

Torn leaned back in his chair. "You acknowledge there's a risk, and we don't believe it's low. It's like rabies: If you get bitten by a dog, you probably won't get rabies, but if you do and it's not treated before symptoms manifest themselves, you die. Same with patents. Disclosure may or may not be a problem, but by the time you find out, it's too late to fix it."

"But ten million dollars is a lot of money for a right of first negotiation."

Torn looked at Saya and then back at Janet. "The alternative would be to go to a straight license for a twenty-five-million-dollar up-front fee plus a running royalty."

"No. Our client wishes to test it first."

Torn leaned forward. "I personally question whether any such testing is necessary at all. I've told Saya already I think even considering it is being too generous."

Janet ignored his comment. "I assume it's refundable?"

"No. It needs to be nonrefundable given that we'd be locking up the technology for several months. We would ask the same of any potential licensee."

"It would be a right of first negotiation for a worldwide license?"

Torn nodded. "Yes, that's what Raijin is proposing. I apologize if that wasn't clear."

Janet looked down at her tablet. "Sorry. I see you have 'worldwide' here in the term sheet. Assuming CPV were to agree to this, and to be clear, they haven't yet, three months is too short. We would want a year to negotiate."

He looked at Saya, who said, "I think that we could agree to six months. If the parties are making real progress at the end of six months, we would continue the discussions. But one year is too long to lock up our technology." Saya and Torn were in sync.

Janet seemed relieved. "China PV probably can live with that, but we'll need to confirm internally."

"Of course."

Then she added, "Also, we'll want a month to test the technology."

Torn laughed heartily and slapped his knee for added effect. "You want time to reverse engineer it even before you receive a license? As noted in the term sheet, we can agree to one day of testing. Saya or another representative from Raijin will be present at all times during testing."

Janet pursed her lips. "Torn, that's offensive to my client. No, China PV doesn't intend to copy the technology. It just wants enough time to thoroughly test it."

He leaned back with a smirk. "Look, Janet, the technology either works or it doesn't. One day is more than long enough for testing. In fact, Mr. Li can confirm the technology works tomorrow at the demonstration." Saya remained stone-faced although every fiber of her being wanted to agree to a month, or indeed agree to anything, to get the money in the door. The only thing holding her back was her trust in Torn.

"Well, we'll need to discuss internally how much time CPV needs for testing. But do not accuse my client of being a thief."

From Janet's indignant tone, Torn suspected the negotiations weren't going quite how she'd envisioned. He leaned forward. "You can think about it all you want, but one day is eminently reasonable. And I'm not accusing anyone of anything. It was a question. Unless you can provide a reasonable explanation why CPV needs more than a day, let alone an entire *month*, to 'test' the technology"—he added air quotes with his fingers when he said "test"—"we have no choice but to assume the worst."

Mr. Li leaned over and said something to Janet in Chinese.

She looked up and took a deep breath. "China PV will consider the appropriate amount of consideration, but it would be easier for it to agree to ten million if instead of a right of first negotiation, it can subscribe for shares in Raijin."

Torn sat back and put the back end of his pen to his lips. He and Saya had discussed this issue in advance and this was her cue. "That's an interesting point. I discussed the possibility of CPV making an investment in Raijin recently with our tax advisor. She indicated that issuing shares in exchange for the ten million dollars may be better for Raijin from a tax perspective. However, it raises valuation issues we'll need to consider internally."

Janet looked at Mr. Li and then back at Saya. "China PV understands that. How much of a valuation are you considering?"

"Pre-money, one billion dollars," Saya said without hesitation. Although she believed Raijin Clean was worth at least that much, she could say it with a straight face only because Torn had made her practice.

Janet gasped and Mr. Li straightened up to listen more carefully, not sure if he'd heard right. Now it was Janet's turn to sit back and fold her arms. "That's ridiculous. We'd get only one percent of Raijin for ten million?"

Torn smiled and put his hands on the table. "And that's a great deal, Janet, given the nature of the technology. An argument could be made that the company is worth multiples of that. Keep in mind, CPV's primary goal has been to receive a license and not to invest in the equity of Raijin."

Torn was thinking to himself how well prepared he and Saya were. They'd taken the time to discuss in advance the various possible twists and turns the discussions could take and how to choreograph the negotiations.

"Yes, but the terms need to be fair," Janet said somewhat plaintively.

Saya smiled. "They will be. For its ten million, CPV will receive convertible preferred shares, just as Raijin's other investors have, *and* a license for an up-front license fee of an additional fifteen million and a running royalty."

"What about a convertible note?"

Saya looked at Torn, who replied gently, "Well, Raijin would consider a convertible loan that CPV could either forgive as partial consideration for the up-front license fee or convert into common shares of Raijin at the then-effective valuation."

"What do you mean, 'partial consideration?'"

"Stop being coy, Janet. The up-front license fee has always been twenty-five million. Ten million is just for the right of first negotiation."

Janet swallowed and replied, "CPV never agreed to twenty-five million." Mr. Li touched her arm and looked at her. Janet said, "We'll consider that."

Mr. Li again said something to Janet in Chinese.

"Mr. Li is ready to see what his colleagues have been raving about." Janet sounded somewhat relieved that the negotiations were over for now.

Saya said, "Great. Then let's meet at 9:00 a.m. tomorrow."

Baggage

荷物

"Let's talk about something festive, like our divorce." God, he wanted a drink.

They had been eating mostly in silence at a French restaurant in Roppongi Hills. He'd almost canceled after the expressway attacks, but he hadn't seen Yukie in more than a year, and the kick in the pants from his children gave him even more reason to want to move the divorce discussions forward. When he actually saw her, however, he'd suffered a panic attack and almost left.

Yukie, looking tired and drinking even more than usual, stopped mid-chug. "Torn, you know I don't want to discuss that." She held in her other hand a lit cigarette, smoke rising from the tip in a series of curls.

As usual, he was drawn in by her huge dark eyes that reminded Torn of a Japanese anime character. Her eyes were so large that he once told her she had cow eyes. He'd meant it as a compliment, but she'd found it hilarious.

They always spoke in Japanese because Yukie didn't particularly like speaking English.

He brushed a nonexistent piece of lint off his pants. "Well, this current state of limbo is not good for either of us. I want to move forward, and I'm sure you do too."

"Torn, you promised we wouldn't talk about this when you asked me to dinner. I'm fine with the way things are."

Torn put his fork down and leaned in. "Yukie, I made no such promise... and you're the one who asked me to dinner."

She quaffed her second full glass of wine. "Whatever. I distinctly remember you suggested it. But you'll probably just say I must've been drinking at the time and then forgot!" Several people at surrounding tables turned to look at them.

He suppressed the urge to ask, "Would I be wrong?" Instead, he responded, "That's not fair. I haven't brought up your drinking once tonight. Although now that you mention it..." His voice trailed off and he decided not to remind her she'd already had two Tom Collins before she'd ordered a bottle of wine for herself.

Yukie sat back in her chair. "I'm sorry for raising my voice. I know things can't go back to the way they were."

"I don't think either of us would want them to. We were miserable and fighting all the time."

"We didn't fight that much. And I was happy," she said softly, almost in a whisper, while looking at the wineglass she had again filled to the top.

"Well, I wasn't, and it's not sustainable unless we're both happy. Look, I waited to file until recently because I was hoping we could do this amicably."

She stiffened. The "until recently" was not lost on her, but she didn't want to inquire further. Denial was one of Yukie's strengths, and the divorce papers had yet to be served on her. "I have no intention of divorcing you because I don't believe in it. More importantly, you—and only you—live in my heart. There's no substitute. I can't just stop loving you and move on."

He sipped his sparkling water. "Well, it's a process. It's not easy for me either."

"I understand you feel you can't move back. But can you please give me more time?" She took another drag on her cigarette and blew smoke across the table, waving her other hand through the noxious stream, as if that would make it go away. "Sorry."

"How much more time do you need? I don't think this is about time, Yukie." *You're just holding me hostage*, he wanted to add, but didn't.

She looked down at her napkin and replied slowly, "I don't know, Torn. But I think our priority should be Sean and Sophia. A long drawn-out litigation wouldn't be good for them."

"I agree. That's precisely why we should settle amicably and move on. That would be better for everyone than this current purgatory."

"Speak for yourself. I'm happy being the international lawyer's wife, even if you aren't around. I'm proud of our accomplishments and don't want to be the sad, lonely divorcée." She emptied the wine bottle, turned it upside down in the ice bucket, and took another long draught from her glass.

"So, being sad and lonely is acceptable as long as you remain married?"

She looked at him over the top of her glass. "Torn, don't be mean. Can we *please* talk about something else?"

As he sat looking into her eyes, memories of their early romance came rushing back to him. He thought again what a shame it was that it hadn't worked out. *If she weren't such a raging alcoholic, it could've worked*, he thought for the millionth time. And he hated it when she smoked; it gave her bad breath and she always seemed to be coughing or complaining about an ulcer that never seemed to go away, and the secondhand smoke made him cough, too, and got into everything around her.

"Sure."

She looked down, and he stared at the plant behind her.

Yukie finally broke the silence. "So, I hurt my back trying to dig a tree root out of the garden."

"Are you all right?" He was genuinely concerned. He wanted her happy and healthy. The idea of divorcing her when she was ill made him feel even more guilty and she knew it. And he knew she knew.

Sounding melodramatic, she said, "It's nothing. I've returned to work and can walk the dog again. Not that you care."

What happened to her fearlessness? Nothing used to faze her. When did she become such a victim? Do I turn women into victims? he thought to himself. More silence.

"So, how's Sean? I haven't heard from him in a while." Torn was failing miserably at sounding cheerful.

"Reiji?" she asked.

He rolled his eyes. Yukie knew perfectly well he was talking about their son, but she always insisted on calling her children by their Japanese names.

"He's OK. I rarely talk to him because he's living in the dorm and seems to be studying all the time or doing *iaido*," a Japanese sword-fighting martial art.

Torn chuckled. "That's not all he's doing. He seems to be dating a lot too."

Yukie looked down at her hands. "He doesn't tell his mother those things."

"Because he knows you won't like anyone he dates."

"That's not true. I keep an open mind."

Torn looked sideways and said in a more sarcastic tone than intended, "That's not his view, given the way you treated his last girlfriend."

Yukie continued to look down. "She's not a nice person."

"I liked her. Perhaps you didn't approve of her because she was dating your precious son."

Yukie came from an old samurai family, the Ishikawas. They traced their lineage back a thousand years. One prominent ancestor had been a *Hatamoto*, a "guardian of the banner," a retainer in direct service to the Tokugawa shogunate of feudal Japan. He had ruled over an obscure region of northern

Honshu, the largest Japanese island. Although she thought of herself as a modern liberated woman, Yukie was quite traditional in some ways, including being a walking Japanese stereotype of the possessive mother who thinks no woman is good enough for her son.

Yukie was about to cry. "He's *our* precious son! Torn, are you trying to start a fight?"

He held up a hand. "No, no. I'm sorry. I just don't want to see you cut out of his life because you're intolerant of his girlfriends. It's his life and his choices."

She sat up straight and looked him in the eyes. "He's nineteen! I'm his mother—I have a right to express my opinion."

Torn took a deep breath and responded calmly, "Sometimes less is more. He's not stupid and will find his own way. My mother told me she intentionally held her tongue when she disapproved of my girlfriends because she knew it would drive me straight into their arms."

Yukie didn't take the bait. "I'm not your mother."

Torn smiled. "Thank God."

"Torn!"

"Sorry, that was uncalled for."

Just in the nick of time, the waiter asked if they'd like dessert. Torn declined and Yukie ordered a cognac.

She took a drag on her latest cigarette and stubbed it out. She exhaled to the side in an effort to keep the smoke out of his face.

Torn asked, "And how's Sophia?"

"Haruka?"

He was so annoyed at Yukie's intentional obtuseness that all he could do was nod affirmatively.

"She's doing well. You should know. You saw her over the weekend, didn't you?"

"I know. Just checking."

Yukie lit another cigarette. "She's getting so tall. And I don't like her doing kendo. It's not ladylike. I'd rather have her do tea ceremony and *ikebana*," flower arrangement. "They're refined."

He was surprised that Yukie, who used to fashion herself a modern and unconventional Japanese woman, would criticize their daughter for diligently pursuing a passion. "Well, she's been doing kendo since junior high, was captain of the kendo team in high school, is captain of her kendo team at college, and is great at it. Her coach said she is the best he's ever trained. There's little downside to being athletic and good at a martial art, particularly for a girl. Besides, it's better that she channel her energy through a disciplined marshal art than beating bullies to a pulp on the playground like she used to do in grade school. And if Sean can do *iaido*, why can't Sophia do kendo?" Sophia was quite accomplished at *iaido*, too, but *iaido* is more of a refined art like aikido rather than a sport.

One might say that the Japanese invented helicopter parenting, although they never called it that, and the coddling and over-protectiveness drove Torn nuts. He felt it suffocated children and prevented them from becoming creative and independent. But he also felt guilty for leaving his kids with their alcoholic mother, because it had just made things worse. After he left, Yukie clung to them more as a crutch for herself than to protect them.

"Well, I don't like it. She's almost as tall as Reiji and so muscular. It's fine for Reiji to do it. He's a man."

"Don't be ridiculous," he sneered. "It's the twenty-first century. She's beautiful, smart, and tough. As her father, I don't even want to think about the men who must be interested in her."

Yukie replied, "You're *oyabaka*," a crazy parent who can't think objectively about his children.

The waiter brought the cognac.

Torn took a deep breath as the waiter walked away. "Is it money that you're worried about? If it's money, I'm sure we can work something out. Your lifestyle won't change." It was abrupt, but Torn was tired of the Kabuki theater.

"What do you mean?"

He threw his napkin on the table. "Come on, Yukie, let's stop wasting each other's time!"

"No. Money's not the issue. You've been more than generous, including paying the mortgage and the children's tuition, and I know you'd do the right thing if we got divorced."

"Well, thank you for acknowledging my generosity."

"I mean it. I have my own income, yet you continue to pay for everything. I appreciate it."

He paused and thought of something. "Have you even told the neighbors or your employees about our separation?"

"No, they think you're in the US on business."

He smirked. "That's some business trip."

She again looked like she was about to cry. "Very funny, Torn. I'm not ready to decide and it needs to be my decision. How many times do I need to say it? And you know how people feel about divorce in Japan. It's not like the US." She paused. "Anyway, you know you can't win in court if I refuse to divorce."

He sighed. She was right, at least for now. Japan was not a no-fault jurisdiction. His lawyer had said that unless Yukie agreed to a divorce, he would need to wait at least six more years before a Japanese court would grant him a divorce. He was hoping the act of filing would convince her how much he wanted a clean break.

"We'll see. We're not functioning as a couple and should move on."

She put a hand on her forehead and looked down. "Gosh. I'm just asking for a little more time!"

He almost spat out the water he was drinking. "You've already had more than two years!" He was trying not to yell, but several heads again turned to look at them.

"Don't yell at me. It can take more than two years to recover from the death of a close relative. I feel like I'm experiencing the same thing."

"I'm not dead."

"Perhaps that's worse."

"So now you wish I were dead?"

"Torn, leave me alone." She started crying and excused herself to the washroom.

After returning, she took out a pack of cigarettes, lit one with her lighter, took a deep drag on it, and said, smoke coming out of her mouth and nose, "You seem happy, work's going well, and you have plenty of time to ride your motorcycle and fly fish. Isn't that enough? What more do you want?"

She picked up the snifter of cognac. "You know, we could've worked things out if you'd just told me what you wanted after the first time you moved out."

He felt like he was in the Twilight Zone. It was all he could do to remain calm. "I did. But you wouldn't even let me sleep in the same bed."

She shouted, "No! You never asked for my permission or said you wanted to change. Or I would've worked with you!" People were looking at them again.

"That's simply not true. You never think you're wrong or need to change. Your definition of 'work things out' is that I change into what you want."

"Torn, my heart is still open to you. No matter what horrible things you've done to me and the children, my heart is still open."

He shook his head. "Yeah, it's all my fault, I'm sure. Don't be such a drama queen."

"I can't talk anymore. My heart is breaking." With that, she extinguished her cigarette in the snifter, stood, and walked out, her stockings making a brisk swish-swish sound.

CHAPTER 12

Beta Test
ベータテスト

Saya punched a code into a touchscreen mounted next to a large stainless steel door. When prompted, she placed the fingers of her right hand on the glass. A small opening appeared, revealing what looked like binoculars. She put her eyes up to the lenses. The door slid open.

Torn trailed the others into the dark room. Two technicians sat watching eight large monitors streaming video and displaying gauges showing voltage, watts, amperes, temperature, and other metrics. In front of them was a wall made of thick, shatterproof glass through which could be seen another room.

Behind the technicians in the second of three rows of observer seats sat two Japanese men. Next to them sat Tamayo Watanabe and Asahi Susono, her executive assistant. Tamayo, wearing a rose-red dress and ruby necklace, clutched a red purse in her lap with red gloved hands. She stood as Torn arrived and, still holding her bag, said with a smile, "We are just observers today because, as you know, Wakkanai is a shareholder of China PV and a potential investor in Raijin Clean. We are diversifying into renewable energy and will want your help when we invest. Mr. Harden said you would be perfect for this matter."

Torn suppressed a frown. "It's great to see you again, Watanabe-shacho. Unfortunately, we can't represent both Wakkanai and Raijin in the same transaction. I can refer you to another firm that can handle the matter."

Tamayo frowned. "Well, perhaps they could help us with Project Ibis as well. We can't work with a lawyer with divided loyalties."

"I'm sure we can work something out," he responded, gritting his teeth. Torn was furious at Vince for putting him in this position despite having explained that Hilsberry couldn't represent Wakkanai in negotiations with Raijin Clean.

Mr. Li, the CEO of CPV; CPV's General Counsel; and Janet Wang, CPV's outside lawyer, sat in the front row. Torn, who had seen the demonstration before, took a seat in the third row behind Tamayo, Asahi, and the two men from the Agency for Natural Resources and Energy.

The ceiling of the second room was ten meters high. A thin horizontal divider closer to the ceiling than the floor separated the room into upper and lower chambers. The divider was made of a material Torn knew from the schematics to be a special ceramic mesh interlaced with copper. The top chamber had what looked like metal coils embedded in the ceiling and walls with thin tubes sticking out of the ceiling. Eighty long, thin copper spikes, evenly spaced apart, hung from the divider into the bottom chamber. Twenty thick copper rods, each a meter high, also evenly spaced apart, emerged from the copper floor of the bottom chamber. The streaming video showed each of these components from different angles and a large wheel they could not see through the glass.

Saya, holding a remote control, stood facing her guests, her back to the technicians and the safety glass.

Now in her element, she took control of the room. "The first step is to force warm, moist, dirty—one secret is what makes it dirty!—compressed air into the upper chamber, and then cool the air very quickly. This results in the creation of a cumulonimbus cloud in which ice particles—or 'graupel'—form. The graupel sink as warmer air rises, causing friction. The friction creates an electric field generating static electricity above the ceramic and copper mesh divider. The thick copper rods protruding from the copper floor of the lower chamber and the copper spikes hanging from the divider will conduct the static electricity, concentrating the electric charge. Any questions?" She repeated her comments in Japanese, which she continued to do throughout her presentation, for the benefit of the people from Wakkanai and the Agency for Natural Resources and Energy.

No one said a word because everyone was excited to see the demonstration.

Smiling, she continued. "At the same time the rods and spikes are conducting the static electricity, the electric field generated by the cloud in the upper chamber creates a positive field along the copper floor of the lower chamber. As the electric charge is conducted through the copper spikes hanging from the divider and the two fields attract each other, we add a secret ingredient. The resulting chemical reaction causes lightning to form between each cluster of four copper spikes hanging from the divider and its corresponding copper rod on the floor. Each rod on the floor of the lower chamber collects the energy from the lightning generated from the cluster aligned with that rod. We control the entire process with our proprietary artificial intelligence technology."

All of the spectators except Torn were completely lost.

She pressed a button on her handheld device and the protective glass darkened. Then she pressed another button and the lights dimmed. "I've darkened the glass because the lightning is dangerously bright. Don't worry, though, you'll be able to see all of the action," she said with a flourish of her remote control.

Looking over her shoulder at the upper level in the second room, Saya pressed another button. A grayish mist filled the upper level. After pressing another button, the coils glowed slightly and the mist in the upper level darkened. Nothing happened for a moment, and then, one after another, in such quick succession that it was impossible to follow each flash, bluish white lightning bolts erupted from each cluster of four spikes hanging from the divider. Each bolt lit up one of the heavy metal rods on the floor of the lower level. They were all glowing.

Despite the thick protective glass, the noise was deafening. Saya yelled over the din, "All of this instantaneous power is captured by the heavy conduction rods on the floor and transmitted for storage through ultra-heavy-duty electrical circuits to our unique energy storage system, which includes supercapacitors, located in another room."

She pressed another button on the remote control, and the number of lightning bolts gradually decreased until there were none. Only silence remained.

Saya smiled triumphantly as she surveyed her audience. She had seen this reaction before—the reaction of people who have just seen someone walk on the moon for the first time. Even Torn, who had seen it before, looked amazed. The only person whose expression hadn't changed was Tamayo's. She sat stone-faced, revealing no emotion.

No one spoke, so Saya pressed on. "Once the system starts, it needs no outside energy to operate because the energy from the batteries can be used to restart the system."

Mr. Li said something in Chinese to Janet, who interpreted. "Mr. Li wishes to know how the system can create more energy than is used to operate it."

Saya pointed at one of the monitors. "The secret is in the magnetic generator shown on this screen. The magnets on the wheel you see are neodymium. They are arranged in the shape of three arrows, the points of which meet in the center of the wheel, with empty space between the arrows. Combined with the magnet above the wheel, this arrangement keeps the wheel moving. The only limitation is that the magnets eventually lose their magnetic power, which is why we have two magnetic generators. We can cut from one to the next without disrupting the power generation process. While we're using one magnetic generator, we can be charging the magnets for the other one."

Janet asked, "How do you magnetize the depleted magnets?"

"We magnetize all of the magnets with a generator using just one percent of the lightning's energy by passing electric current through a capacitor to deliver a large impulse current to an inductor, which develops a large H field. We use the H field to magnetize the magnets."

"How are you saving the rest of the energy?"

"Through our ESS, we store up to twenty-five megawatts of energy for five years, which, depending on consumption rates, will power more than twenty-five thousand homes for a year. Our ESS suffers almost no energy loss and the batteries last for thirty years. No other ESS comes close!"

"ESS stands for energy storage system?"

Saya nodded.

Janet continued, "How much usable electricity can be generated by your system?"

"Our little system here can produce approximately one hundred megawatts a year or enough to power one hundred thousand homes for a year."

"That's incredible, if true." Janet was struggling to contain her enthusiasm.

Saya grinned. "Oh, it's true all right."

Torn noticed that Janet wasn't interpreting Saya's answers.

Janet interpreted another question from Mr. Li. "Is your system scalable?"

"Yes, absolutely. We could easily build a one-thousand-megawatt plant. And our ESS is scalable without breaking the bank.

The entire system can also be used at the micro or home level. So, there're both industrial and consumer applications. In fact, we have a mobile miniature unit as well."

Janet said, almost gushing, "Mr. Li can't wait to test your system."

Saya looked at Torn, who smiled at her, as if to say, "We've got 'em now."

Torn looked at the back of Janet's head. "He's welcome to and only need wait until we have completed the filing of our patent applications. If he wants CPV to have the right to test the system before anyone else, it will cost only ten million."

Janet translated another question from Mr. Li. "Is it not true that fusion could be a major competitor of yours?"

Saya laughed. "Well, the joke about fusion has always been that it's thirty years away and always will be. Do you remember that movie *Chain Reaction*, with Keanu Reeves and Morgan Freeman? Well, that movie came out more than thirty years ago and we're still waiting for fusion to work... and it's still thirty years away.

"My technology is ready—here and now. Everyone could have a unit for home use. Utilities themselves could become obsolete, at least as a source of home energy. The possibilities are endless. For example, people usually think of electricity generation and passenger cars as being the producers of pollution and greenhouse gases. But they produce less than half of such gases. The majority comes from industrial energy use, and that demand is growing at an astronomical rate."

Janet looked up from her tablet. "Why?"

"As the developing world modernizes, the equivalent of a new city roughly the size of New York is being built each month in China, India, and Africa and, according to some projections, will continue to be built each year for the next forty years. That means we need to address the pollution and gases generated by the production of steel and concrete, which will be needed in ever greater quantities as our urban areas expand and multiply. My technology will enable us to produce cement and steel and, indeed, any other commodity, without emitting greenhouse gases or pollution."

Mr. Li said something to Janet in Chinese.

"Mr. Li strongly believes we can work something out," Janet responded, resigned to the fact that, after what she'd just seen and heard, her client no longer had any leverage. She guessed Mr. Li was prepared to pay multiples of what Raijin was asking.

I Feel the Earth Move Under My Feet

鯰が暴れると地震が起こる

It started slowly, just as the sun setting behind Mt. Fuji bathed the conference room in a golden glow. At first, Torn could barely feel the up-and-down motion. An associate slowly looked up from a Raijin Clean patent application she'd been working on and said quietly and matter-of-factly, "*Jishin*," glancing around as if she were searching for its source. She sought confirmation from the others in the room that she wasn't imagining things.

Torn looked at her and nodded. He sat waiting for it to subside. Instead, the up-and-down motion strengthened, a swaying motion joined in, and the building began to creak. A painting fell from the wall. Time slowed.

He stood, walked to the cabinet, opened it, pulled out white safety helmets and flashlights, and distributed them to Saya and two patent attorneys who had been asking her questions about her technology. He had trouble walking because of the swaying. Chairs were sliding around the room.

Donning a helmet and looking out the window, he saw the giant twenty-story crane on the other side of the elevated expressway swaying back and forth, the tip of it making ever larger arcs through the air. Mesmerized, he hoped it wouldn't fall in their direction. On the third swing, the lattice boom snapped off near the platform and the crane fell for what seemed like an eternity before crashing into the almost completed new green office tower, rending a multi-story gash. Tons of glass rained down on the crowded sidewalk below, scattering pedestrians in all directions.

They all stared out of the window in disbelief. Torn, quickly realizing that he needed to focus on his lawyers and staff, sent an email from his phone to "TK All":

"PUT ON YOUR HELMETS AND GRAB YOUR FLASHLIGHTS NOW! IF YOU LEAVE, TAKE THE STAIRS."

Each office and cubicle was equipped with a helmet and flashlight.

They were at the three-minute mark as the earthquake continued strengthening.

Their office building, Artesian Garden Tower, resembled a giant terrarium because its entire outside surface consisted mostly of thick green glass. Now it screamed as it swayed back and forth like it was about to disintegrate into a useless heap of steel and glass.

Torn turned to Saya and his associates. "I need to check on the rest of the office. Each of you needs to decide what's best for you. If you decide to leave, don't take the elevators."

With that, he raced out of the conference room and into the inner office space, using his magnetic key card to open the locked door separating the internal offices from the conference rooms. The building shook and swayed so much it would've been a real struggle to open the door with a regular key. The door slammed shut behind him as the building swayed in the opposite direction from its last swing.

He checked each cubicle and office. Barely able to walk, he had to hold on to cubicle countertops and doorjambs as he made his way down the path between attorney offices and the cubicles used by staff. As he stumbled his way around the office, books, tchotchkes, keyboards, laptops, desk lamps, paintings, photographs, deal tombstones, telephones, coffee mugs, and almost anything else not a fixture, slid off walls, desks, and shelves. Gypsum board and light fixtures fell from the ceiling.

He asked each person he encountered if they were all right and told anyone without a helmet to put one on. Most people were under their desks silent or crying with some nervous giggling mixed in. Some said they felt "seasick" from all the swaying.

He saw a partner visiting from the San Francisco office sitting at his desk working and laughed. Only someone from earthquake country would do that.

Torn asked, "How're you doing, Ken?"

"Great. I've got to get a brief out. I've been in a lot of earthquakes, but this is by far the worst. As soon as I find out how big this quake is on the Richter scale, I'm going to bill our clients my usual hourly rate multiplied by that number for working through this craziness!"

Torn laughed again and told Ken to put his helmet on.

"So my head will be preserved when the building collapses, crushing my body like a pancake?"

"Something like that. Just put it on to set an example for our staff." With that, Torn went to check on the rest of his team.

Halfway through the office of approximately 170 lawyers and 50 staff, the earthquake started to subside. It had completely stopped by the time he had checked on everyone.

He tried to call Sean and Yukie but couldn't reach them. So, he texted them, but they didn't respond. He texted Sophia, who was back at the University of Washington, that he was safe and sound and trying to reach her mother and brother. Both Kiwako and Mayumi texted him, asking if he was safe. Kiwako was in San Francisco, where she spent about half the year to be close to her children. He assured her that he was fine, then responded to Mayumi: "I'm relieved you're safe. I'm fine and will touch base later."

Building security announced over the PA system that hiding under a desk in the building was safer than going outside.

He went to his office, which had floor-to-ceiling windows, and looked down at the street below. Hordes of people crowded the sidewalks. Obviously, they believed it was safer outside than under their desks.

A large aftershock hit.

Sitting down to check the news on his laptop, Torn glimpsed a flash out of the corner of his right eye and turned to look toward Chiba Prefecture on the other side of Tokyo Bay. A giant ball of fire shot into the air, then another and another. A few seconds later, an even larger fireball followed by a huge plume of smoke rose into the afternoon sky. Moments passed before loud booms arrived as the sound of the explosions finally reached him.

He opened his browser and clicked on the local news, which showed scenes of chaos and carnage all over the metropolis, including the fireballs he'd just witnessed and the crane he had seen topple minutes ago. According to the news, the balls of fire emanated from an LNG terminal that had blown up after the earthquake. *Of course. What else would it be?* he thought.

Torn stood and looked out the window before leaving his office. He noticed the large red antenna on top of Tokyo Tower leaning at an angle to the right. He had much to do but suffered paralysis for several seconds as it sank in that a giant quake had ravaged the city he loved, threatening—possibly already taking—many lives.

He returned to the conference room and peered out the window at the scene below. Part of the elevated expressway had collapsed, tipping off its supports onto the right lane of a three-lane surface road, crushing the cars in that lane. He could see the sides of squashed cars sticking out from under the fallen expressway.

Pedestrians choked the sidewalks and automobile traffic created complete gridlock.

Torn received a text from an associate writing that she was stuck in one of the building's giant shuttle elevators, which had stopped on its way up to the thirty-fifth floor, where Hilsberry's offices were located. He also received an email from his office manager, Tadashi, indicating all subways and trains had stopped, and no flights were taking off or landing at the airports.

A young Japanese associate burst into the conference room, exclaiming, "I'm so sorry I abandoned everyone. I was afraid the building would collapse." The associate had run downstairs when the earthquake started. Then, ashamed of abandoning his colleagues, he had walked back up thirty-five flights of stairs.

Torn almost laughed but instead shook his hand. "There's absolutely no need to apologize. Under the circumstances, each of us needs to decide what's best for them and their family and there's no shame in that."

Saya, watching the news on her laptop about the earthquake and the resulting tsunami and LNG terminal explosions, looked up. "They'll never restart those nuclear reactors after this. And, of course, my technology doesn't have a propensity to blow up."

Torn was preoccupied by recent events. "You're welcome to stay until the trains start moving."

She frowned. "Are you listening to me? The reactors shut off after Fukushima will never be brought back online after this. The Japanese government is going to need my technology more than ever to replace the lost nuclear power and reduce greenhouse gas emissions from oil and gas."

"We can discuss that later. We're going to get some food for those remaining in the office."

"Ugh. Never mind. I can find my way out."

"Are you sure? It's probably safer here, and it's pretty much pandemonium outside."

She saw the genuine look of concern on his face. "I live only thirty minutes away on foot. Why don't you join me?"

"Thank you, but I need to stay until everyone else can go home."

The gravity of the disaster finally started to sink in. Impressed with Torn's handling of the situation, Saya smiled. "I understand. Then I'll stay here as the government recommends and enjoy your fine dining."

"Good. Do you want anything from the *combini*?"

"Whatever you get for everyone else."

"I'll be back in a few."

Torn normally would have sent one of his staff, but he didn't think it was fair to ask someone to take a risk he wouldn't. His office manager, Tadashi, had already volunteered, so they left together. On their way to the stairwell, they noticed that the two large glass doors at reception were cracked and stuck open outwards toward the elevators. They were designed to open only inwards and built out of super-strong Plexiglas that shouldn't crack. But Torn and Tadashi continued on. There was nothing they could do about it now.

People leaving the building filled the stairwell. Everyone was civilized and courteous. Halfway down, a strong aftershock knocked the lights out. Several people screamed. Many people had flashlights or used smartphone flashlights to illuminate the stairs.

Rain and a floor flooded with thirty centimeters of water greeted them in the cavernous lobby. The sprinkler system had malfunctioned, spraying water everywhere. Torn looked up and saw a giant shuttle elevator, slightly askew, stuck in the glass-enclosed elevator shaft. People were sitting on the elevator floor, their backs against its glass walls.

They went to a large convenience store across the road. At first, they felt like idiots with their helmets on, but they were not the only ones wearing protective headgear. Merchandise had fallen out onto the sidewalk through the store's broken windows. One of the store employees was picking up the merchandise and another was cleaning up the glass. A passerby picked up a box of granola bars from the sidewalk, went into the store, and lined up to pay.

The pickings were slim. They grabbed whatever they could find, including chips, jerky, cup ramen, and candy bars, and joined the long queue. The entire building and everything in it started shaking. People looked around and several exclaimed "aftershock," but no one left the store. Tremors would continue for the next several days, and each time Torn's phone would buzz and flash a warning about an aftershock moments before he felt it.

By the time they returned to Artesian Garden Tower, the sprinklers in the lobby were off and the lights were on. Torn was relieved to see the stuck elevator back on the ground floor. They hauled their provisions up the stairs to the thirty-fifth floor, passing more people heading down. Their thighs burned and they breathed heavily as they climbed flight after flight of stairs, inhaling the stale, warm air in the stairwell created by the people coming down.

Halfway up, Torn's phone buzzed twice with texts from both Yukie and Sean. They were safe. Yukie was home but Sean was walking home from school, a five-hour trip on foot. He texted Sean, promising to see him first thing in the morning.

Everyone cheered when Torn and Tadashi delivered the food to the conference room. The import of their safe return from an otherwise mundane expedition to the convenience store had been magnified tenfold by the emotional stress everyone felt due to the massive earthquake and aftershocks. Shortly thereafter, building security announced that the elevators had started moving again. Torn laughed at the irony. Had they waited only ten more minutes, they could've taken the elevator back up.

The conference room was crowded with people watching news about the earthquake, tsunami, explosions, fires, collapsed buildings, and general devastation. Some were trying to reach their families by phone while waiting for the trains and subways to start moving. Someone found a few cans of warm beer and several bottles of wine to enjoy with the snacks from Torn and Tadashi.

The spouses of some of the staff started to arrive to await the trains. Everyone ate except for Torn, who was busy taking care of his colleagues and their spouses and communicating with the firm's senior management.

Mayumi texted that she was walking home from the office and asked if he wanted to join her for dinner. He said he couldn't because he had to look after his staff. "I understand," she responded, with a smiley face. "You're a great boss! Let me know if you can get together later."

Intimacy

深まる関係

"I'll show you out. Bring your helmet and flashlight. Consider them a gift," Torn said to Saya after the trains had started moving and everyone else had left the office.

He accompanied her out of the building and started to say goodbye, but she grabbed his arm. "Can you please walk me home? I won't be able to get a cab."

He agreed, because he thought making sure she got home safely at a time like this was the right thing to do, particularly after the attacks. But he didn't completely trust his motives.

They walked in silence for a while. Saya felt safe with Torn despite the throngs of people on the sidewalks, some of whom were drunk and loud. He looked like a giant compared to those around them, and she could tell he was deliberately slowing his gait so she could keep up.

At one point, seeing mopeds riding on the sidewalk, Saya said, "These bikers on their pathetic little bikes are so inconsiderate. I guess you couldn't drive on the sidewalk even if you wanted to. That monster would take up too much space."

Torn laughed. "I see you've become quite the big bike snob since our ride."

"Speaking of which, did the police return your bike?"

"No, but I have another one."

Several minutes later, they arrived at the serviced apartment building where Saya had been staying since Torn suggested she stay away from her regular apartment until the police found their attackers. He turned to her and said, "Well, you made it. I hope you can get some rest."

Saya looked up at him. He could have sworn her green eyes sparkled in the moonlight. "Why don't you come up for a drink?"

He didn't think that was a good idea but couldn't help himself. Smiling, he said, "Sure."

As the CEO of a start-up in which she had invested all of her money and that generated no cash flow, Saya's normal apartment was small and her serviced apartment was smaller. The wall of the building next door greeted her when she opened the drapes.

She offered him a seat on a small sofa, poured two glasses of red wine, and sat down at the other end of the sofa. "Torn, I want to tell you something, but you're going to think I'm crazy."

His pulse quickened and he felt tightness in his pants. He loved this stage of a new relationship when the limerence, a word he loved, was blooming. Playing it as cool as he could, he raised an eyebrow. "Yes?"

She leaned forward and looked into his eyes. "I really think someone's following me."

He paused, deflated, surprised, and concerned. "What makes you think that?! Did you tell the police?"

She took a drink and then held her large wineglass with both hands. "Yes, I called the female cop who interviewed me after we were attacked. But I have no proof. I feel"—she hesitated—"for lack of a better word, a presence. The police said they can't do anything unless I can identify the stalker."

Torn drained half his glass. The wine tasted good and warmed his body. He stood and started pacing, still holding the glass. "How often has it happened? Have you felt this *presence* since the attacks?"

"Please sit down. You're making me nervous."

"Sorry." He complied. She filled his glass again.

"Several times, I think. I feel like someone's following me to and from the office and sometimes during the middle of the day when I'm walking outside." Anticipating his next question, she said, "And yes, I've been followed after the attacks too."

"Have you seen anyone?"

She thought for a moment. "Only glimpses, but they seem to blend into the crowd or disappear when I try to spot them. It could be my imagination, but I've never been this paranoid before."

"Do you have any idea what the person looks like?"

"My impression is the stalker isn't very large. Almost like a woman. Maybe that's why he or she is difficult to spot. But I'm really not sure. And there's something else. The frequency of hacking attempts on our servers has increased dramatically. I feel somehow the two may be connected, particularly after the attacks."

"Do you know where they're coming from?"

"Evidently Russia."

"Russia? Have you asked Kroll whether they can look into the stalking and hacking? I know you used them to investigate me before you engaged us. They work on cyber security matters too."

"No. I'll discuss it with them. Our IT guy has been working with our vendor on the hacking issue and so far, there have been no breaches."

"If it's helpful, I can introduce you to my friend, Mak. He's a partner at Longstreth, a Kroll competitor."

Torn emptied his glass, placed it on the table, took one of her hands in both of his, and looking genuinely concerned asked softly, "Why didn't you tell me before, Saya?" He knew he was overstepping his bounds but he couldn't help himself. He was sick with worry.

She withdrew her hand. "I've burdened you enough, Torn. Let's change the subject."

As she refilled their glasses, the power went out. Saya found a large decorative candle and lit it with a match, making her apartment feel warm and cozy. They felt like the only two people in the world.

Torn took a drink, sat back, and said, "Tell me about yourself."

"What do you want to know?"

"Tell me about your family."

"I grew up mostly in Arizona. My mother and younger brother still live there. My mother's Japanese and my father's American, white. They met when my father served with the US Air Force in Japan and she worked as an interpreter for the Japan Self-Defense Force. They married and moved to the States. My dad became an airline pilot after his stint in the military, while my mom taught Japanese."

He smiled. "Sounds like a nice family."

"Except my father left my mother for a flight attendant when I was young. It was hard to forgive him for leaving her alone in a foreign country. She did her best to raise us, but she suffered from depression and alcoholism. I often felt like the parent in the family, making sure my mother didn't drink herself to death and protecting my kid brother from her moodiness and neglect. How about you?"

Torn paused to digest what she'd said. "That does sound rough. My background is similar, except it was my father who was Japanese. I grew up in Alaska. No siblings. My father died when his fishing boat went down during a storm in the Bering Sea. I was sixteen. My mother was a successful lawyer. So, financially we were fine. But I missed my dad, and still do," he responded in a somewhat clipped manner. He really didn't want to talk about it. "What was it like growing up in Arizona?"

"We lived in an all-white community. I played a lot of tennis and was usually tanned. People often thought I was Native American or Latina. Sometimes they'd ask me what tribe I was from or if my family moved from Mexico." She laughed at the memory. "They usually didn't know I was half Japanese. But you know how it is. No matter where you go, you don't quite fit in. But it is fun to be able to slip in and out of two such completely different cultures seamlessly like a shapeshifter."

She paused. Then: "So why was your father in Alaska?"

"He had three older brothers, all of whom became hand-line giant tuna fishermen in Aomori like their father. So, my dad decided to go to Alaska, where he could do his own thing. He said he wanted an adventure, but all he knew how to do was fish."

"How'd you get the name Tornait?"

"Mom liked it because it's an Inuit spirit you can call upon for help in times of need. My mom's family believes there's native Alaskan blood in the family, even though no one can identify a specific ancestor. So, they think they understand the local culture. The problem is, as I later found out, some Inuits believe a tornait is actually an evil spirit that can possess or hurt people." He laughed.

Torn asked more questions about her life. He had a gift for putting people at ease, and she opened up about her upbringing, her brother, her schooling, her research in graduate school, and how she came to found Raijin Clean. She laughed when she described how she had met Vince through his VC firm and how difficult he could be.

Smiling, Saya asked, "So what's the 'M' stand for?"

"'M'? Oh, my middle initial? It's Masao. My father liked it because it means sincere, faithful, trustworthy."

"I like that name." She touched his knee. "You seem very trustworthy."

And sincere, but I guess not faithful, he thought to himself.

Before he could respond, Saya asked boldly, "I don't see a wedding ring. Are you not married?"

He paused and took another drink. He had the feeling she knew the answer already. "Legally, I'm married. But we've been separated for more than two years. It's next to impossible to divorce in Japan unless both parties agree, and I have a recalcitrant spouse."

She sipped her wine. "Any children?"

His face lit up. "Two. Sean and Sophia." He told her how they were the best and most important things in his life. He spoke with pride and lovingly about Sophia's kendo, Sean's *iaido*, their skiing and fly-fishing trips together, and Sean's and Sophia's scholastic achievements. As he spoke, he felt closer to Saya and was starting to let his guard down.

"Do your children know what they want to do when they grow up?"

Torn laughed. "Sophia can't decide whether she wants to be an MMA fighter or an astronomer."

"Perhaps they're not mutually exclusive."

"Well, I tell her I'll support her in any of her endeavors, although I would prefer not watching my daughter mercilessly beating her opponents."

"You don't like watching her win?"

"Of course I want her to win, but she exhibits this scary rage. You can see it build in her eyes, which become flat and focused as she gets close to a match."

"Where do you think the rage comes from?"

Torn, surprised by the question, reflected on the recent conversation he'd had with Sean and Sophia over dinner. "Well, I'm sure the discord in our house and slow disintegration of our marriage didn't help."

Saya changed the subject. "What about Sean?"

"He fantasizes about being a fly fishing guide. But he likes business and I suspect he could end up at a start-up somewhere."

"Well, at least they have options."

Torn was finishing his third glass of wine when Saya said, "So, you must have some girlfriends."

The apartment shuddered briefly. They both looked around but neither of them moved. People living in Japan don't get excited about earthquakes until things start falling, particularly if it's an aftershock.

She filled his glass and he took another drink. His head was spinning. Her comment was disarming. The stress from his practice and managing the office, the motorcycle chase, the arrest and ongoing investigation, the earthquake—it all came crashing down on him. After all they'd been through, he didn't want to lie. He was tired of lying to women and needed to talk to someone.

"I date."

She laughed. "And?"

He shifted his weight in his chair. "One is younger and one is closer to my age."

Saya leaned toward Torn, holding her glass with both hands and putting her elbows on her legs. "How did you meet them?"

"The younger one texted me after I'd met her at a party. The older one contacted me out of the blue seeking my help to sell her business. We'd dated in college but ended up on separate paths. At our first dinner, she told me she was recently divorced and... well... one thing led to another."

"Why do you need two girlfriends?"

He laughed. "I don't *need* any girlfriends. It's just..."

"Just what?"

"Well, technically, I'm still married, so..."

"No need to choose?"

"Something like that." He felt his face turning red.

"Well, that's convenient."

"It's complicated. My wife's an alcoholic and we have had issues for years, which is why I moved out. Mayumi is aggressive, smart, independent, sexy, and loyal. But our relationship has been on and off because she's got a borderline personality that keeps me walking on eggshells. She refuses to acknowledge my family or talk about them, which isn't sustainable long term, and I don't need that kind of dysfunctionality in my life. Kiwako is stable and an adult. We have a lot in common and I can talk to her about anything, including my marital situation and my kids. But she's out of the country more than half the year. And even if I were divorced, I'm not ready to settle down again."

Saya rolled her eyes. "You're not ready to make a commitment."

"Touché!" He tried to smile. "Let's just say I don't want to jump from one relationship to another."

She laughed. "So, you put your toes in two?"

It was his turn to laugh. "Guilty as charged."

Before she could probe further, Torn asked, "No special person in your life?"

She gazed at her wineglass. "I was engaged in graduate school. But he called it off because I was spending all my time on research and starting my first company."

"I'm sorry to hear that."

"Don't be. Not having a relationship has been great for my career and Raijin Clean, but it does feel odd in this day and age to be in my late thirties and only have had one relationship in my life." She laughed nervously.

As if on cue, the lights came back on. Without a word, Torn got up and headed for the foyer to put on his shoes.

"You're leaving already?"

"I better go."

She kissed him on the cheek at the door. At first, he stood stone-faced. Then he grabbed her and kissed her on the lips. She hugged him tightly.

On his way down in the elevator, he kicked himself. *Limerence. Yeah, right. What a jackass.* While it had been cathartic to tell someone about his problems, one of the last people in the world he felt he should've spilled his guts to was Saya.

His phone rang. It was Mak. "Torn, Mayumi called looking for you."

"I'm just leaving Saya's apartment."

"Dude, seriously? I don't mean to be a dick and I know you've got a lot going on, but you need to clean up your women situation. I'm certainly no fuckin' saint, but how would you feel if they were two-timing you?"

Relieved, Torn thought. "It's not like that. She's a client."

"All the more reason not to put yourself in harm's way. Why did you need to go to your beautiful client's apartment at this time of night?"

"She asked me to walk her home."

Mak sighed into the phone. "Riiiggghhht. How convenient. Buddy, I'm sorry for moralizing here but think about your situation. You're under investigation, potentially for murder. You told the police she's only a client, right? And I hope that's true. If it is, you need to keep it arm's length all the way. No conflicts of interest. It's too messy. You're also in the process of getting divorced. You don't need Yukie using evidence of infidelity with a client against you, man. Think about the publicity. It's bad enough she could potentially hire a PI who could find out about Mayumi and Kiwako quickly. Plus, you have a rule, a very sound one, against sleeping with clients."

Torn couldn't argue with Mak's logic. For a host of reasons, he knew he should be avoiding what legal ethics rules called "the appearance of impropriety."

"Mak, I know I have issues. Okay?"

"Acknowledging you're fucked up doesn't mean you're not fucked up. It's just the first step to fixing the problem."

Torn sighed. "Don't worry. I've got this under control."

"I hope so. Talk later. I've got info for you."

Torn now felt even more stressed, angry, and disappointed with himself. He needed to let off some steam and knew just whom to call.

"Hi, honey. How're you doing?"

Mayumi whispered throatily into the phone, "I'll be better after you fuck me."

Jet Lag

時差ボケ

As usual, Torn fell asleep as the plane left the ground; something about the white noise of the engines during taxiing and takeoff put him out every time. He just couldn't stay awake. He always passed out for several minutes, coming to when he heard the tone indicating the seatbelt sign had been turned off.

After his short nap, a young Japanese flight attendant asked if he wished to change into the comfortable pajamas and slippers provided in first class, which he did. She took his suit and hung it in a closet near his seat. Then she placed a tablecloth on the dining table she pulled from under the large video screen in front of his seat and brought him some sparkling water and a coffee.

When she took his dinner order, he selected the "Western Cuisine" over the "Japanese Cuisine." There was much better Japanese food in Japan. He chose spiny lobster as an appetizer and roasted lamb for his main course. For dessert, he said no to the port and cognac and the fruit and the cheese plate and yes to the parfait and coffee. After dinner, he worked on the Share Purchase Agreement for Project Ibis, the M&A deal he was working on with Vince for Wakkanai Drilling, watched a movie, and walked around and stretched. Then it was time for some shut-eye.

As if reading his mind, one of the three flight attendants asked if he wanted her to make his bed. Since there were only two passengers in first class, she offered to make his bed on an internal seat across the aisle from his window seat so he could leave his laptop, smartphone, headphones, e-reader, magazines, and shoes where they were. After she'd made his bed, complete with sheets and a blanket, he took a nap. He later rose to work at the window seat. He also had one of the two toilets in first class to himself. It was like his own flying apartment.

He and Mayumi once had sex in a first-class bed after the lights had gone out. It was very exciting and yet romantic at the same time, but not as exciting as when they sat in the back row of economy and had sex on the Sapporo to Tokyo flight at the end of a ski weekend. That was a pure unadulterated adrenaline rush. The flight time was only an hour and thirty-five minutes and the plane was relatively full.

They had started with kissing and petting under blankets, culminating in a mad dash to one of the heads behind them. Mayumi couldn't have been more wet, and Torn climaxed quickly as she sat on the sink with her legs spread as widely as the small toilet would allow. The scariest moment was when they left the toilet because you never knew when someone might be waiting to use it. Torn had exited first in case he needed to make an excuse, as if he would've been able to protect Mayumi's honor under those circumstances. They were giggling after they'd returned to their seats and high-fived each other.

When Torn first started flying overseas he loved international travel, even when flying economy. After several years of flying somewhere overseas at least once a month for business, however, the excitement had worn off, and he often experienced hot flashes and felt claustrophobic and melancholy during the latter half of a long-haul flight. Even lying on a spacious bed in first class he found himself thinking dark thoughts about his past, present, and future. His family situation was a disaster, he was not proud of being an adulterer regardless of his dysfunctional relationship with Yukie, his relationships with Mayumi and Kiwako were exciting and ego-boosting but superficial and unsustainable, Saya coming into his life had complicated things even more, he loved his job but he spent most of his time in tubes hurtling through the sky and cooped up in boxes on the ground, rarely seeing the natural light of day, he knew he couldn't keep up the frenetic pace of work his practice demanded, and yet he didn't know how to pull back on the throttle of his life at full tilt. Now someone wanted to kill him, he could go to jail, and he could lose his job. He could lose everything.

As his mood darkened, he tried to focus on the positives. Thanks to his lawyer, Saki Katayama, the police had returned his passports and permitted him to fly to New York for a semi-annual firm Leadership Team Meeting. But they had demanded a detailed itinerary and required that Saki "guarantee" his return. Saki told him he should interpret the return of his passports and that the police had yet to charge him with any crime as positive signs. He wasn't so sanguine, however, since they had yet to catch his attackers and seemingly had no leads.

He prayed for the lights to come on, signaling that the plane was only two hours from landing. He wanted to get out of the plane as soon as possible, but he wasn't looking forward to the jet lag: waking up at 3:00 a.m., being emotional over unimportant things like life insurance commercials, forgetfulness, including forgetting people's names and having telephone conversations he didn't remember (jet-lag-induced Alzheimer's, some people called it), saying things out of character as if his internal filter were broken, like the time he told a lawyer he barely knew across the table during a break from negotiations that his shoes didn't match his suit, doing things he wouldn't usually do like straightening the paintings in his hotel room, leaving stuff lying around like the time he left his wallet and passport at an ATM, making him careless when driving like when he got off his bike and walked away without putting the kickstand down, and making bad decisions like deciding to stay out all night and drink because wherever he was at night was the morning or middle of the day wherever he'd come from. As a result of these experiences, when jet-lagged, he spoke only when necessary, he didn't make any important money or personal decisions if he could avoid it, he religiously checked for his wallet and passport, and he didn't ride his motorcycle.

While still fighting his depression, the lights came on and the flight attendants served breakfast. After the captain announced the plane would start its final descent, Torn put his laptop and other things in his carry-on luggage, checked emails and texts one last time on his smartphone using the in-flight Wi-Fi service—he already had a text from Mayumi asking if they could meet that night—and settled in to enjoy a novel. He felt the large Dreamliner begin its descent toward Haneda International Airport. He had thirty minutes to read in peace.

The flight landed on time at three fifteen in the afternoon on the day after it had left New York. First off the plane, he walked briskly to Immigration; he was almost running because he wanted to get outside into the natural air and light as soon as possible, even if for only a brief moment before getting into his car. He didn't take any escalators, instead walking up and down stairs and walking next to, not on, automated walkways. He wanted to get his blood circulating after sitting and lying down for seventeen hours, including time sitting in the car to the airport, the airport lounge, and the airplane.

While waiting for his luggage, he texted his driver that he'd be out shortly. He then texted Sean, trekking in India with friends during a university holiday; Sophia, at college in the US; Kiwako, home in San Francisco; and Mayumi, in Japan, that he'd arrived safely. Then he started checking emails again, including the rare voice mail, the recording of which was delivered by email. He found it odd Saya hadn't texted or emailed.

Torn's driver met him as he exited customs. The driver took Torn's luggage and led him to the Maybach. They headed for the office. He had yet to tell his driver he'd moved into a hotel, which had not raised any questions since Torn generally walked to work. Once in the car, Torn finished checking emails, including emails about due diligence for Project Ibis and patent applications his team had prepared covering more of Raijin Clean's technology.

He texted Saki Katayama, who indicated she'd heard nothing from the police and recommended they let sleeping dogs lie.

Next, he called Mak.

"You said you had some information?"

"Yes, sir. Still digging into Tamayo Watanabe's past. Wakkanai definitely is involved in the Northern Okhotsk Project, or they want to be. They're one of the three bidders to supply the platforms, other drilling equipment, and piping. They'll also be able to invest. This project is worth potentially more than a billion dollars to Wakkanai."

Torn looked out the car window at the cobalt-blue water of Tokyo Bay. "What about the Agency for Natural Resources and Energy?"

Mak responded, "Japan was planning to reactivate the more than fifty nuclear reactors shut down after Fukushima, but after this latest quake, there will be even more public resistance to restarting any of the nuclear reactors. And wind and solar power can't fill the shortfall. So, we'll need to continue to rely on oil and natural gas, which means Japan won't meet its targets under the Paris Agreement on climate change. They're desperate to find alternatives."

Torn moved his phone to his other ear. "And the Chinese?"

"China doesn't have the nuclear reactors Japan has. So ChinaPetrol is using China PV to diversify into renewables to help solve China's dirty coal problem, but they know wind and solar aren't the answer. So, they're looking for a silver bullet, just like the Japanese."

"Thanks, Mak."

Torn next called Mayumi, because if he didn't call her now there would be hell to pay later. She answered immediately, as she almost always did.

"Hello?" He could hear the work tension in her voice.

"Hi, sweetheart. How're you?"

"I'm fine. Did you get my text about tonight?" It was almost an accusation, as if she were asking, "What took you so long to respond?" He felt like he should apologize for "responding so late," but he didn't. Mayumi's expectations were unreasonable. She had a knack for making him feel like he was late responding if he didn't answer the phone on the first ring.

He really just wanted to get some work done and return to the hotel for some peace and quiet. Torn used the one excuse he knew she'd accept. "Yes, I'd love to see you tonight, but I need to work. I have a lot to get done, and I'm not much fun when I'm thinking about work."

With less tension in her voice, she said, "I understand. I know that work takes priority. I'm the same way. If I have a deadline, I can't enjoy myself when I'm on a date, and, in fact, I start to resent the person I'm with because I'm worried about stuff I need to get done."

Worked like a charm, he thought. Anything else would just irritate her.

He hung up and looked out the car window at the expressway soundproofing wall blocking the view of the city, thinking again that it seemed odd he'd yet to hear from Saya. Usually, she responded to emails and texts right away. He was starting to feel uneasy. They had exchanged emails quite frequently while he was in New York. He was waiting for her comments on the draft contract he'd prepared to grant a right of first negotiation to China PV, but she'd gone silent during his flight. Part of that made sense because he boarded the flight when it was the middle of the night in Japan, but he was surprised he hadn't heard from her since the beginning of Japan's business day. He decided to send her an email saying he'd landed and ask whether she'd heard from CPV.

He wouldn't receive a response.

Lights Out

消灯

In the morning on the day of Torn's return to Japan, a light rain pelted western Tokyo under a gray sky. Saya, dressed casually, drove to Raijin's research facility, which was located in the foothills of Tokyo, and parked in the outside parking lot. She arrived earlier than anyone else to finish some paperwork before scheduled meetings with her staff.

She walked up steps to the building, which was located on a knoll above the parking lot, and entered through a side door she unlocked using the usual security protocol.

She was thinking about Torn. She felt warm all over when her thoughts wandered to their evening together. Not only had he saved her life during the motorcycle chase, but he remained genuinely concerned about her well-being. He'd even suggested before the police had that she move out of her apartment just in case.

He had come up with creative ideas for protecting her technology in the event she became unable to carry on its development. Saya knew it was Torn's job to develop workarounds for his clients, but he seemed to worry more about her problems than even she did. She also had witnessed the compassion with which he'd treated his staff and her during and after the earthquake.

And it had been so sweet of him to walk her home and spend time with her that evening. She thought, *He probably doesn't know how much I needed him to be with me that night.* Even Saya herself wasn't aware how stressed and vulnerable the attacks on the expressway and the sense of being followed had made her feel. Or how much Torn's presence calmed her nerves.

For the first time in a life she'd spent looking out for herself and others, including her mom and little brother, and later her employees, she realized how nice it was to have someone looking out for her. And not just anyone, but someone strong and smart. And although his personal life seemed to be a mess, she found it endearing and disarming that he'd been so open with her about his women problems, even if he had loosened up only after she'd plied him with wine. But at the same time, the dysfunctionality of the private life of the always serious and professional Torn Sagara surprised her, and the overlap with her father set off alarm bells.

Could she trust him in a relationship? Clearly, he had commitment issues. Could he change? She never imagined that a man so successful and in control of his professional life and so caring and thoughtful could have such a complicated personal life. Still... it was an opportunity and she was skilled at bringing order to chaos. She laughed at herself.

Lost in thought, the usually observant Saya didn't think anything of the van parked across the street that she'd passed when turning into the parking lot. She didn't see the footprints in the mud between the bushes around Raijin's building. She failed to notice the holes drilled in the foundation of the building where the concrete met the ground. She had no way of knowing that someone had bribed an employee at Raijin's security company to gain access to the building or that explosives were attached to each joist on every floor.

As she rode the elevator up to her office, she remembered needing to call Kroll to see if they could find the stalker or at least determine whether there was one. She felt more certain than ever that someone was following her.

She exited the elevator on the fourth floor of Raijin's small building, every centimeter of which she had designed. The full-size prototype and related equipment and servers occupied the basement and the first two floors, a research lab filled the third floor, and the fourth floor was office space. She walked down the hall and used a key card to open the door to the inner office space, comprising an open area with numerous cubicles and three private offices, one in the right-hand corner.

Saya walked past the cubicles and unlocked the glass door to her corner office with a conventional key. She entered the office and sat down at her desk facing four monitors. Beyond the monitors, she had a view of the western part of Tokyo through floor-to-ceiling windows on her right and left that met at the corner of the building. A beautiful oak tree blocked part of her view to the right but also protected her office from the direct rays of the sun.

Gazing out the window, she marveled again at the Tokyo metropolis below, which, although she could see only a small part of it, stretched all the way from the western foothills of the Kanto Plain to Tokyo Bay in the east. As she sat admiring the view, Saya thought about how well the latest technology demonstration had gone and the very positive feedback she'd received from CPV and the Agency for Natural Resources and Energy. They obviously were very interested in supporting her work financially. She had yet to hear from Wakkanai; perhaps she didn't need them now with CPV willing to invest, as evidenced by their verbal agreement, just two days after the demonstration, to a right of first negotiation and request for a written contract.

When she first reviewed the draft agreement Torn had prepared, she was again surprised that he'd convinced China PV to agree to the ten-million-dollar fee for the right of first negotiation. When he had first suggested it, she thought he was crazy. But in some ways, he knew Raijin's business, and understood the energy market, better than she did.

As Saya turned to her computer to work, she heard a loud rumbling and turned to look out the window again, trying to locate the cause of the sound. The sprawling metropolis was the last thing she saw.

The explosives detonating in the foundation caused the rumbling. The charges set on the joists exploded a fraction of a second later. Each floor pancaked onto the one below, and the tons of concrete and steel of the roof collapsed into the fourth floor, including the space that moments ago had been Saya's office, smashing and completely crushing everything below it, except for Saya and anything else blown out the windows.

Before she could register what was happening, a charge attached to a joist under her office exploded. The flash blinded her, and the explosion hurtled her through the floor-to-ceiling window. The shock wave from the explosion shattered the thick window and propelled the jagged pieces of safety glass with such force that several were buried into nearby trees and the exterior of a building across the street.

Saya felt the initial blast wave, then sailed straight through the giant hole where the glass window had been a moment before the hole itself disappeared as the building collapsed. Fortunately, she avoided hitting the thick glass of the window because the force of the blast blew it out only milliseconds before her body reached where the glass had been. The blast concussion ruptured her eardrums and rendered her unconscious by the time she reached open air.

She would have fallen straight to her death on the asphalt below, but instead, she landed in the middle of the large oak tree. She regained consciousness briefly before hitting the first of three large branches as she fell to the narrow strip of grass ringing the base of the tree. The branches broke her fall, but the first also broke her right arm and clavicle, the second broke two ribs when the left side of her chest landed on it, and the third caught, and momentarily held, the calf of her left leg below her knee. The weight and force of her falling body twisted that knee violently in its socket. When she hit the ground, the impact of the right side of her head on one of the grapefruit-size rocks arranged in a circle around the tree knocked her unconscious. Her right leg landed on two other rocks, shattering the kneecap and causing multiple fractures, including a compound fracture, to the tibia.

While Saya lay on the ground bleeding and unconscious, someone was ransacking her apartment. They weren't going to stop there.

News Travels Fast

悪事千里を走る

"Are you there, Sagara-sensei?" asked Detective Taniguchi, a genuine note of concern in his voice. He had called Torn to inform him of the destruction of Raijin's building and the burglary of Saya's home.

"Yes," Torn responded. It was almost a whisper. He pulled himself together and cleared his throat. "Where is she?"

Taniguchi pulled up Torn's email address on his office laptop. "I'll send you the hospital address. She's in a coma in the ICU. The doctors intend to keep her comatose until the swelling in her brain subsides. I have stationed guards there and will let them know you're coming. Prepare to be shocked when you see Brooks-san." Taniguchi paused before adding, "Obviously, it's not just you they're after, which is what we thought initially. I'm not even sure you're the main target. I know you must be upset and exhausted from traveling, but I have to ask: Who do you think is responsible?"

It was 10:00 p.m. on the day of Torn's return to Japan, and he'd been working since he got off the plane. The combination of the distressing news about Saya and exhaustion meant the gears of his mind moved slowly as if gummed up by a viscous liquid. It took him a moment to clear his head and respond. When he did, he was slow and deliberate as he organized his thoughts.

"Blowing up Raijin's building and killing Brooks-san could stop development of her technology. But why would someone put a tracking device on my bike if the real target were Brooks-san? How would they know she'd be on the back?"

"Haven't you been advising Brooks-san and her company?"

"Yes, we have."

"What about?"

"Mostly about intellectual property issues."

"What does that mean?"

Torn grabbed a bottle of water and walked to the window of his hotel room. He explained that Hilsberry had been advising Saya how to protect her inventions using patents and trade secrets and assisting with preparation of the patent applications. He also explained that patents provided a twenty-year right to exclude others from using the patented technology in exchange for full public disclosure, while trade secret protection was forever so long as the technology was kept confidential.

Detective Taniguchi, a seasoned detective trained to see all angles from a perpetrator's point of view, thought for a moment before replying, "So, if the perpetrators wanted to stop development of the technology, they'd want to prevent you from completing the patenting process."

"Right. Blowing up the prototypes and killing Brooks-san would only slow down the technology's development if it were in the public domain."

"The question remains: Who would want to stop the development of her technology?"

Torn, his mind moving more quickly now, replied, "It could be anyone in the fossil fuel, renewable energy, or even nuclear power industries. Her lightning technology is as reliable as fossil fuels but produces no greenhouse gases. It's far more reliable than solar and wind power, which depend on Mother Nature, who is notoriously fickle; sometimes the sun just doesn't shine and the wind doesn't blow. It takes up much less space than wind farms and doesn't require the clearing of huge swaths of land like solar power. And it won't harm any animals, let alone the huge number of bats and large birds, like eagles, that wind farms kill, or desert animals like tortoises that solar farms kill, or fish that dams kill. It also doesn't create an eyesore on the horizon like wind farms and doesn't leave any nuclear waste. So, all of those energy producers would feel threatened."

Taniguchi put his elbows on his cheap metal desk, which was empty except for a laptop, his notebook, and a pen. "But who specifically might be obsessed with her technology? Who knows about it?"

"Well, there's Brooks-san's parents, who live in America, and Raijin Clean's employees. Then there's Raijin Clean's angel investor, Vince Harden." A light bulb went off in Torn's head as he said Vince's name. "And Eagle Technology Capital, a VC investor in Raijin. There are also potential investors like China PV, which is majority owned by ChinaPetrol, a giant SOE controlling much of China's energy market. And Wakkanai Drilling, a Japanese publicly traded corporation in the oil and gas drilling and mining industry. Harden also is the Vice Chairman of Wakkanai. Then there's the Agency for Natural Resources and Energy, whose representatives attended the most recent demonstration of the lightning technology together with representatives of China PV and Wakkanai."

To Detective Taniguchi, much of what Torn just said might as well have been Greek. Although bright and inquisitive, he knew nothing about venture capital investing and had very little familiarity with anything outside of Japan. "What's an angel investor and a VC investor?"

"An angel investor invests at the early stages of a start-up's development, often shortly after the founder and the founder's friends and family. Angels are typically rich individuals. A VC investor is usually a venture capital investment fund that invests in later rounds of financing. The fund is often owned by several silent partners and managed by a professional investor in technology companies."

Taniguchi ran a hand through his cropped hair. "Sagara-sensei, would an investor try to shut down something they're investing in? And do you think a Japanese or Chinese government agency would really go to such lengths to suppress technology that may be good for the country?"

Torn looked at the dark night sky. It was still raining, and he could see neither stars nor the moon. "I guess an investor might try to destroy a company it's invested in if the investor thinks the destruction of the company would result in a gain to the investor outweighing any risk. In this case, the risk would be both financial and the risk of going to jail. So, for example, I can't imagine the employees, who are receiving salaries from Raijin, doing anything to harm their employer unless someone's got a screw loose or they expect some huge gain, financial or otherwise—and I'm not seeing any such potential gain—from Raijin's demise.

"The angel and VC investors receive stock in exchange for their capital contribution. Their motive is purely financial. They don't generally have a strategic interest in the technology or the business. The big payoff for the investors comes only when the company goes public or someone buys it. In this case, however, Vince Harden, the angel, said Raijin's technology could put him out of business, which means he has a conflict of interest. He claimed he was joking. I don't know if that makes him a suspect. But I'm sure he understood the disruptive nature of the technology before investing."

He took a drink of water before continuing. "As for the Chinese and Japanese governments and potential corporate investors China PV and Wakkanai, I'm not a conspiracy theorist, but it wouldn't be the first time a government or large corporation tried to suppress information to gain some strategic advantage. And since they're all involved in the energy industry, they each could have a reason for wanting to bury Raijin Clean's technology. But again, the risk of going to jail is high. On the other hand, the risk of getting caught fails to prevent criminals from committing heinous acts every day."

"Exactly, but we need proof."

Torn thought, *He's got a knack for stating the obvious.* The truth was they had no idea who was behind the attacks and were engaging in mere conjecture. Torn didn't know that the police had started whittling down the list of possible suspects or that his name was still on it.

His brain finally firing on all pistons, Torn asked, "Not to change the subject, but have you checked the serviced apartment Brooks-san has been staying in?"

Taniguchi's old metal chair creaked when he leaned back. "Yes. They tore it apart. Clearly, they've been watching her every move."

Before Torn could respond, Detective Taniguchi said, "Sagara-sensei, one more thing. We'll be guarding Brooks-san, but you need to protect yourself. Whoever blew up Raijin Clean's building and ransacked her home most likely is still after you."

"I'll be careful."

"You should consider moving again, and don't tell anyone where you're staying."

Torn finished his water. "I'll think about it. By the way, have you contacted Brooks-san's family?"

"I've informed her mother."

"I'll give her a call as well."

After hanging up, Torn saw that Vince had tried to call. He pressed callback.

Vince answered, impatient and haughty as ever. "Torn, I heard about the explosion. I can't reach Saya."

Torn said dryly, "Hi, Vince, how're you?"

"I'm fine. Did you hear me?"

Torn thought, *Yes, I heard you, but there ain't no way I'm telling you where she is.* "I'm trying to track her down."

"She needs to leave Japan immediately. What're you doing to find her?"

"I'll be talking to the police first thing in the morning."

"OK, buddy. Keep me posted."

At this point, he didn't trust Vince as far as he could throw him. Still, Vince was right about one thing: Saya needed to get the hell out of Japan.

Life Flight

避 難

Torn fought back tears when he saw Saya in the intensive care unit. He had slept little the night before because he'd been on the phone to Saya's parents, Saki, Mak, and a few hospitals in the States. He'd also prepared and sent an email to Detective Taniguchi and Prosecutor Tsujikawa, copying Saki. Sleep-deprived, and extremely jet-lagged, he closed his eyes and took a deep breath.

Her face was intact and relatively injury-free with only a few scrapes and minor cuts. But she was unconscious, with a breathing tube in her mouth and a feeding tube in her nose. Her right arm was in a cast, and although he couldn't see it, a metal plate and screws held her clavicle together. Needles for intravenous drips had been inserted in veins in the crux of her left elbow and the back of her left hand. Her left leg was in an inflatable cast, and a modern version of an Ilizarov Apparatus, which looked like a round erector set attached to her leg with Styrofoam-covered screws, stabilized her shattered right knee and leg.

Placed in a medically induced coma, her body temperature had been lowered to aid with the healing of her brain injury. Torn could hear the "breathing" of the mechanical ventilator and the beeping of the machines monitoring her vitals. Saya lay in one of several beds surrounding a nurses' station like spokes to the hub of a wheel. The configuration enabled the nurses to monitor the ICU patients around the clock.

The sights and sounds were unpleasant, but the assault on Torn's mask-covered nose from the stench of sweat, stool, and blood permeating the close quarters of the intensive care unit was even worse. He desperately wanted to do something for her but felt powerless. Once he recovered from the initial shock of seeing Saya's comatose body, however, he remembered Vince's admonition.

Dressed in a dark suit and light-blue tie, he removed his mask and tracked down the ICU doctor for Saya in his office. In his haste, he barged in and blurted out, "How long will she be in a coma?"

Dr. Kumakura, a short, squat man with thinning hair and no neck, sat behind a modern white desk wearing a white lab coat and spectacles. He looked up from his computer screen. "I'm sorry, but who are you and to which patient are you referring?"

Torn took a deep breath. *I need to calm down.* He pulled out his business card holder. "Oh, how rude of me. I'm Saya Brooks's attorney, Torn Sagara. Very pleased to meet you. The police let me in. They informed the hospital that I would be visiting."

The doctor stood stiffly, and they exchanged business cards in the traditional way.

Torn remained standing while Kumakura sat down and leaned back in his chair. "Ah yes, a Detective Taniguchi and a Prosecutor Tsujikawa called. They said to expect you."

Wow, thought Torn. *Saya's getting the royal treatment from the police. Having a former prosecutor representing you has its advantages.*

"What's the prognosis?"

Kumakura perked up. "The swelling in her head's coming down. As soon as the MRI shows significantly reduced swelling, we should be able to start bringing her out of the coma and weaning her from the ventilator. I hope to start in two weeks at the outside." He seemed very proud of himself.

"How long will it take to bring her out?"

"It depends, but she's young, and other than her injuries, she's generally healthy, so I don't expect it to take more than a couple of days."

"When can we move her?"

The smug look on the doctor's face vanished and he sat up straight. "Move her? Why would you want to move her?"

"Her family has their reasons."

Losing his calm, the doctor said firmly, "She can't be moved for at least a month. Even after she's brought out of the coma, the recovery process will take months." Almost as an after-thought, Kumakura said, "Besides, the police won't let her go."

"Well, we're flying her out tomorrow," Torn asserted force-fully while still being polite and formal.

Kumakura was beginning to panic. This ran counter to everything he'd been taught, not to mention standard hospital procedure. He stood, came around from behind his desk, and looked up at Torn. "You can't do that!" He looked around to see if he was attracting too much attention because the door to his office was still open.

Torn smiled and went into full lawyer mode. "Actually, Kumakura-sensei, I don't mean any disrespect, but we can, we have the authority to do so, and we will. Prosecutor Tsujikawa and Detective Taniguchi have already approved it. I'll send you a copy of a letter of authorization from Brooks-san's mother. We'll need your help getting her prepped and into the ambu-lance. The international transport staff will take it from there."

Kumakura, mouth open, stared at Torn. Clearly, he wasn't used to being told what to do.

Torn continued. "Also, we'll need a copy of her medical records, including X-rays and any CT and MRI scans. If you could burn them to a couple of disks by first thing tomorrow morning that would be most helpful."

Medical care wasn't Torn's concern. Japan had excellent medical care, but he knew whoever had tried to kill Saya would try again once they learned she was still alive. And the media had been reporting on the explosion nonstop for twenty-four hours. So far, the police hadn't confirmed whether there were any victims, but Torn believed the perpetrators probably took the lack of transparency about the status of victims as a sign that Saya remained alive. They would be searching for her.

Kamakura asked, "Where are you taking her?"

"That's confidential."

Kumakura pushed his glasses up to the bridge of his nose. "But she needs to be kept intubated and in a coma for now."

"Yes, of course."

"Also, in light of her injuries, she should be kept at sea level."

"The plane's air pressure will be adjusted accordingly."

Kumakura furrowed his brow. "Is the plane properly equipped?"

"Yes. It's an air ambulance with state-of-the-art life support equipment."

It was a Gulfstream G650ER, capable of traveling close to the speed of sound for over 7,000 miles. Torn had arranged for the air ambulance through Mak, whose firm had assisted with other such evacuations. Mak had also made arrangements to have Saya admitted to a hospital in Arizona close to her mother.

Torn wasn't sure how much safer Saya would be in the US. If the bad guys were a government or a multinational corporation, they would be able to find her anywhere. However, he suspected that at the very least, she would be somewhat safer in the US given that the attacks had all occurred in Japan. Besides, Saya's parents wanted her treated in the US where they could easily visit her.

Kumakura said somewhat officiously, "This is highly unusual. I'll need to confirm with the president of the hospital."

"Please hurry. Brooks-san has a plane to catch."

Kumakura straightened up. "I would feel better if I could be with Brooks-san when she is taken to the airport."

"Of course. You're welcome to accompany her in the ambulance." Then Torn leaned in and looked Kumakura in the eyes. "And Doctor, as I'm sure Prosecutor Tsujikawa and Detective Taniguchi have told you, confidentiality is of utmost importance." *In particular, I don't want that asshole Vince to know where she is*, he thought to himself. He wasn't sure why he felt that way. It was just a hunch.

"Yes, Sagara-sensei, I understand." Torn smiled. Kumakura's use of the word "sensei," reserved for professionals, including doctors and lawyers, but which Japanese doctors notoriously tried to reserve to themselves, was tacit acknowledgment Kumakura knew that the hierarchy had changed. Torn was in charge of Saya's fate now. "As a doctor, I want to ensure the health and safety of my patient."

"Of course. Thank you for your understanding."

Loud and Clear

受信完了

Dear Mr. Sagara:

We represent Ms. Saya Brooks. Before the tragic explosion resulting in Ms. Brooks's current comatose state, she granted you power of attorney to act as the President and CEO of Raijin Clean, Inc., and appointed you the sole trustee of her living trust, both to become effective in the event of her incapacity.

We have determined that she has indeed become incapacitated. Therefore, enclosed please find:

(i) a memory stick;

(ii) Japanese power of attorney for you to act as the President and CEO of Raijin Clean, Inc.; and

(iii) trust documents, including a trustee appointment letter, creating a living trust for Ms. Brooks and appointing you trustee of such trust.

The power of attorney and trust documents both become effective on the date you sign the enclosed copy of this letter. Therefore, if you agree to your appointment as the trustee of Ms. Brooks's living trust, please countersign the enclosed copy of this letter and return it to my attention. Ms. Brooks may revoke the power of attorney, your appointment as trustee, or both, at any time.

Ms. Brooks said that you would know the password for the memory stick because you understand how she conceptualizes her technology.

Please do not hesitate to contact us should you have any questions.

Sincerely,
Scott Miller
Partner

Torn stared at the memory stick in his hand, having no idea what the password could be. He closed the door to his office and inserted the memory stick into his laptop's USB port. A message appeared that the driver software for the memory stick had been installed. He opened a list of drives and clicked on "Removable Disk." The only file on the disk was a PDF file named TMS, which he guessed stood for Tornait Masao Sagara.

He clicked on it. A password prompt window opened on one of his monitors. He tried "perpetual motion," "lightning," "lightning in a bottle," "magnets," "ESS," "energy storage system," and several other words and phrases. Nothing worked. He wondered, starting to grow frustrated, *Why would she assume that I'd know the damned password?*

Taking a deep breath to calm himself, he turned to the power of attorney, reading it in disbelief. Saya had granted him all of her rights and powers as the Chief Executive Officer and majority shareholder of Raijin Clean. He was stunned and was not at all sure that was a good idea. It was one thing to advise Raijin Clean on its important legal matters. It was quite another to run a company, any company, let alone a start-up that Saya, someone he was falling for, had passionately built from scratch. Also, he knew her lightning technology could change the world, and he didn't want to be responsible if the venture failed.

He sat back in his large, comfortable black office chair, his head sinking into the headrest, with the power of attorney in his hand, thinking about Saya. Taking another deep breath, he closed his eyes and recalled his first telephone call with her, their first meeting, their intellectual property protection strategy sessions, the technology demonstrations, the financing negotiations they had worked on together, their wild motorcycle ride, his arrest, the earthquake, her comments about being followed, spilling his guts to her over drinks at her temporary apartment, negotiations with the Chinese, the explosion, and seeing her comatose. Turning to his laptop, he typed in "Bottled Lightning." The PDF document opened revealing a hyperlinked nine-digit number on one line and "Zeus#1" on the next line. He recognized the number as being a link to a private video on a secure website Saya had often used to provide information about the more mundane aspects of her technology.

Torn clicked on the number, opening the video website in his browser. He typed in Zeus#1 in response to the password prompt. A video loaded and Saya's smiling face appeared. Her lipstick had a fresh sheen. She looked very pretty and happy. He was struck again by how green her eyes were, even in the video.

"Hi, Torn. You're watching this video because I'm either dead, perish the thought, or I've been legally incapacitated, as the lawyers say, which I guess is marginally better than being dead."

Torn choked up and paused the video for a moment. He put the fingers of his right hand on the screen as if attempting to touch her. Then taking another deep breath, he clicked "play."

"I've instructed my lawyer," and then, smiling, "—and you know how much I like instructing lawyers—to deliver a memory stick, a power of attorney, and trustee documents to you by courier if either event occurs. Sorry for all of the cloak and dagger, but as you know, I'm a stickler for confidentiality."

For good reason, Torn thought.

She looked down, needlessly straightened the collar on her dark-green dress and looked back into the camera. "But at least I dressed up for you! After all, I want to look my best in case this is the last time you see me alive!" She laughed nervously.

Oh God, Torn thought.

"Before I get started with the business side of things, I want you to know how much I care for you." She paused, looked down and then back up. "Oh heck, I might as well say it. What do I have to lose at this point?"

With that, Saya leaned toward the camera and smiled. "Torn, I love you. Maybe your mom gave you the right name after all. Because you help people and you've possessed me." She shook her hair and laughed as she leaned back. "There, I said it. I've never said that to anyone but my family. It's so liberating to be able to say it to someone, even if it is by video and even if you may never see it. I know you've got a "complicated"—she made air quotes with her fingers when she said "complicated"—personal life, and I probably shouldn't trust you with my heart, but I can't help myself."

Torn paused the video and slumped in his chair, tears welling up in his eyes. He put his head in his hands and almost cried. *I finally meet someone who might be the one and now she's in a coma. Or is that just the grief talking? Fuck me*, he thought. But he was working and knew he had no time for self-indulgence or self-pity.

He straightened up, wiped away the tears, and clicked "play" again.

Saya paused and looked down. When she looked up, she wiped away a tear, eerily echoing him. "At any rate..." Her voice cracked and, clearing her throat, she started over. "At any rate, down to business. Whether you like it or not, you've been appointed the trustee of a trust that holds my shares in

Raijin Clean. You also should've received a power of attorney granting you all the rights that I have as president and CEO. You now have complete control over Raijin Clean. Lucky you. Just know I can take back those rights at any time, assuming I'm alive." She giggled nervously again.

"As you might've guessed from our discussions, developing the Raijin technology and seeing it put to good use, if I may be so bold, for the benefit of humankind is the most import-ant endeavor in my life. As a result of recent events, how-ever, including our harrowing motorcycle ride and my sense of being followed, I've come to believe that certain people or institutions or countries or all the above may not share my goals and, in fact, may be hostile to them and to me person-ally. I know you lawyers like to define things, so perhaps we should define these hostiles as the 'Bogeyman.'"

Well, the Bogeyman is real in this case, Torn thought.

"In the spirit of 'just because you're paranoid doesn't mean they're not out to get you,' I've decided to take steps to ensure that all of my technology is put into the public domain, even if I'm not around to oversee that process. Which is why I am appointing you as the trustee of the trust holding my shares and granting you a power of attorney making you acting pres-ident and CEO of Raijin Clean."

Torn felt honored, and more than a bit humbled, that she would put so much faith in him.

"I've given much thought to how best to accomplish that disclosure, including simply having the technology dissemi-nated on the internet or sent to 'scientists,' like in the movies, or in a free app people can download onto their smartphones. I know that this is analogous to open-source software, not protected by copyright. However, I'm not that egalitarian. I want my company to thrive for the benefit of my family and the company's shareholders, employees, customers, suppliers, and partners." She paused for a moment and then said, "And for your benefit, Torn, so don't let me down."

No pressure there, he thought.

"And unlike most original open-source software, which is not ready for prime time, my technology works well enough now to commercialize it, even without further development.

"Also, I'm not sure if disclosure for use by anyone at no cost will result in its broad application. I'm concerned the technology might get 'lost' somehow and not be properly funded or developed if no one owns it. Even Tesla didn't open up its technology to competitors until it had a patent portfolio. That patent portfolio enabled it to extract certain promises from its competitors in exchange for the right to use Tesla's technology. In other words, there's a quid pro quo that makes competitors take Tesla's technology seriously. Likewise, Raijin Clean needs a proper patent portfolio to attract capital and the best engineers."

Torn thought, *Wow, she speaks in paragraphs like a lawyer.*

As if knowing what he would think, Saya said, "Sorry to drone on. In conclusion, I've decided to take your advice and patent everything, even the chemical mixtures and formulation process. No trade secrets. Patent everything. And I mean everything. That's one of the reasons I need you to stay involved, and the other being that there's no one I trust more. This way my technology will be completely disclosed to the public, and Raijin will have patent protection long enough to give it an ample head start over its competitors."

Torn paused the video and thought about what he needed to do. Patenting would be easy, provided he knew all the technology, but only Saya knew all of it. She'd been very careful about not giving anyone else, including him, full access, particularly to the chemical mixture and formulation technology. Then it dawned on him she'd probably thought of that as well. He clicked "play" one last time.

"Obviously, you'll need access to all of the technology to complete the patent application process. So, I took your advice. Well, at least part of it. I have deposited in a safe deposit box at a certain bank a memory stick containing an encrypted copy of the designs, diagrams, and other information related to the technology we planned to patent. I also deposited in another safe deposit box at a second bank a memory stick containing an encrypted copy of the designs, diagrams, formulae, and other information related to the chemical mixtures and formulation technology we planned to protect as trade secrets. As you suggested, I put the decryption keys for both memory sticks in a third safe deposit box at yet another bank.

"However, instead of giving copies of the keys to all three safe deposit boxes to my lawyer, or splitting the keys up among three different people as you had suggested, I taped them to the inside of your other bike's gas tank!" She laughed again and clapped her hands together gleefully. When she raised her hands, Torn could see her freshly manicured fingernails with fingernail polish matching her eyes. No longer nervous, her laughter was uninhibited and infectious.

Torn started laughing, too, and reached out and touched the screen again as if to caress her face.

Still laughing, she exclaimed, "I really enjoyed sneaking into the garage and putting the keys in your gas tank! I've been such a nerd all my life, so it was fun to do something naughty! I think our motorcycle ride and sneaking into the garage of your office building may be the most exciting things I've ever done in my life! I need to get out more, I know!" She pulled out some facial tissue and dabbed at her eyes, teary from laughing.

Torn thought, *How in the hell did she get my keys?*

"I know that may seem a bit melodramatic, and it's not a long-term solution. But you're the only one I trust to make sure my inventions get protected, disclosed, and commercialized, and that was the best way I could think of to protect the keys to the safe deposit boxes. And I figure that if something is going to happen to me it's going to happen soon, because to prevent it from getting to market the Bogeyman needs to act before the technology is commercialized."

I'm not sure why she trusts me so much, thought Torn.

Again, as if reading his mind, Saya leaned into the camera. "We've worked together for years, and no one other than me knows my business or the energy industry better than you. Besides, you saved my life! And you were so open and honest with me about your personal life, and that was after you fed me at your office and walked me home after the earthquake. Do you have any idea how wonderful you can be when you put your mind to it?" With that, she threw her head back and laughed again.

"By the way, I was able to open your gas cap because I had a pirated key fob to your bike. Remember when you gave me the spare keys to your bike before the cops put us in the patrol car and asked me to have them sent to your assistant for her to arrange to get your bike fixed once the police released it? You seemed to believe your bike might get out before you did!" She laughed. "Anyhow, the keyholder for the K 1200 LT had a key fob to your other bike too. I had my IT guy copy your key fob to a blank remote. I had an extra key to your K 1200 LT made too, because I didn't know which key I'd need. I didn't even know you had another bike until you told me about it on the night of the earthquake. And that was after I'd returned your keys. Pretty sneaky, I know. But please don't be angry with me. It's for a good cause, and I did it to protect my technology and because I trust you. I know I already said that, but it's true!"

Torn realized he didn't know Saya had such a wild and mischievous side to her, but her demanding a motorcycle ride should've been a sign.

"I hope you haven't sold your bike! But given how you treat your bikes better than most men treat their wives, I'm pretty sure you'd never part with it. In fact, I'm surprised you leave your bikes in a garage instead of keeping them in your bedroom where you can sleep with them!" She laughed her lovely natural laugh again.

"Seriously, though, Torn, if you're watching this video, unless what happened to me was the result of an accident or natural disaster, you really must be careful. If their beef is with the technology, which would be my guess, they will come after you next.

"I know I'm asking a lot, and you certainly have a right to decline your appointment as trustee and acting president and CEO. But I'll make it worth your while. If you accept these responsibilities, in addition to paying Hilsberry's legal fees for your teams' work for Raijin, you'll receive a fee for acting as trustee, a salary for acting as president and CEO, and shares equaling five percent of the equity of the company on a fully diluted basis, which will vest over five years. Assuming the technology is worth what we both believe it's worth, all that will make you a very rich man.

"Well, there you have it. You know what to do, or you'll figure it out."

Saya leaned into the camera again. "And remember, I love you." She blew a kiss and laughed as the video faded to black.

He leaned back in his chair, interlocked his fingers behind his head, and closed his eyes. His brain was on overload. All he could think was, *I wish I had as much confidence in me as she does.*

Then he opened his eyes. *And I love you too*, he thought.

Exodus

脱出

The envelope was too small and skinny to contain a bomb. "It could have anthrax in it, however..." he said out loud to himself. But then he thought, *I must be getting really paranoid.* It wasn't the first time something had been delivered to him anonymously at the office.

He had been staring at the black screen of the monitor after Saya's video ended when Mamiko, his executive assistant, walked in with the envelope. It had no return address.

He examined it closely while turning the envelope over several times in his hands. Only his name was printed on it. He held it up to a light above his desk and saw inside what looked like one folded sheet of paper, but he didn't see anything resembling powder floating around inside. Curious, he carefully opened the envelope with a letter opener and, as he expected, found only a single sheet of paper inside.

He removed the piece of paper and opened the first of three folds. There was no letterhead. Then he opened the fold at the bottom, exposing the lower two-thirds of the sheet of paper and a note printed in Japanese: "Stop helping that bitch! It will not go well for you or your family if you stay involved."

Torn used an encrypted app on his smartphone to call Sean. He hoped it would prevent anyone who might be listening in from hearing the conversation. While waiting for his son to answer, he pressed the intercom button on his office telephone and asked Mamiko to come in.

Sean answered the phone as Mamiko walked into Torn's office. "Hi, Dad."

"Sorry, Sean. Hold on just a sec." Torn put Sean on mute.

"Mamiko-san, please scan this letter and its envelope and send password-protected PDFs to me right away. Send me the password in a separate email. Then, have the originals sent to Katayama-sensei by bike messenger, with instructions to give them to her former colleague at the metropolitan police. She'll know what I'm talking about."

"Will do." Mamiko closed his office door behind her as she left.

Torn unmuted the phone and put his elbows on his desk. "Hi, Son. Sorry. I had to ask Mamiko-san to do something urgent for me. Now, I need you to listen very carefully."

"What's up? Sounds serious."

"Deadly serious." *A little melodramatic*, Torn thought to himself even as he said it. "I want you to take your mom and go to the cabin."

"In Alaska? Why? What's going on?"

"You remember that building that got blown up?"

"The one out past Hachioji? Yeah, why?"

"Well, it was owned by a client, and I just received a threatening letter from someone."

"In Japanese or English?"

"Japanese, why?"

"It narrows down who the perpetrator might be," Sean said with conviction.

Ah, my son the detective, Torn thought. "Maybe. The sender might be Japanese, but it could also be someone disguising themselves as Japanese. Who knows?"

Sean replied, "I'm not sure if someone who's not Japanese would go to the trouble of sending you a note in Japanese. They'd have to get someone to translate it unless they were really good at Japanese. I assume it's not a bad Google translation, right?"

Trying to be patient because he didn't want to panic Sean, Torn said, "Fair point. No, the Japanese is good contemporary Japanese. Anyway, I need you two to get to the cabin right away. Tell your mom to get out of the house and on an airplane today. You go with her. And don't go home first. You can meet her at the airport. Use my credit card. I'm sending you my card information now. I'll call your sister too, and have her meet you in Anchorage."

"OK, I can pick Mom up."

"No. As I said, don't go home. Meet her at the airport. She needs to leave the house now. These people are very dangerous. I can send you guys anything you need later. Send me a list of what you want."

"Got it. Where should we stay if we can't get a flight?"

"At an airport hotel so you can get on a flight first thing in the morning. Stay on the executive floor where there is more security."

"This is kind of extreme, Dad."

"I know it's weird. But they blew up a four-story building with my client in it." He almost added that he should've had them leave before now. But then he'd have to tell Sean about the attacks on the expressway, and he didn't want to worry him even more.

"I have school and..."

"Son, just do it. You can attend classes remotely."

Sean laughed. "From the cabin? It's in the middle of nowhere. You do remember we have to fly in and land on a lake to get there, right? In fact, we have to fly to McCarthy, refuel, and then fly to the cabin. Also, there's no Wi-Fi access or mobile service there."

"It's a good opportunity for you to practice your flying. Your grandmother is a great pilot. Also, she has a sat phone you can use. I'll send you two more sat phones as well. Then you and

Sophia can each use one for school and your mom can use one to communicate with her business and family. You'll be able to use them to create instant hotspots too."

"What will I tell my teachers?"

"Tell them your grandpa died in a tragic fishing accident in the Bering Sea, which is true."

Sean sighed. "Yeah, when you were a teenager. Dad, are you serious?"

Torn raised his voice slightly. "What did I say, Sean?"

"Deadly serious. I heard you."

"Exactly. I'm not screwing around. But I'm joking about your teachers. I'll let them know you'll be traveling for a while for family reasons but will keep up with your studies and attend classes online to the extent you can. Whatever you do, don't tell anyone where you're going and tell your mother not to tell anyone."

"Are you going to be OK? Maybe I should stay here with you."

"No. Take care of your mother and sister."

"OK. Will do."

"Let me know whether you can get on a plane today. And remember, don't tell anyone where you're going, and I do mean anyone. Not your girlfriend, Stephanie, or your best buddy or any relatives. I'm counting on you."

"It's Margot. I love you, Dad."

"Sorry. I love you very much, Son."

After hanging up, Torn turned off the automatic cloud storage syncing function on his phone. Whoever was behind the motorcycle attacks and this letter was too sophisticated for him to take any chances uploading anything to the cloud. Using the same secure app, he texted Yukie to expect Sean's call and that she was in danger and needed to leave the house immediately. He instructed her also not to tell anyone where she was going.

She responded that she was on the phone talking to Sean. She ended with, "This is crazy."

Next, he called Sophia on the same secure app. It was late in the afternoon on the previous day in Washington State. She was in the library studying when he called. She put up even more of a fuss than Sean, but finally agreed to go to the cabin for "just a week."

He called his mother in Alaska. She readily agreed to meet Sean, Yukie, and Sophia in Anchorage before flying them to the cabin.

He then hurriedly left his office. His first instinct was to fly out with his family, but he didn't want to lead anyone who might be following him to their location. And he wouldn't be able to help the police find the perpetrators if he were stuck in the Alaskan wilderness.

Checking his emails while waiting for the elevator, he saw a list of emails caught in his spam filter with a note prompting him to "Release," "Block," or "Permit" those emails. Typically, he blocked most emails snared in his spam filter, but one of them caught his eye. In the subject line was the English command, "Stop helping that bitch!" He thought to himself, *I've got you now,* and clicked Release to send it to his inbox.

Still in the elevator, he checked his inbox for the released email, which read, in English, "We know where you live, where your wife lives, and where your son lives."

He didn't recognize the email address or domain name.

He could feel his blood pressure rising, but was relieved the email didn't mention Sophia, Mayumi, or Kiwako. He texted Sean as the elevator doors opened: "You and your mom need to leave now!"

Sean responded almost immediately: "Leaving the dorm now. Mom's leaving home soon."

Torn texted Sean back: "Keep me posted."

After exiting the elevator, he attached the threatening email to another email and sent it, via Hilsberry's secure email system, to Miriam Yeu, the global head of Hilsberry's IT department, copying Saki Katayama, with a note:

CONFIDENTIAL: DO NOT FORWARD

Miriam,

Can you determine who sent this email or at the very least its country of origin?

Regards,

Torn

Torn also attached both the email and the PDFs of the letter and its envelope to another email, which he sent to Saki and Mak with a note reading:

CONFIDENTIAL

Saki and Mak,

See the attached email, letter, and its envelope.

My assistant, Mamiko, is sending the original letter and envelope to Saki for her to give to the police. Perhaps the police (Detective Taniguchi?) can determine who sent the letter and/ or email or at least the country it came from.

Mak, you should look into it too.

I'll forward the password separately.

Regards,

Torn

Torn walked to his bike, pulled the toolkit from the right-side case, and searched through the tools until he found the screwdriver handle and an assortment of drivers. He stuck the longest driver into the handle and twisted it until it locked.

He opened the gas cap, which automatically unlocked when he got close enough with the key fob. After opening it, he inserted the screwdriver into the opening and fished around in the dark. Sure enough, he felt a slight weight on the screwdriver. After pulling out about forty centimeters of a black plastic strip, he felt resistance and heard a clank on the inside of the gas tank. Three keys, one right after the other, emerged as he continued to slowly pull on the plastic strip. But more plastic strip remained in the gas tank. He kept pulling and finally retrieved what looked like a small plastic bag folded and refolded several times into a five-centimeter square and covered with several strips of duct tape.

Torn wiped off the keys and the plastic bag with a rag he kept in his toolkit. He gently removed the duct tape and tore open the plastic bag, which contained a small sheet of paper. On the sheet were the names of three banks, their branch addresses, and safe deposit box numbers.

After reconfirming that the cloud syncing function on his smartphone was disabled, he took a photo of the piece of paper with his phone and sent the photo to himself using the firm's encrypted email app. When the app asked if he wished to password-protect the photos, he chose "Yes" and sent the password to himself in a separate email. He then deleted the photo from his phone (and emptied the "trash") and put the keys and the piece of paper in a zippered pocket inside his backpack, which he stowed in the bike's back case.

Torn drove his motorcycle home while listening to "Crossroads" by Cream. So many foreigners had left Japan because of the earthquake and so many Japanese had abandoned the city to escape the aftershocks that Tokyo had an eerie *Walking Dead* feel to it. The streets were devoid of cars and pedestrians. The overcast sky added to the general air of malaise. He half expected to see zombies walking among the rubble.

CHAPTER 21

The Cat

我が猫

At home, Torn packed an extra suit and other clothing and toiletries, then drove to the Andaz Hotel, where he had decided to stay after checking out of the Hotel Okura. Again, he didn't tell anyone except Taniguchi where he was staying. After parking his bike, he checked his phone while waiting for the elevator to take him to the fifty-first floor to check in.

He had six missed calls, a voice mail, and four text messages from Sean. The first text read, "We got seats to Seattle on ANA, leaving at 6:09. Flight NH 178."

Followed by, "Dad, call me right away. Mom went back home."

And then by, "Mom's not answering her phone."

The final one read, "Still haven't heard from her. She's not answering her mobile phone or home phone. I'm worried and going to check on her." The time of that text was six minutes after four, two minutes ago.

Torn dialed Sean without listening to the voice mail.

When Sean answered, he sounded panicky. "Mom was in a cab on her way to the airport, but she texted that she was going back to get the cat. I told her you would take care of Buttons but she wouldn't listen. I'm going home to check on her."

"Sean, get on the plane. I'll check on your mom. I'm sure she's fine."

"But I'm worried about her."

"Me too, but she'd never forgive me if something happened to you."

His phone buzzed and Torn saw Mak's name on his screen. "Dad, she's my mom."

"I know, but there's nothing you can do that I can't, and I'm closer anyway. I'm leaving now. I'll let you know as soon as I find her. Do both your mom and me a favor. Get on that plane."

After hanging up, Torn hailed a cab to Yukie's house. He would've taken the bike, but he wanted to return Mak's call and read any incoming texts or emails.

The cab driver said through the safety glass separating the front and back seats, "The expressway is still closed due to earthquake damage. We'll have to take surface roads."

Shit, that'll take an extra fifteen minutes, Torn thought to himself. "Just hurry, please."

He pressed Mak's number.

Mak answered on the first ring. "Torn, I'm gonna go out on a limb here and say the same people who had this nasty email sent to you probably ordered the attacks on the expressway and the blowing up of Raijin Clean's building."

"That's my theory. 'That 'bitch' must be a reference to Saya," responded Torn.

"I took the header from the email you sent me and ran it through a tracing tool. It was sent through a source host located in Komsomolsk-on-Amur. That's in the Russian Far East, dude. The Russians manufacture airplanes and nuclear submarines there, or at least they used to."

Torn thought, *Well, that's a start.*

"I just sent you a link to the results. And there's one more thing."

"What's that?"

"Either they're really trying to throw you off track or they're rank amateurs. If they'd just used Gmail or Outlook, the email header would tell us only the location of the source host in the US, which wouldn't be very helpful because that just tells you where Google hosts email servers for Gmail accounts or Microsoft hosts email servers for Outlook accounts. If I were going to send you a nastygram, I'd send it from a Gmail or Outlook account and then close the account. It'd be hard to trace the email beyond the source host without a court ordering Google or Microsoft to provide more information about the account user."

"So, it's some stupid Russian?"

Mak sighed. "Well, given that Komsomolsk is in the middle of bum fuck nowhere, it's easy to think that some stupid Russian pickled in vodka sent that email. But Russians engaging in spamming typically are very tech savvy. They wouldn't be stupid enough to send an email from a source host in Russia. They'd route the email through several source hosts so the recipient couldn't trace their location. The sender could be someone in Brazil, for example, who routed the email through the Russian Far East to completely throw you off their track. Or, as I said, it could be a rank amateur. Do you know anyone in Russia? Did you piss someone off there? Fuck their wife?"

"Not that I know of."

"Generally, you know if you're fucking someone's wife."

"That's why I know that's not it. China PV doesn't do business in Russia because there's little demand for renewable energy there. Its parent, ChinaPetrol, on the other hand, must do business in Russia since it's China's biggest oil company and Russia is rich in oil and natural gas.

"Also, Wakkanai Drilling, which is bidding on the Northern Okhotsk Project, may be doing business on the Russian mainland. Russia also is rich in precious metals, and Wakkanai sells drill bits, piping, rigs, and other equipment to oil, gas, and mining companies. Can you find out what they're doing in Russia, if anything?"

"I'll check it out."

"Thanks. By the way, what's with the hyphens?"

"What?"

"You said Komsomolsk-on-Amur. Sounds like a hyphenated name. Seems pretentious for a Siberian town."

"Well, first of all, Siberia is technically to the west of the area Russians consider the Russian Far East. And second, Russians hyphenate place-names as a matter of course. They even hyphenate non-Russian place-names like New York and Buenos Aires. Komsomolsk-on-Amur gets its name from its location on the banks of the Amur River, which flows into the Pacific, but no one in Russia calls it by its full name. People just call it Komsomolsk."

"Never heard of the Amur River. Is it big?" asked Torn.

Mak laughed. "Most people outside Russia, Mongolia, and China haven't heard of it. But it's a huge river that starts in Mongolia and flows to the Pacific, forming much of the border between China and the Russian Far East. Most people haven't heard of the Russian Far East either. It might as well be on another planet. Look it up."

After hanging up, Torn found Mak's email with a link to a geo-location map of Komsomolsk-on-Amur showing the location for the source host of the email he'd received and the following information:

Country: Russian Federation
City: Komsomolsk-on-Amur
Latitude: 50.5670331
Longitude: 136.9658947

He then looked up the Russian Far East. He was surprised at its size. It stretched from North Korea to the Arctic Sea in the north and almost all the way to Alaska in the east. It was an area larger than Alaska, Western Canada, and the US Pacific Northwest—including Northern California—combined, but only a little over six million people lived there. He was also surprised at its vast natural resources, including fish, oil, natural gas, wood, diamonds, iron ore, coal, gold, silver, lead, uranium, and zinc.

As the cab approached Yukie's house, Torn received a separate email from Miriam Yeu confirming the information Mak had sent. She also added:

"Just in case, I checked our hacking log. There has been a tremendous increase in the number of attempts to hack into our system. The source seems to be Komsomolsk, Russia. I'm not sure if the two are related, but if not, it's an odd coincidence."

He looked up from his phone as the car came to a stop and was alarmed to see both the gate in the wall surrounding the grounds and the front door wide open.

Homecoming

帰宅

Torn sprinted through the wrought iron and wood gate into the courtyard and ran along the stepping-stone path, up the steps to the porch and through the door, all the while yelling Yukie's name at the top of his lungs. He proceeded through the foyer into the house without taking off his shoes; he had no time for cultural niceties, even though wearing shoes in the house is verboten in Japan. He hurriedly checked the bedrooms on the first floor, all three of which had been ransacked.

The bedding had been torn off the beds and the mattresses turned over. Books, papers, clothing, money, mail, photographs, and jewelry covered the floor. He checked the toilets, the laundry room, the smaller bathroom, and the master bathroom with the large his-and-her showers, his-and-her sinks and vanities, and tiled jacuzzi bathtub. The vanities above the sinks had been emptied and torn off the wall. The contents of the drawers and cabinets below the sinks, including medicines, toiletries, towels, and cleaning supplies, had been thrown on the floor.

It wasn't until he reached the stairs that he noticed the blood. He paused for a moment. There was blood on the railing, on most of the steps, bloody shoe prints much larger than Yukie's stocking feet, her usual footwear when at home, and a bloody stripe sloping upward along one wall. He ran up the stairs two steps at a time to the second floor while calling Yukie's name. He was panicking and almost screaming but managed to avoid stepping in the blood on the steps.

Checking the kitchen, he found a large bloody carving knife and knife block on the floor with several smaller knives, one bloody, scattered around the block. *Not good*, he thought. But he needed to keep looking for her.

He checked the living room, the dining room, the guest bedroom, and the connecting bathroom. All had been turned upside down. Depending on the room, books, knickknacks, magazines, electronics, towels, fine china, silverware, food, and other household items lay spread over the floor.

In the living room, someone had knocked down the glass display case holding the Ishikawa family's authentic long and short *katana*—samurai swords, with their beautiful black and blue sheaths—but had left the swords. They had been in Yukie's family for hundreds of years. He found Yukie's purse in the living room, its contents spilled on the floor, and more blood in the hallway.

He ran upstairs to the den, home office, and toilet on the third floor. Still yelling her name, he was almost hoarse by now. These rooms also had been pillaged. Paper, memory sticks, pens, mobile phone chargers, and other office supplies were strewn all over the floor. Two laptops had been removed from their docking stations and the monitors lay smashed on the floor. But there was no blood in either room, the hallway, or the toilet, or on the railings or walls in the stairwell between the second and third floors.

He looked out of the window over the green canopy of the cemetery to the west and saw Mt. Fuji. It was a particularly beautiful day, in contrast to the dark scene in the house.

He remembered that they had built the house here primarily because of the peace and quiet afforded by the kids' park and verdant, wooded *jinja*—Shinto shrine—across the street, and the large cemetery on the side. The shrine and cemetery had the added advantage of preventing anyone from building in front of their corner lot at the end of the road and blocking their view of Mt. Fuji.

He ran down the two flights of stairs, almost slipping twice in his motorcycle boots, which he hadn't changed in his rush to find a cab, trying again to avoid stepping in the blood on the steps or touching the blood on the railings. He found a bloody handprint on the wall at the bottom of the stairs. In his haste, he hadn't noticed it earlier. He didn't want to admit it, but the print seemed to match the long delicate fingers of Yukie's right hand. He found more blood on the inside door handle and on the inside gate handle.

Emerging from the courtyard, he yelled at the taxi driver to call the police and an ambulance, then heard sirens before the driver had time to pull out his phone. He stopped for a moment, not knowing which way to go.

Memories of playing with Sean and Sophia on the swings came back to him as he looked at the park. He looked up at the *jinja* and remembered the entire family, dressed in festive kimonos, going to the little wooden shrine with the large bell at the top of the hill to ring in the new year and watch the sun rise on New Year's Day. As he turned toward the roundabout with the cherry tree in the middle marking the end of the road in front of the ancient cemetery, he recalled teaching his kids how to ride a bicycle on the quiet road in front of their house and how sibling rivalry had pushed them to overcome their fears and learn to ride without training wheels.

He raced into the cemetery, running down a short tree-lined path between lines stretching to his right and left of skinny ancient Japanese tombstones standing like sentries, arranged one after the other with little space between. He saw smatterings of blood here and there on the path. He crossed the arched wooden bridge over an hourglass-shaped koi pond, where Sean and Sophia used to love to feed bread to the giant carp, catch frogs, and chase red dragonflies with gossamer nets. He noticed blood on the first post of the bridge's railing and the bridge itself. He kept running until he reached the ruins of the five-story pagoda where he and Yukie used to go sometimes in the evening to talk and enjoy the fireflies.

Two lovers had burned the pagoda to the ground in a suicide pact more than three centuries ago. A massive oak tree, the largest in the cemetery, marked the spot where only the foundation stones remained. It had a huge trunk and numerous giant branches stretching out in all directions like the legs of a monstrous brown and green octopus. Several of the branches were propped up with poles like crutches because the limbs were too long and heavy to support their own weight.

Yukie, shoeless, lay on her side on a large granite slab with grass growing around its edges. She was warm but lifeless. Blood had pooled onto the stone beneath her. He checked her pulse. Nothing. Her eyes were wide open as if staring at something. He looked up in the direction her eyes seemed to be pointing and saw Buttons watching him from her perch on one of the oak tree's giant low-hanging branches.

What's in a Name

名前の重み

Torn kissed Yukie, closed her eyes, and covered her with his motorcycle jacket. Then he sat on the ground and held her hand while waiting for the police to arrive.

When Buttons came down from the tree and curled up in his lap, he started crying for the first time since his father had died. He cried for Yukie and for Sophia and Sean. He cried for himself.

By the time the police arrived, Torn had regained his composure. After speaking with them briefly, he called Sean, who was about to board his plane.

"Son, you need to come home."

"Did you find Mom?"

"Yes, you need to come home."

"Dad, tell me."

"I'd rather tell you when I see you."

"Dad, I need to know."

Torn didn't respond, barely able to hold it together.

"You need to tell me."

"Son, your mother's gone."

"What do you mean, 'gone'?" Sean asked, voice rising.

Torn suspected Sean knew the answer.

"She's dead, Son. Murdered."

For a long moment, Sean didn't respond.

"You should've let me go home. I could've protected her."

"No. It wouldn't have made a difference, and you might've been killed too. Your mother wouldn't have wanted that."

"I'll see you at home, Dad," Sean responded without emotion.

Torn had considered letting Sean's plane depart without telling him because he wanted him out of Japan. But he knew no matter what he said, Sean would have immediately returned once he learned of his mother's death. He also knew that, despite the risk, Sophia wouldn't stay away either.

Torn then called Sophia. This time he didn't withhold any information. And he didn't sugarcoat it. Sophia paused and then screamed and cried. After calming down, she said haltingly through sobs, "Oh, Dad, I'm so sorry you had to be the one to find her." Overcome with grief, she paused again. "And that you were alone when you did."

Torn, on the other hand, was relieved he—not one of his kids—had found Yukie's body. "Your brother is upset with me because I didn't let him go home to pick up your mom."

"You did the right thing, Dad. We could've lost them both if Sean had gone home."

Sophia landed in Tokyo two days later.

Detective Taniguchi was able to have the autopsy expedited. But Yukie's home, now a crime scene, couldn't be used for the wake. So, her body was delivered to her parents' house.

Yukie's parents were deceased and her older brother, Kenji Ishikawa, now owned the family home. Her body, dressed in a *yukata*, an informal kimono, rested on a futon in a large tatami room of the old house with dry ice placed on her stomach over the *yukata* and around her body, which was covered with a thick sheet. A white cloth covered her face. The entire house smelled of the incense her family kept burning day and night.

Before Yukie's body had arrived at the Ishikawa home, Torn drove to the airport with Sean to pick up Sophia. He didn't ask his usual driver to take them because he wanted as few people as possible to know his family's whereabouts. The police, now providing full-time security, sent a patrol car to accompany them to the airport. Sean said barely a word until they had reached Haneda International Airport. "Dad, I know it's not your fault."

"Son, it's not your fault either. It was my decision."

"Whoever killed Mom needs to pay."

"They will, Son, they will. We need to let the police do their job."

When Sophia saw them outside of customs, she hugged each of them tightly, crying softly.

Sean had been stoic after learning of his mother's death but became inconsolable when he saw Yukie at his grandparents' house. Sophia, however, barely shed a tear when she first saw her mom, although she did hold her mother's cold hand for quite some time. Torn attributed it to exhaustion and jet lag, but he worried about Sophia's lack of emotion.

That evening, Yukie's family and friends visited the house to pay their respects. Everyone brought food and drink. They sat around the body eating, drinking, and talking. Many of them touched and talked to Yukie, and about her, as if she were still alive. At times people cried, at times they laughed.

After the last guest had left, Torn stayed up with his children as they kept vigil until they finally fell asleep in their respective bedrooms. When he found himself alone with Yukie and his thoughts, he began crying again when the weight of regret and guilt overwhelmed him. Buttons, who had barely left the room since Yukie's body had been brought in, sat in his lap and started to purr.

Throughout the night, he felt aftershocks from the big earthquake of just a few days before. But no one else in the house seemed to notice, or if they did, they didn't get up.

The next day, Torn and his brother-in-law, Kenji, left the house for a meeting at the Grand Hyatt Hotel. The police insisted on sending an officer.

At the Grand Hyatt, Torn and Kenji went to the hotel business center, where they met with the go-between facilitating the arrangements with the Buddhist temple for Yukie's funeral and burial of her ashes. The police officer sat outside the conference room's closed door. The go-between was also assisting with the negotiation of Yukie's *kaimyou*, her posthumous Buddhist name. Torn wasn't looking forward to the discussion. He'd already overruled one of the temple's "for the benefit of the family" suggestions, which he suspected the temple made because it wished to avoid press about the burial of a murder victim married to a "foreigner." He figured they would've refused altogether if Yukie's family didn't have a plot there.

Yukie's homicide was not her family's fault. But because of the "bad karma associated with a murder and because most victims' families felt ashamed," the temple had recommended a small funeral with close family members only. When Torn's family discussed it, Sophia had said, "She's our mother. If we hide the fact that she was murdered, the people who did it will succeed in silencing us." End of discussion.

To Torn's surprise, Yukie had written a will designating the *kaimyou* she wanted, and it was impressive. Comprising nine characters, very long for a relatively young woman, it included "charity," "purity," "water," "kindness," "significance," "fragrance," "chrysanthemum," "heavenly," and "grand dame." It was a bold request that reminded him of the Yukie she had been before.

It would not be easy to convince the temple to grant such a name, and it would be expensive. The temple would resist because of Yukie's relative youth, her lack of significant "noble accomplishments," and her marriage to someone with a foreign name. Sure enough, those were the issues the go-between, Akemi Matsuo, said the temple had raised. She also said the "donation" for such an illustrious posthumous name would be nine million yen, or one million yen per *kanji* character. The temple had probably assumed such an amount would end the discussion. It had not.

After taking his seat, Torn said in formal and polite Japanese, "Matsuo-san, thank you for coming. Yukie's family appreciates your efforts. We are hoping you can convince the temple to allow Yukie to receive the *kaimyou* designated in her will. As you know, she was murdered while trying to protect her family." While perhaps an exaggeration, she had returned home to rescue a family member. "As her husband I may be biased, but there is no more noble way to die."

Yukie's brother sat ramrod straight on the edge of his chair, nervously sipping green tea.

After an awkward silence, Matsuo-san explained in a whisper, "I appreciate Sagara-sensei's honesty and the Ishikawa family's sincerity, but I'm afraid convincing the temple might be difficult."

"Difficult" in Japanese was a polite way of saying impossible.

Torn looked at Kenji, who was staring at his clasped hands, and then back at Matsuo-san. "I'm hoping we can resolve this issue amicably. I want to introduce you to someone who can explain the public interest at stake here."

Growing pale she asked, "What do you mean, 'public interest'?"

Torn pulled out his phone. "I'll let my lawyer explain. Like me, she's a *bengoshi*." He paused for effect. "And was a prosecutor for several years. For the sake of a six-hundred-year-old temple known for the purity of heart of its priests, please listen."

He dialed Saki Katayama, set his phone to speaker, and put it in the middle of the table.

"Hi, Torn," Saki's disembodied voice said cheerfully in English.

"Hi, Katayama-sensei." And then switching to Japanese, "I have with me Yukie's older brother, Kenji Ishikawa, and the go-between for the *kaimyou*, Matsuo-san."

Saki, switching to Japanese, said, "Hello, it's a pleasure to meet you both. My condolences to you, Sagara-sensei, Ishikawa-san, and your family."

Matsuo-san looked around, and then said stiffly, "It is nice to meet you, Katayama-sensei, but I don't think your participation in this meeting is warranted. It's a personal matter between the deceased's family and the temple."

Saki, sounding less cheery, responded, "I'm participating in this discussion at the request of Sagara-sensei to facilitate a constructive resolution, for everyone's benefit."

Matsuo-san furrowed her brow. "I'm not sure I understand."

"That the temple may not be aware of some of the legal issues here is exactly Sagara-sensei's concern. He's unsure whether the temple understands there could be unintended consequences if this matter is not resolved soon. Clearly, the Ishikawa family would be shamed if there's no *kaimyou* for the deceased at her funeral."

Matsuo-san frowned. "It's not that the temple won't grant her a *kaimyou*. They're merely concerned about whether the *kaimyou* she requested is appropriate given her relative youth and marriage to a foreigner."

Torn bristled.

Kenji, not used to this kind of confrontation, looked down at his hands again. He would have happily agreed to a lesser *kaimyou*, but Torn insisted Yukie deserved what she had requested.

"I'm sure Sagara-sensei and Ishikawa-san have explained why such concerns are unfounded. First, Sagara-sensei is not a *foreigner*."

Torn thought, *And it shouldn't fucking matter even if I am.*

"He's a Japanese citizen and his children are too. Second, the temple is aware that the deceased died protecting her family, correct?"

"Yes, but..."

"The Ishikawa family wants the temple to continue to enjoy its unsullied reputation without problems from the media or the government..."

Matsuo-san's voice softly cracked. "I'm not sure I follow you."

"Well, the deceased has two college-age children traumatized by the horrific murder of their mother. There's no way to know how they'd react if they thought their murdered mother, their widowed father, or they themselves were being discriminated against in their own country. Young people can be impetuous, and grief can make them even more so. Also, the deceased's children have been educated at American schools, and their father is a lawyer. They may be more open to taking legal action than the average Japanese, to say nothing of what they might say on social media."

Matsuo-san's jaw dropped. "The temple will not appreciate being threatened."

"No one's threatening," Saki said calmly. "I'm just explaining the risks so you can discuss the issues with the temple and advise it appropriately."

"The temple has its own counsel and can handle such a matter," Matsuo-san said icily.

"I have no doubt. But the press likes to sensationalize these things. No one wants to see a headline like, 'Temple Discriminates Against Mother Who Gave Her Life to Save Family' or 'Temple Discriminates Against Murdered Mother and Grieving Children.' Also, in my experience, once the media shines a spotlight on this type of matter, government investigations often follow."

At this point, Matsuo-san was almost hyperventilating. "I'm— not—sure—why—the government—would get—involved."

Saki continued unrelentingly. "Well, such investigations are not necessarily related to the story. For example, the tax authorities might conduct an audit. I once prosecuted a tax evasion case against a religious corporation like the one that manages the temple's assets. Friends at the prosecutor's office specialize in such investigations."

Matsuo-san looked ill. Somehow, she managed to say, "The temple has a long and good relationship with the tax authorities."

"Relationships can change. I'm sure the temple doesn't wish to be audited. I don't mean to be rude, but I must attend another meeting. Matsuo-san, thank you for your attention. I have faith the temple will do the right thing. Ishikawa-san, again, please accept my condolences. Sagara-sensei, I will talk to you later."

With that, Saki hung up.

Matsuo-san looked down and smoothed out her wrinkle-free skirt, then took a deep breath and looked up. "I'm not sure that was constructive."

Torn, who had been leaning back in his chair while Saki was talking, sat up straight. "As Katayama-sensei said, we thought you and the temple should be aware of our concerns. Also, we understand this is not an easy decision. So, we're prepared to donate an additional one million yen to the temple, and to pay you an additional one million yen for your trouble."

Bowing his head, Yukie's brother held out an envelope with both hands. "This is in appreciation for your kind assistance on behalf of our family."

Looking surprised, Matsuo-san hesitated, then accepted the envelope with both hands. "I understand well the position of the Ishikawa family. The temple will appreciate the family's discretion and generosity, as do I. The next step will be a face-to-face meeting at the temple. My suggestion is that only Ishikawa-san and one other sibling attend, since I understand your wife's parents are deceased and that you, Sagara-sensei, separated from your wife some time ago."

Torn agreed that only Kenji and his younger brother should go. This was helpful advice and a good sign Matsuo-san would advocate for the temple to grant the requested *kaimyou*. He didn't want to push his luck by demanding an audience for himself or his children, although what he really wanted to do was burn the temple to the ground for its greed, arrogance, and racism.

The Wake

通夜

The morticians arrived early the next morning. They applied makeup to Yukie's bloodless face. One commented she looked remarkably "healthy," which Torn found ironic since she was *fucking dead*. He kept his thoughts to himself.

They dressed her in a formal white kimono with the right side crossed over the left, customary for the deceased, instead of the left over the right, customary for the living, and a white *obi*, a wide belt around the midriff. Her hands were clasped, holding Buddhist prayer beads over her chest. They placed her body in a plain cypress casket, packed in dry ice, and added a pair of sandals and the six coins needed to cross the River of Three Crossings. The casket had carvings of peacocks on one side. Its lid contained a shuttered window above Yukie's face.

The morticians closed the shutters and placed the coffin into a Japanese hearse resembling an El Camino-Cadillac hybrid with a sleek black front end and a gilded, ornate, portable shrine on top of the truck bed. The gaudy mobile shrine's black lacquer and gold carvings gleamed in the sunshine.

The hearse transported the casket to the temple for the wake. Yukie's family traveled separately. Accompanying the body was considered bad luck because the deceased might take the rest of the family to *ano-yo*, "the other world."

The morticians placed the casket in front of an elaborate three-tiered arrangement of flowers, lanterns, candles, and sculptures, with a small shrine on the third level. The arrangement, representing paradise, ran the entire width of the large hall. They placed a large, black-framed portrait of Yukie in front of and slightly below the entrance to the shrine.

In addition to the terraced fields of flowers behind the casket, flower arrangements filled the hall, each with a long, flat piece of wood bearing the name of the sender. Given the prominence of Torn and Hilsberry & Carter, several major Japanese corporations, including Wakkanai Drilling, and government organizations sent flowers. Torn noticed that even Vince had sent flowers.

Torn spent the morning with his children at Yukie's family home. At mid-afternoon, his brother-in-law drove them to the temple. Torn's feelings bounced from sadness to guilt to anger to regret to numbness. Because of him, Yukie had been murdered over something that had nothing to do with her. But there was nothing he could do about it now.

By now, news of Yukie's murder, the leveling of Raijin Clean's building, the ransacking of Saya's apartment, and the expressway attacks on Torn and Saya had been leaked to the press. The tabloids speculated as to how Torn had survived the attacks on his client and his wife relatively unscathed. Barbara Zimmerman, Hilsberry's Chairwoman, called from San Francisco to offer her condolences, but he suspected the firm might pressure him to resign if negative press coverage continued. For now, he was focused on getting through the day.

After the guests, all in mourning clothes, some wearing black kimonos, were seated, a maroon-robed Buddhist priest with a clean-shaven head knelt in front of the casket and started chanting a sutra. Every so often, his young assistant struck a bronze prayer bowl with a lacquered mallet, causing a delicate bell tone to ring out. One by one, Yukie's family members got up to pay their respects at the middle of three incense altars in front of the casket.

Using the thumb and first two fingers of their right hands to pick up granular incense from a bowl, they held the incense to their foreheads and then dropped it onto a burner. Then they prayed with their hands clasped in front of their faces and bowed to the portrait. Some held prayer beads.

Other guests followed the family three at a time to pay their respects at one of the altars, each bowing to the family before placing a pinch of incense onto the burner. The smoke from the burning incense at each altar looked like slender dancing apparitions snaking upward.

Torn noticed Mayumi standing in line. Her attendance was a surprise since he hadn't invited her or even spoken to her since Yukie's murder.

Mayumi's presence made him nervous, but at the same time, he appreciated her thoughtfulness. He couldn't help noticing how provocatively she was dressed; even in expensive mourning clothes, her white blouse was open to reveal cleavage. No other woman showed skin below the neck. Some even wore black gloves.

Then he saw something that doubled his anxiety. Kiwako, dressed elegantly in a black kimono with black obi, stood in another queue. *Fuuuuuck*, he thought. *This could get ugly*. Kiwako had returned to Japan the day before Yukie's murder, and he'd told her about the wake. Now he regretted it, because Kiwako would've had the good sense to stay away had he not mentioned it.

His girlfriends didn't know each other, neither knew the other existed, and Torn wanted to keep things that way. He had a feeling Yukie's passing might be a catalyst for what Mak had warned him about.

After the last mourner had offered incense and the chanting of the final sutra had ended, the guests departed, each receiving a thank-you gift, but not before Mayumi tracked Torn down.

She smiled her big, beautiful smile. "Konnichiwa, Torn-sensei. Surprise!" Then her smile evaporated and she looked down sheepishly, holding her purse in front of her with both hands.

Torn stiffened. "It's thoughtful of you to come."

She looked up searchingly. "I'd like to take you out tonight."

An appealing offer, titillating in its inappropriateness. Time with Mayumi would help him relax. Still, he felt uncomfortable with his family and Kiwako around. "Thanks for asking, but I need to stay with my kids."

Mayumi was about to say something when Kiwako appeared. He felt a sudden tightening in his chest and an overwhelming desire to run away. Instead, he decided to take charge of the conversation.

"Hello, Kiwako. It's so nice of you to come," he said more loudly than he'd intended. "Let me introduce you to my friend and former colleague, Mayumi Ino. She's head of compliance at Germanic Bank." He was rambling but plowed ahead. "Mayumi, this is my *kohai*, Kiwako Meyers. She was a year junior to me in college. She deals in antiques and has stores in San Francisco, Tokyo, and Bangkok." He wanted to keep talking, even though he suspected he was fooling no one.

Kiwako smiled. "Yes, I remember. You told me about her the night she tried to call you."

Torn had difficulty breathing.

To describe Mayumi's demeanor toward Kiwako as frosty would be like describing an ice age as minor climate change.

Mak came to the rescue. "Torn, it's time to take Sophia and Sean to dinner."

Torn felt like a drowning man catching a rescue buoy. "Right. Please excuse us."

Mayumi and Kiwako each expressed their condolences again. Mayumi hugged Torn tightly and Kiwako kissed him lightly on the cheek.

Shortly after Mak led Torn away, he received a text from Mayumi: "Are you fucking her?"

"No," he lied.

"Do you still love me?"

He sighed. "Yes, sweetheart."

"I love you too. I'm sorry for being so thoughtless. Funerals make me crazy."

Not just funerals, he thought.

Kiwako texted him later: "She's young."

He didn't know how to respond. Torn, his children, and Yukie's family went to a restaurant for a light meal. Two police officers sat at a nearby table.

Torn turned to Kenji. "How was the meeting with the temple?"

"They listened politely but were non-committal. They asked us to agree to a second choice in case they couldn't grant the *kaimyou* Yukie wanted."

"What did you say?"

Kenji looked nervous. "I declined, as we agreed. I'm not sure it was the right decision. Our family will look bad if the temple fails to grant a *kaimyou* before the funeral tomorrow."

"I know it's a gamble. But rejecting her request would reflect even worse on the temple, given that Yukie was murdered. Everyone will think the temple must have refused to agree to the *kaimyou*. The press might pick up on it too. I'm sure Matsuo-san informed the temple of the risk. It's not a risk they will take when the alternative is receiving ten million yen."

After dinner, Sean said he didn't want to leave his mother alone. So Torn, Sean, and Sophia returned to the temple to spend the night with Yukie's body. The police, however, allowed them only thirty minutes, after which they returned to the Andaz Hotel, where Torn's children were staying in rooms next to his. Yukie's brothers said they would remain with Yukie's body and keep incense burning through the night.

Ashes to Ashes

灰は灰に

The next day, Torn and his children put on their mourning clothes and returned to the temple for the funeral. On the way, Torn received a text from Kenji: "The temple agreed to the *kaimyou*." Torn felt vindicated. The only other thing he could do for Yukie was to protect their children.

At the temple, much of the entire wake ceremony was repeated. But the group was smaller, consisting mostly of family and close friends, and the atmosphere even more formal and somber.

After the ceremony, the mourners filled the casket with flowers from the three-tiered arrangement, being careful to leave Yukie's face exposed. The morticians then nailed the lid shut with a stone. The pounding of the nails into the coffin signaled a finality Torn had not been willing to acknowledge until then. His mind knew she was gone, but his heart wouldn't accept it. He felt like crying, but he couldn't break down now; he needed to hold it together for Sophia and Sean.

Torn, his children, and Yukie's brothers loaded the casket into the hearse for the trip to the *kasoba*, crematorium. Mourners followed in buses and cars. A patrol car trailed Torn, Sean, and Sophia, who rode with Kenji. Torn sat in the passenger seat, his children in the back. He faced forward and put on sunglasses so his children wouldn't see his tears.

The crematorium had four classes of chamber. Yukie had joked at her father's funeral that the fourth-class room consisted of a dirt floor, an open fire pit, and torches. The first-class chamber had huge bronze outer doors with giant brass handles. Inside those doors were stainless steel inner doors whose steel handles were covered in black rubber. A white-gloved attendant opened the outer and inner doors and pulled out a long ceramic tray resting on a frame that slid on rails.

Pallbearers placed Yukie's casket on the tray. The attendant opened the shutters to expose Yukie's face one last time. Torn's children stroked their mother's dark hair and kissed her goodbye. Sean placed a cherished wooden amulet he'd bought in Guatemala in the casket. Finally, Torn kissed Yukie's forehead and silently thanked her for blessing him with two beautiful children.

The white-gloved attendant closed the shutters and gently pushed the casket into the chamber. She shut and locked the inner doors, which closed with a vacuum-seal sound. She shut and locked the outer doors and handed the key to Kenji, the Ishikawa family's most senior representative. She led Kenji to the right side of the chamber and instructed him how to operate the furnace. He pulled a large lever down, and the fire started with a whoosh. The noise from the furnace grew until it was a soft muffled roar.

Well, there's no denying it now, thought Torn. He was surprised by how much of a struggle it was to accept the fact that she was really gone.

Yukie's relatives and close friends went upstairs to a large private room with tatami mats and low tables for the funeral meal. They sat on floor cushions and ate out of elaborate lacquered bento boxes with compartments of rice, fish, meat, vegetables, tofu, pickled plums, and a small sweet. Some people drank beer, sake, wine, or all three.

Torn, sitting next to Sean and Sophia, was suddenly famished. He removed the lid from his lunch box and looked at the courses. He split the disposable chopsticks and dug into his food, noticing with relief that his children were also eating.

In the middle of the meal, Torn's phone rang.

"Hello, Sagara-sensei. Do you have a moment?" Detective Taniguchi's tired voice asked. He was calling on an encrypted app.

Torn noted the detective had addressed him as "sensei" instead of "san." Detectives generally paid that kind of respect only to prosecutors. He suspected Taniguchi was treating him with such deference because his lawyer, Saki Katayama, was a former prosecutor.

"We're at the crematorium having lunch"—which struck Torn as a darkly funny thing to say—"but I'm glad you called." He got up and left the dining room, but not before Sophia glared at him for taking the call.

"I'm so sorry to bother you, but could I trouble you to meet me outside by the gate?" he asked gently.

Torn looked at his phone in surprise before putting it back to his ear. "I'll be right out."

He found Taniguchi, wearing sunglasses and smoking a cigarette, beside a long white paper *chochin*, lantern, hanging near the gate to the gravel-covered parking lot. Black *kanji* decorating the *chochin* pronounced this as a place where souls embarked on their final journey.

Taniguchi pulled out a small metal case that fit in the palm of his hand, opened the lid, and meticulously stubbed out his cigarette. He closed the lid and returned the case to his pocket.

He took off his sunglasses, bowed to Torn, and said, "I thought you'd like to know we tracked down the taxi driver. He still had your wife's luggage. You were right. Mrs. Sagara had called Metro Taxi to order a cab."

Torn nodded and waited for more information.

"The driver said they were on their way to Narita when she asked him to take her back home because she'd forgotten something. When they arrived, he noticed a large black sedan across the street. Mrs. Sagara told him to wait and that she'd be right out. Shortly after she went into the house, two men in black wearing masks and baseball caps appeared at his window and ordered him to leave."

"He panicked and drove away. But I guess his conscience got the better of him because he soon made an anonymous call to the police. That's why we showed up so quickly. He was so scared that he went to his parents' home in Miyagi Prefecture, which is why it took time to find him. He was mortified to learn of Mrs. Sagara's murder and offered his sincerest apologies and condolences to her family."

Torn, squinting from the bright sun, took a moment to respond as he considered what he'd just heard. "So, the men spoke in Japanese?"

"Yes, the driver said they growled at him in gutter Japanese. They didn't seem to be foreign, but he couldn't see their faces. Sagara-sensei, can you tell me again why you think they went to your house?"

Torn felt a heavy weight on his chest. He cleared his throat. "As I said, I don't know for sure. The only thing I can think of is they were looking for information about Raijin Clean's technology. They probably blew up Raijin's building in an attempt to stop the development of Brooks-san's invention. They might also be trying to gather any materials that could be used to replicate it."

But both Torn and Taniguchi knew of another reason; Torn had not changed his domicile registration. By law, within two weeks of moving out of Yukie's house, he should have deregistered in Sagami Ward, where Yukie's house was located, and registered in Minato Ward, where his new apartment was located. He kept telling himself he would do it after they divorced. If he had done so, the perpetrators wouldn't have found Yukie's house when they looked up where he lived. There was no other explanation. They wouldn't have been able to follow him there because he hadn't been back in over two years.

As if reading his mind, Taniguchi said, "You can't blame yourself for her murder."

They both knew that was only partially true.

"Sagara-sensei, I know this is hard for you to discuss right now, but do you have any media explaining the technology?"

"No." Which was technically true. The ability to access information and possession of such information were two different things. He didn't trust anyone except Mak at this point, and just in case his phone was tapped or there was a mole within the police force, Torn wanted whoever was listening to think he was in the dark with respect to Saya's technology.

"I've studied the technology extensively, but I don't have all the information in my head necessary to recreate the invention. The prototypes were destroyed, and no one can rebuild them without having all of the technical information describing Brooks-san's inventions."

He didn't mention he had access to that information. No one else knew he had such access and no one else had access, not even Saya's trusts and estates lawyer. That was dangerous for the company, because if something happened to Torn before Raijin could build another prototype and file the remaining patent applications, the technology would be lost. He needed to get a working prototype built and the applications filed fast.

Taniguchi looked Torn in the eye for an awkwardly long period of time before saying, "I see. Pardon me for asking before the funeral's even over, but why do you think Mrs. Sagara ran to the ruins of the five-storied pagoda?"

Torn had been mulling over that question ever since Sean had asked it too. All he could think of was Yukie loved that spot because she thought it was romantic: two inseparable lovers, one married, one much younger, stuck in a rigid society with no way to be together other than in death. *Total corn*, he thought, but part of him also found it endearing.

"I'm not sure. But she loved that spot. Maybe she panicked after realizing the taxi was gone and ran to a place where she felt safe." Almost as an afterthought, he asked softly, "I understand she was stabbed twice?"

Taniguchi lit another cigarette. "Yes, evidently she surprised the killer in the house. She fought back though. The DNA tests revealed that not all the blood in the house was hers, and that the blood on the largest carving knife in the kitchen wasn't hers. Some of it belongs to someone else."

Torn stepped to one side to avoid the stream of secondhand smoke wafting his way. "Well, she was a marathon runner in college and was tough, that's for sure. Did they chase her into the cemetery?"

"It's not clear. But we found no footprints other than yours and hers around the foundation stones. They might have had their hands full getting the injured guy out of there."

Torn thought for a moment. "Have you had any luck tracking down the sender of the threatening email?"

"Unfortunately, no. As you know, the email arrived from Russia and we have no way of getting information from the Russian service provider. We've put in an inquiry through Interpol. But the Russians aren't responsive to such requests unless there's something in it for them, and in this case, I don't see why they'd be inclined to help us."

Detective Taniguchi was silent for a moment. "Sagara-sensei, I have to tell you something. I want you to know that given what happened to your wife and Brooks-san, we're now convinced you were attacked on the expressway, but officially we must continue the investigation. There's still the question of whether you used reasonable force in defending yourself by forcing the biker into the wall."

Torn felt his blood begin to boil. "Detective Taniguchi, there's a bullet hole in my motorcycle!"

"Yes, I know, but someone in the Mercedes shot at you, not one of the Yankees. So, it's not clear the Yankees were working with those in the car."

Torn was incredulous. "Is it really possible they weren't working together? I've been riding motorcycles for years without incident. You expect me to believe that all of a sudden I'm the victim of two unrelated attacks on the same day?"

Taniguchi, struggling to walk the line between common sense and the dictates of the police department, looked sideways, took a long drag on his cigarette, and pursed his lips. "Sagara-sensei, we also believe it's unlikely, but thus far we have no proof of a connection other than that the two events happened one after the other on the same day. And of course, it's the prosecutor, not the police, who ultimately will decide whether to dismiss or prosecute this case."

Torn wanted to grab the detective by his thick-veined bureaucratic neck, but Taniguchi was right: Only the prosecutor's office could ultimately decide what to do with Torn's case. And he needed the police on his side. So, he said with all the sincerity and appreciation he could muster, "I understand you're only doing your job, Detective. My family and I very much appreciate your efforts and protection. As you know, my children will be leaving Japan again for safety reasons. I hope you find the perpetrators soon. They can't return until you do."

"Thank you for your understanding, Sagara-sensei. Katayama-sensei is well-respected by the police and the prosecutors, and she speaks highly of you. We'll do our best to clear up these matters as expeditiously as possible."

Torn, still fuming, managed to bow before returning to the dining area, where he sat down, only to find he'd lost his appetite.

An hour later, a representative of the crematorium said they were ready for the *honeage*, the bone-gathering ceremony. Everyone returned to the cremation chamber and gathered around the furnace doors. Kenji returned the key to the white-gloved attendant. She opened the bronze outside doors and the stainless steel inside doors. Using a metal hook, she pulled the ceramic tray out of the furnace. The tray still radiated heat and was covered with white bones and ash. Many of the bones, including the leg bones, arm bones, ribs, pelvis, and cranium, were clearly identifiable.

The attendant then moved the tray to the bone-gathering room next to the cremation chamber, with Yukie's relatives in tow. A marble urn sat at one end of the tray. The attendant pointed out that the bones were in very good shape and many had survived cremation because the deceased was relatively young and healthy. Torn wanted to roll his eyes.

Using a special pair of unusually long chopsticks, one made of bamboo and another of willow, signifying a bridge between two worlds, the attendant picked up a neck bone she said was shaped like a Buddha sitting cross-legged. Torn didn't see the resemblance but kept his opinion to himself.

After the Buddha bone had been placed to one side, Yukie's family lined up on both sides of the tray. Using the special chopsticks, relatives on either side of the tray picked up a bone together and placed it in the urn. This was the only time Japanese ever picked up anything together with chopsticks, and why they never handed food from chopsticks to chopsticks. In addition to being bad karma, it brought back memories of funerals past.

Torn's hand was steady as he picked up a bone with Kenji. By now Torn was calm. He would continue to mourn Yukie's death, but he knew she was gone. The three steps of nailing the coffin lid, placing the coffin in the furnace, and putting the remains in the urn helped him accept the loss. He was proud that Sean and Sophia, though teary-eyed, got through the process too.

After the relatives had gone through the lines once, the attendant put the remaining bones and ashes in the urn, placed the Buddha bone on top of the other bones, and put the lid on. Then she placed the urn in a box wrapped in a large silk cloth, which she handed to Sean, the oldest son. The police drove Sean, Sophia, and Torn back to the hotel. Sean held the precious box in his lap throughout the ride. The urn would later be interred in the Ishikawa family plot.

He handed the urn to Torn when they reached the hotel, but Sophia asked to keep it in her room. Torn gently passed her the box with her mother's bones and ashes.

Self-Centered

自己中心的

"Torn, what in the hell's going on? Where's Saya? According to the news, the police aren't saying whether there are any victims from the explosion."

Without thinking, Torn responded icily, "I was hoping you could tell me, Vince."

It was the day after the funeral, and Sean and Sophia had just left for Alaska to stay with their grandmother at the family's remote cabin. They were devastated by their mother's death, and Torn didn't want to leave them alone. But it was too dangerous for them to be in Japan, and yet, he needed to stay to help the police find the perpetrators.

"That's not fair. I can understand why you might be suspicious of anyone connected to Saya, and I may be difficult sometimes, but I'm not a monster. Besides, what do I have to gain from blowing up a company in which I'm an investor?"

Torn, trying his best to think straight, said slowly and deliberately, "Only you know, but perhaps to protect your oil drilling equipment distribution business? You're the one who told me Saya's technology might put you out of business. And by the way, why didn't you tell Tamayo we had a conflict of interest? Why did she expect Hilsberry would represent Wakkanai in connection with its planned investment in Raijin when I clearly told you we couldn't?"

Vince sighed. "Torn, I was joking. And besides, I hedge all the time. That's why I invest in competing technologies. As for the conflict, I did tell her. She's old. Maybe she forgot. But I'm being thoughtless. You've been through a lot. Let's start over."

Ya think? Torn didn't believe a word Vince said.

"I'm sorry to learn of your wife's death. I should've mentioned that first, but I've been worried sick about Saya."

"Sure ya have," Torn almost said sarcastically, but catching himself he remained silent.

"How're you and your family holding up?"

Torn thought, *Where's the Vince Harden I've come to know and love? Because you ain't him.*

Pulling himself out of his dark hole, he stood and paced in his office. "You're right. I'm not being fair. I don't know what to think. The funeral was yesterday, and we're taking things one day at a time." He still believed Vince might be behind all of the carnage, but he had no proof.

"May God protect you. Do the police have any leads?"

"Not that I know of."

"Do you know anything about Saya?"

"No. The police won't tell me anything. I think she may be dead," Torn lied.

"What makes you think that?"

"I received documents from Saya's lawyer appointing me acting CEO and president and giving me a proxy on her shares in Raijin Clean."

Silence. Finally, Vince asked, "What do you plan to do with Raijin Clean?"

"What do you think I should do?"

"Continue her work. She would've wanted that."

Torn stopped and looked out the window at workmen clearing rubble from a fallen building.

Vince filled the silence. "So, I guess your first step will be to complete the deal with CPV?"

"Both the small and large prototypes were destroyed. We can't rebuild them without access to all of the technology, and some important aspects seem to be only in Saya's head. No one is going to invest in a start-up if the founder is dead. Unless we have all the technology."

"Her lab guys can't piece it together?"

Torn walked to the window and looked at the harbor. "Unlikely. She intentionally withheld certain information so no one could steal it from her."

He didn't tell Vince that he had picked up the memory sticks hidden in the safe deposit boxes or that Torn's colleagues were already hard at work preparing patent applications to cover all of her technology. His next step was to get another prototype built, which he also wasn't about to share with Vince.

"What about my ten million dollars?" Vince asked.

"Perhaps we can salvage the energy storage system technology and recoup some losses from that. But I can't guarantee anything. The creditors will come first anyway."

"Have you spoken to ETC?" Eagle Technology Capital was the other major investor in Raijin Clean.

"No, but when I do, I'll tell them the same thing."

Vince sighed again. "Fuck."

Torn smiled. "Look on the bright side. We'll close Project Ibis tomorrow, which will make Tamayo very happy with you, and your businesses are safe from the ravages of Raijin's technology."

"You're right. I win whether Raijin's technology takes off or not." Vince paused. "So, the police aren't making any headway at all in the investigation of your wife's murder?"

Obsess much? thought Torn. But he said, "I haven't heard anything yet." And then, against his better judgment, he added, "But I'm going to do everything I can to help the police catch whoever killed her and Saya."

"We don't know yet for sure Saya's dead."

Torn stopped and looked at a photograph of his children on his desk. "Doesn't matter. Whoever did these things will be. Japan still has the death penalty and they use it."

"It's understandable you'd want revenge. But remember..." Vince spoke slowly and deliberately for effect, "...good thoughts, good words, good deeds."

"Vince, no offense, but that's not even Christian. It's Zoroastrian." Torn was in no mood for a sermon.

Vince laughed. "Very good! Same difference. Anyway, you know I'm right. You don't want to stoop to their level. You need to think of your children."

"Same difference? Really, Mr. Born Again?" Torn knew he was being impertinent. "I am thinking of my children. Anyway, they can take care of themselves."

"I'll let that slide. Of course they can, if they're anything like their old man. But you don't want them to lose another parent. I can understand why these events would put you in a dark place, but you know that God loves you, right?"

"Vince, I'm not religious, and if I were, I'd be having doubts about God's love right now."

"It doesn't matter. The Lord loves you anyway, and I will be praying for you and your family. You should leave things to the police."

"Right, because they've done such a wonderful job protecting my client and family so far." Torn paused. He knew he was being too emotional.

"You're right that the perpetrators need to be caught to make sure you're all safe. But why did the Japanese police contact me?"

You motherfucker, Torn thought. *Now I know why you called me in a panic about Saya, acted all nice to me, and keep pressing about the investigation of Yukie's murder. You're only concerned about yourself because you think the police are on to you.*

He took a deep breath and focused on the immediate question. "Well, I'm not sure what you want to know, but the police are investigating the motorcycle chase, which I'm sure you saw in the news, the explosion, the ransacking of Saya's apartment, and Yukie's murder." He didn't mention the threatening email and letter he'd received because they hadn't been revealed publicly yet. "They've interviewed me several times and interviewed all of Raijin's employees. The police are also interviewing Saya's family, her neighbors, and anyone who's done business with Saya or Raijin. Interviewing Raijin's investors would make sense under the circumstances."

"Do I need a lawyer?"

"I don't know whether you *need* one, but my advice is that you consult with a lawyer before responding to the police."

"That's why I'm talking to you."

Torn was pacing again. "As much as we'd like to, neither I nor Hilsberry can represent you in this matter. First, even though I acted in self-defense, I'm still a suspect in connection with the expressway attacks—I'm sure you heard that one of the motorcyclists who attacked us died. We also have a conflict of interest because we represent Raijin Clean and you're possibly a suspect in the expressway attacks, the destruction of Raijin's building, and my wife's murder. In addition, as I mentioned, I'm acting CEO and hold the proxy for Saya's shares. That puts me personally in direct conflict with you, an investor in Raijin Clean."

"Can you refer me to a good Japanese criminal defense attorney?"

"I don't know anyone, but I can ask my attorney, Saki Katayama. I'm sure she can refer you to a good criminal defense attorney who speaks English well. I'll have her get in touch with you directly."

After his call with Vince, Torn checked on the Project Ibis team to see how the pre-closing was progressing, then went for a walk outside to clear his head. He was admiring the view of a tree-lined street from a pedestrian bridge when Kiwako called.

"Hi, Torn. How're you and the kids doing? I'd ask how the funeral was but I know it couldn't have been fun."

He smiled. "Hi, Kiwako. It's sweet of you to check in. We're surviving."

"What are you up to today?"

"I'm outside getting a breath of fresh air."

He thought what a breath of fresh air this normal conversation was compared to the psychotic texts he'd received from Mayumi after the wake. Mayumi never once asked about his children, consistent with her desire to deny their existence.

"Shouldn't you be with Sean and Sophia?"

He debated whether to tell her about the kids. He knew that he needed to tell someone other than his mother in case she couldn't get ahold of him for some reason. Even though he had told Mak, he wanted his mother to be able to reach someone in a closer time zone, and he knew Kiwako would return to San Francisco soon.

Seeing no one else around, he said, "Kiwako, I need to tell you something in complete confidence."

"Sounds serious. What is it?"

"Sean and Sophia are in Alaska with my mom."

"You're trying to keep them safe. Makes sense."

"Exactly. They'll be there until the police catch Yukie's killer. They have Mak's contact information, but my mom needs someone else to contact if she can't reach me."

"You can give her my details. I'm happy to do it."

"You can't tell anyone where they are."

"Mum's the word."

"Thank you very much."

"I'm only doing it to help Sean and Sophia... and because I love you, Torn."

"I love you too, Kiwako."

"Then stay away from Mayumi." And with that she hung up.

Head Spin

混乱

Torn spent all night preparing for the Project Ibis closing, returned to the hotel for a quick shower, and was back in the office by 6:00 a.m. Orchestrating simultaneous closings in Hilsberry's offices in Asia, Europe, Africa, and North America, and the offices of local counsel in India, was like herding cats. But so far, things had been going about as smoothly as possible.

Around 3:00 p.m., Wakkanai authorized the first of a waterfall of wire transfers to purchase the shares of the various subsidiaries of Zephyrus Oil & Drilling being acquired in different jurisdictions. The wire transfers would take several hours to complete as each receiving bank came online in its particular time zone, but the closing was essentially done, pending confirmation from the seller of receipt of each wire transfer and physical transfer of the share certificates.

Shortly after the first wire transfer in Japan, Mamiko buzzed Torn. "It's Asahi Susono-san of Wakkanai again. He says it's urgent."

Torn had already spoken to Susono, Tamayo Watanabe's executive assistant, several times over the past twenty-four hours about closing matters and was not surprised he was calling again. "Put him through." He had his headset on and had been standing all day to stay awake. He started pacing.

"Sagara-sensei, I know you're busy, but Watanabe-shacho asked me to tell you we've terminated Harden-san. She notified him a few minutes ago."

Torn stopped pacing and closed his door. "On what grounds?"

"The board has lost confidence in him."

"But he's the one who negotiated a great price on this deal for Wakkanai."

"True, but he may have received a kickback from Twain Advisory."

A light bulb went on in Torn's tired head. "Do you have any proof?"

"Not really. Which is why we don't intend to press charges."

Torn started pacing again. "But the deal terms with Twain were better than with Sakurajima." He thought Vince's behavior had been suspicious as well, but it could be chalked up to Vince being an impatient businessperson not wanting to wade into the weeds.

Susono sucked air through his teeth. "As you know, Harden-san fired Sakurajima and brought in Twain without a beauty contest like the one he made you go through. And Wakkanai believes that even though Twain agreed to a lower success fee, Harden-san was willing to accept no discount and no cap on their due diligence and consulting fees. You were the one who insisted on getting a discount and capping those fees."

Torn frowned. "That's it? Just because he hired a new financial advisor and didn't really push for a discount or cap on certain fees?"

Susono lowered his voice to almost a whisper. "Well, there's also a concern he might have been planning a coup."

Another light bulb went on in Torn's head, but he didn't see any proof for that either.

"What makes you think that?"

"Harden-san is always looking for the bigger, better deal, and he told someone he thought Wakkanai needed to make management changes. Watanabe-shacho learned of his comments and decided to fire him."

Ah, the real reason, Torn thought. He closed his eyes and rubbed his temples. "How'd he react when she told him?"

"He threatened to sue. But don't worry, we have a local employment law attorney who can handle the defense. At any rate, she wanted you to know in case he calls you for help. Wakkanai doesn't want Hilsberry representing him."

Torn gave a sigh of relief he hoped Susono couldn't hear. He wanted to stay out of this fight. As distasteful as he found Vince, he didn't feel comfortable being adverse to someone with whom he'd worked so closely, and he wanted to avoid being adverse to one of Raijin Clean's major investors.

His other line started blinking. "Don't worry. Wakkanai is our client. Not Harden-san."

"Good. That'll make Watanabe-shacho feel better about you. She was furious when you declined to represent Wakkanai in connection with its planned investment in Raijin Clean. I had to convince her you were doing the right thing and not being disloyal."

"You're right. Thank you for your understanding and support, as always, Susono-san."

No sooner had he hung up than Mamiko buzzed again. "Vince Harden's holding on the other line."

Vince never held for anyone. *This oughta be good,* Torn thought. He started pacing again, but now he was smiling and the furrow in his brow was gone.

"Torn, those bastards fired me. Can you believe it?"

Couldn't have happened to a nicer guy.

Before Torn could respond, Vince added, "And they terminated our Distribution Agreement. They're trying to cut me out of the Northern Okhotsk Project, which is worth at least a hundred million dollars to Harden Industries."

Torn played dumb. "Who?"

"That cunt at Wakkanai. Who else?"

Torn suppressed a laugh. He wanted to ask if that was appropriate language for a born-again Christian but held his tongue.

"I'm sorry to hear that, Vince."

"I'm not looking for sympathy. I want to sue those bastards and buy them out. I have the perfect person to run it."

"Vince, I appreciate you thinking of us, but we can't represent you against Wakkanai."

"Can't you resign?"

"That won't resolve the conflict in this case. We know too much about Wakkanai and your relationship with them."

"Ya know, Torn, I've been good to you. Don't forget, I hired you for Project Ibis."

"And we very much appreciate that. It's been an honor to work with you on this deal. But this is an unwaivable conflict."

"So, find me another lawyer."

"I can't help you there either. The conflict rules won't allow it, but I'm sure your new defense attorney can find someone for you."

"Thanks for nothin'."

Torn heard a dial tone and smiled again. Sitting down, he leaned back and closed his eyes. He was out like a light. A few minutes later, an associate woke him with a question about a wire transfer to South Africa. After addressing that, he called Mak, who had been trying to reach him for the past twenty-four hours.

"Lay it on me."

"Tamayo is eighty-four and the daughter of the founder. Or at least that's what her bio says."

Torn was up and pacing again. "What do you mean?"

"We haven't found any info about college or high school, which is odd for someone in her position. We've hired a local private eye to look into her past because it gets hazy the further back you go. He promised to get back to me by the end of the week."

"Anything else?"

"A photo on Wakkanai's website shows her standing next to a bust of herself, which is next to a bust of her father. In the middle is the corporate seal with what looks like a spaceship in a circle, but I assume it's a drill bit. It's a little North Koreaesque. Anyway, she's evidently grooming her daughter, Miki Watanabe, to be the next president. But by all accounts, Miki is worthless and the real brains behind the operation is Tomohiro Saito, who goes by Tom when dealing with foreigners. He's not related to the Watanabe family. He works closely with Vince Harden, and they like to go to baseball games and sumo tournaments together."

Torn thought perhaps it was true that Vince had been planning a coup all along. "Vince was fired."

"Interesting. From what you've told me, it must be a blessing."

Torn stopped pacing. "Yes, he's got a challenging personality."

"He sounds like a complete dick, and you sound like the enabler of a nasty alcoholic," Mak responded.

Torn turned red. "Are you alluding to my relationship with Yukie?"

Mak paused. "I wasn't thinking about that, but now that you mention it, sometimes I think you would get into less trouble if you were more direct with people."

Torn started pacing again but didn't respond.

Mak continued. "Anyway, Miki's married to Yoji Watanabe, who took Miki's last name to continue the Watanabe line since Tamayo has no sons. Tamayo runs Wakkanai like it's her own privately held company, even though she owns less than one percent of the publicly traded shares. The institutional investors should've forced out management a long time ago given Wakkanai's abysmal returns. But shareholders in Japan are sheep."

"Who's on the board?"

"There're eleven board members, including Vince. Eight of them are career employees and two of those, Miki and Yoji, are related to the chair, Tamayo. It's hard to believe there could be so much nepotism at a publicly traded company. Only three of the eleven are outside or so-called independent directors, but they aren't really independent. Harden Industries was Wakkanai's global distributor for decades before Vince was appointed to the board. And the other two have pre-existing relationships with the career employee directors."

"So, Tamayo owns the board. Why would Vince be interested in buying Wakkanai?"

"Their return on equity has plummeted, and they're hemorrhaging money."

Torn laughed. "Why does that make them attractive?"

"They've got good customers and good technology, but management sucks at running the company and the market cap shows it. One analyst noted that the stock price grossly misrepresents the true value of the company.

"Another problem is this deal you're working on, Project Ibis. The Zephyrus purchase evidently was Tom Saito's brainchild. Unfortunately, Tamayo wouldn't agree to retention bonuses for Zephyrus management or agree to put any of them on Wakkanai's board, even though Zephyrus is comparable in size to Wakkanai. Several senior managers at Zephyrus have resigned as a result. Zephyrus's best salespeople and engineers may be the next to leave. The market isn't confident that Wakkanai, a very domestic Japanese company, can operate an overseas business. They have sales all over the world, but Vince has been handling those.

"Now that he's been shit-canned, they'll be on their own. If Wakkanai can't maintain sales, then the banks financing the purchase price will start to worry Wakkanai won't be able to pay off the loan. And the institutional shareholders have already voiced concerns about how post-merger integration with Zephyrus will be handled."

I'm so glad we're closing this deal today, thought Torn. "You've done your homework, but so far you've mentioned only Wakkanai's problems. I'm still not seeing any hidden value except that Vince probably thinks he could do a better job running the company because he knows the buyers."

"Well, I'm sure that's part of it," Mak replied.

Torn sat down and rubbed his eyes with his fists. "Or maybe he had Raijin shut down precisely because he believes Raijin's technology will make fossil fuels obsolete? With its prototypes gone and its inventor out of the way, perhaps he thought he could protect his own business *and* make a fast buck off buying and then flipping Wakkanai."

Mak paused. "I'm surprised at you, Torn. That's pure speculation, and Vince would be taking quite a risk. There are more obvious reasons for buying Wakkanai whether Raijin does well or not. First, even if Raijin were hugely successful, fossil fuels won't die overnight. The oil industry will still need drilling equipment for years to come. Also, drilling equipment can be used for mining and drilling other kinds of wells, including for water, and the world's running out of clean fresh water. And perhaps the most attractive and least known part of Wakkanai's business is the mining machinery business, including the seabed mining business. Wakkanai is valuing it at basically zero at this point. An analyst wrote that they've got great seabed mining technology but don't know how to exploit it. Perhaps Vince does."

Torn, exhausted and seeing spots, closed his eyes.

After an awkward pause, Mak asked, "Whaddya think, buddy?"

"I can't keep up with this shit."

Hell Hath No Fury

裏切られた女の怨念は恐ろしい

After saying hello to the cop and entering his suite, Torn, exhausted from work, walked down the hall into the spacious living room. He paused and took a deep breath as he admired the panoramic view of the city, with Tokyo Tower—bathed in yellow light—directly in front, and Mt. Fuji's dark silhouette on the horizon to the west. He gazed for a moment through a meter-long telescope near the window at the traffic on the Rainbow Bridge and the ships in the bay before changing into light chinos, a short-sleeved shirt, and hotel slippers.

Mayumi arrived a few minutes before the room service Torn had ordered. She quickly changed into a hotel robe with only a sleeveless sheer white silk blouse and white lace panties underneath.

Torn had allowed her to invite herself over in a moment of weakness. She had given him a hard time about being with Kiwako on the night Mayumi had called. He had lied and reassured her there was nothing between Kiwako and him. And she had given him the third degree about why Saya had been riding on the back of his bike when the attacks occurred. He explained that Saya was just a client wanting a ride, which was true, or at least it was at the time. As usual, he felt a pang of guilt for two-timing Kiwako and Mayumi. The feeling was even stronger now and coupled with fear that his cheating might blow up in his face since Kiwako suspected he was seeing Mayumi.

Despite his fast talking, she'd demanded he prove he wasn't seeing anyone else by letting her come over. Torn had tried to explain it wasn't safe for her to be with him, but she said it was her risk to take. This was just a continuation of their dysfunctional pattern of her being unreasonably demanding and him being unable to say no, in part because he loved her, and in part because he was afraid of what she might do to him or herself if he refused. And while he felt guilty about putting her in harm's way and chagrin for being so weak, the truth was he was happy to see her.

Soon, a young man dressed in a hotel uniform arrived pushing a cart covered in dishes under silver domes. Torn asked him to put the cart in front of the sofa facing the windows so he and Mayumi could eat while watching TV and enjoying the view beyond. The server pulled side flaps out from the side of the cart to make a larger table. In the middle of the tray was a container holding silverware, including authentic hard lacquered chopsticks, instead of disposable chopsticks, and a steak knife. The chopsticks, long, sturdy, and tapered to a point, were for the sushi, sashimi, and tempura. The steak knife was for Mayumi's T-bone.

Torn signed the bill and told the server he would call when he wanted someone to bus the cart and dishes.

They ate dinner while watching the news. Mayumi was happy sitting next to Torn while sipping on her vodka tonic and dining on the food she'd asked him to order.

After dinner, he put green tea leaves in an elegant iron teapot and added boiling water from a small electric kettle. Leaving the tea to steep, he went through the adjoining bedroom to the bathroom to wash his hands. As he rinsed his hands, the doorbell rang and Mayumi went to answer the door. Torn shouted, "Who is it?" over the sound of the running water.

Mayumi shouted back, "It's someone to pick up the dishes!" Torn immediately responded, "Don't open the door!"

Too late. A large brutish man wearing a black tracksuit burst through the door, breaking the chain lock. He knocked her to the floor as he charged down the hall with a large carving knife. An older man with a Japanese afro called a "punch perm," also wearing a black tracksuit and brandishing a knife, followed closely behind.

Hearing the commotion, Torn ran through the bedroom into the living room. Exiting the bedroom as the two men entered the living room, he twisted the telescope off its tripod stand and stepped forward to meet them.

As the first thug came running at him with the knife, Torn stepped next to the coffee table, grabbed the teapot by its wooden handle, and tossed it at him. The hot iron teapot flew through the air, spout over handle, throwing a circle of scalding hot water on the man's face and chest a moment before the teapot and its lid hit him. The man, yelping in pain and surprise, paused and instinctively brought his empty hand to his scalded face. The man behind him also stopped for a moment.

Holding the telescope by the narrow end with both hands, Torn took advantage of their hesitation by swinging it behind him and up like a golfer's backswing and then forward, down, and then up again, catching the first man squarely in the groin. He gasped and his knees buckled, whereupon Torn swung the telescope like a baseball bat, hitting the man in the side of the head and face with the fat end of the telescope. He fell backward, shattering a glass end table next to the sofa.

Before Torn could wind up again, the older man leaped over his partner with surprising agility and tackled Torn, stabbing him deeply in the left shoulder with an overhead thrust. Torn fell backward, shattering the coffee table. His assailant yanked the knife out of Torn's shoulder and drew back to finish the job.

With a blood-curdling scream Torn didn't recognize at first, Mayumi pounced on the man's back, burying between his shoulder blades one of the lacquered chopsticks she'd plucked from the room service cart. Howling in pain, the man jumped up with Mayumi still on his back, holding on with one arm around his neck and her legs wrapped around his waist. Using her other hand, she drove the chopstick deeper into his back while screaming obscenities at him.

The man backed up quickly until he smacked Mayumi hard against one of the windows. Her head snapped back, smashing into the window with a loud thud, rendering her unconscious. She slid to the floor in a heap. The man frantically reached behind his back trying to remove the chopstick she had driven into his left lung.

By this time, both Torn and the first assailant were getting back up, but Torn stood first while the man was still on his knees. Swinging the telescope with his right hand, he brought it down on the man's head like a hammer, knocking him to the floor once more.

The second assailant, now coughing up blood, charged Torn. As Torn fell backward again, with his right hand he caught the assailant's knife hand by the wrist. The man put both hands and his weight on the knife to drive it home. Torn countered with his left hand. But with his left shoulder badly injured and in excruciating pain, he was losing the battle. The knife came down, piercing the right side of his chest.

Just then, Mayumi appeared behind the assailant. Without saying a word, she buried the large steak knife to the hilt next to the chopstick. The assailant crumpled on top of Torn, his knife slicing Torn's right chest open.

Torn pushed the man off. The man groaned and Mayumi, robe open down to her navel and hands and white blouse covered in blood, started beating him over the head with a brass vase. Torn rasped, "I think he's had enough."

"Fuck you, I'll tell you when he's had enough!"

"Mayumi, I need something to stop the bleeding," Torn said weakly.

"Oh, honey. So sorry." She dropped the vase and grabbed two large cloth napkins to staunch the profuse bleeding from his chest and shoulder. He grabbed the napkins with his hands. "Thanks. I'll keep pressure on. Get the police and an ambulance."

Before she could reach for the phone, hotel security burst into the room. Seeing Mayumi standing over a very bloody Torn with her hair disheveled, eye makeup running down her cheeks, hands, open robe, blouse, and bare legs covered in blood, and a knife lying near Torn's left arm, they moved aggressively to restrain her. Torn assured them she was trying to help and, in fact, had saved his life. He told security to make sure the two men on the floor could do no more harm.

They handcuffed the intruders and radioed for the police and an ambulance. One of them got a pillow for Torn's head while the other examined the two assailants. "These guys are barely breathing," said the security guard examining them.

"I hope they fucking die," said Mayumi in a voice that didn't sound quite human.

"They just might," said the guard.

"How's the police officer at the door?" Torn asked in a feeble voice.

"He was unconscious when we found him. One of our colleagues is looking after him. We came up to investigate because the video monitor for this floor went dark. Someone must've disabled it."

Torn barely heard the response as he slipped into unconsciousness.

Bureaucratic Wall

官僚の壁

He felt like he was drowning. He also felt extreme pressure and discomfort, as if his lower abdomen was about to split apart. Opening his eyes, he took a deep breath. It was air. Antiseptic hospital air. His mouth was dry and his throat sore. He tried to move his left arm, but a sling and sharp pain in his shoulder stopped him. Then he tried the right arm. Feeling a tugging sensation, he looked down to see a tube sticking out of the crux of his elbow. He pressed on but pain in his chest stymied him. So, he relaxed his right arm and let his fingers walk slowly under the covers and over his leg toward his crotch, trying not to disturb the needle in his arm or anger his chest.

Thank God. No catheter.

He slowly slid his legs out from under the sheet and blanket, put his feet on the floor, and tried to stand. A wave of nausea washed over him. He remained sitting for a moment to let it pass, took a deep breath, grabbed the IV pole, and tried again. This time he made it, but he hadn't noticed the wires attached to his chest. Standing pulled the wires out of plastic patches stuck to his skin, causing the heart monitor to flatline. Two nurses rushed in.

"What're you doing?!"

"I need to pee or I'll explode," he said slowly, his voice an earnest whisper.

"You'll tear your sutures. We can bring a bed pan or catheterize you."

Torn had a vision of wrestling on the floor with the nurses, trying to prevent them from inserting a catheter.

Using the IV stand for support, he took baby steps toward the bathroom. "Well, I'm up now."

The second and more junior nurse moved to stop him, but the senior nurse said with resignation, "Help him to the toilet."

"How long have I been out?"

"Twenty-five hours."

After relieving himself for what seemed like an eternity, he slowly returned, with the nurse's help, to his bed, where he drank a bit of water through a straw and passed out again.

Torn was eating his first meal the next day when Detective Taniguchi came to visit. "It's good you have an appetite."

"Woke up starving."

Taniguchi pulled a chair to the bed and sat down. Back straight and legs bent at forty-five degrees, he placed his hands on his knees.

"You lost a lot of blood. They put several units into you during surgery. Seventy-seven stitches to close you up. You're lucky to be alive."

Torn, voice still raspy, said, "I don't want to worry my kids. Can you keep it out of the press?"

Taniguchi shook his head. "The press knows about the attacks at the hotel. We haven't disclosed your names, but we can withhold that information for only a few days."

Torn sipped some water. "I hope you don't need any more proof I acted in self-defense on the expressway."

Taniguchi clasped his hands together. "The investigation into the Yankee motorcyclist's death remains open, but I think it's fair to say no one at headquarters doubts you had good reason to believe you and Brooks-san were in mortal danger." He added, somewhat more officiously, "But as you know, we still haven't linked the car and motorcycle attacks, and the prosecutor's office will ultimately decide whether to prosecute. Once our investigation is complete, a prosecutor likely will want to speak with you again."

Torn's heart monitor beeped faster.

Taniguchi paused, looked around, and leaned in. "Sagara-sensei, may I speak off the record?"

"Of course."

"My colleagues and I are very impressed you survived that chase and with the way you took the first Yankee out and intentionally got pulled over to escape the other one. Some former *shirobai* (motorcycle cops) say you must really know how to drive that big BMW."

Torn suppressed a grin. His heart rate slowed. He wanted to say, "You're damn right. I kicked that lowlife motherfucker's ass." Instead, he looked Detective Taniguchi in the eye and said, "Thank you, but I was just trying to stay alive."

Taniguchi looked around again. "I'll deny it if you tell anyone what I just said."

Torn smiled. "I'm sorry, what were we talking about? The drugs must be affecting my short-term memory." Then he changed the subject. "Are the attackers from the hotel alive?"

"Yes, but barely. One's in a coma, quite badly hurt. Also, he has what looks like a pre-existing stab wound."

Torn sat up abruptly, causing pain in his chest and shoulder. "He must be the guy who killed Yukie! He's the one she stabbed!" he tried to shout, but it came out as a loud gravelly whisper. The effort made him cough, causing more pain.

"We have no proof yet, but we're conducting DNA tests. Should have the results in a couple of weeks."

Torn looked down and clenched his fists. "Is the guy who's awake talking?"

"Yes, but he's just a low-level thug from Osaka."

"Who hired them?"

"He said a Korean-Japanese man, but who knows if he's telling the truth. Many thugs blame things on Koreans, particularly North Koreans. The good news is we have a strong case against the two suspects."

"Any luck figuring out who sent me the threatening email?"

Taniguchi's jaw tightened. "Unfortunately, no. Dead end. They're beyond our jurisdiction."

Torn sighed. "Any other leads?"

"Our CSI team is conducting forensic tests on the building debris, bomb fragments, residue from the explosives, even bits of electronics, found at the Raijin Clean building site. We'll see where that leads us." Taniguchi paused and rubbed his chin with his right hand. "And there's one other thing."

"What's that?"

"There were numerous hacking attempts on Raijin Clean's servers. According to Raijin's head of IT, they originated in Russia."

Torn's heartbeat rocketed to 160 beats per minute, and his systolic blood pressure shot up to over 170. "After all these attacks and all this time, the only thing you've figured out is that the attempted hackings originated in Russia? I could've told you that." *Damn Japanese cops*, he thought. *Won't investigate anything unless evidence is handed to them on a silver platter.*

"Sagara-sensei, I understand why you're upset, but give us time."

A nurse came running in. "I'm going to have to ask you to leave."

Taniguchi stood. "My apologies. He seems strong. Sagara-sensei, we should continue this discussion when you're feeling better. I wish you a speedy recovery." Taniguchi bowed to Torn and the nurse and walked out.

The nurse reclined the bed using the remote control hanging at its side, then told Torn to get some rest as she dimmed the lights before leaving the room. Despite being completely exhausted, his mind raced. He pressed the remote control to raise the top half of the bed and called Saki.

She answered, sounding concerned. "I heard about what happened from Prosecutor Tsujikawa. I'm so sorry. But should you be talking?"

Torn replied weakly, "Saki, can you light a fire under the police? They seem allergic to actual investigative work. Does someone else need to die before they'll look into this more aggressively?"

"I understand your frustration, Torn, but Russia is outside their jurisdiction. Don't you have a Moscow office? Is there anyone there with contacts at the police or the prosecutor's office in Khabarovsk or Komsomolsk?"

Torn thought for a moment. "Please contact my partner in our Moscow office, Larisa Anismova. I'll text her that you'll be calling."

"No problem, Torn. Get some sleep."

He hung up and passed out with the phone on his stomach.

A nurse woke him for dinner a few hours later. Ravenous, he devoured the bland hospital food on the tray.

As he texted Larisa to expect Saki's call, Mayumi, looking cute and sexy in a white blouse and powder-blue skirt, walked in.

"Detective Taniguchi said I could visit. I think he likes me."

Torn started to laugh but the pain stopped him. "You're too funny. What man doesn't like you?"

"You have learned so well how to talk to me."

"Sweetie, you saved my life. I can't thank you enough." *She may be a crazy bitch, but she's my crazy bitch.* He had an overwhelming urge to hug her.

She must've felt the same way because she pushed the food tray to the side and put her arms around him, being careful not to disturb any of the tubes or wires connected to his body or put any weight on his wounds. It was an uncomfortable position she could manage for only a moment without hurting him. He could smell her perfume and felt a stirring he hadn't experienced since before the attempt on his life at the hotel.

She pulled away.

Torn felt a pang of guilt. "How're you doing?"

"Much better than you. I have a mild concussion, but I'm out of the hospital."

"Well, follow the doctor's orders."

She smiled. "I'm taking a few days off from work. So, I can come see you every day!"

He grabbed her hand and rubbed the top of it affectionately with his thumb. At the same time, he thanked his lucky stars Kiwako was in San Francisco and felt guilty toward both of them. He didn't know whether he'd be able to juggle their hospital visits if Kiwako were in town, particularly given Mayumi's propensity for popping in unannounced. He had yet to tell Kiwako he'd been stabbed because he didn't want to worry her or make her feel obligated to fly to Japan to see him. He also had to admit to himself he wasn't telling Kiwako about the attack in part because it could lead to the disclosure of inconvenient information.

"The nurse said I could only stay a few minutes. Perhaps next time I can help you with your boredom," she said with a wink.

"That'd be nice." *Who am I kidding?* he thought. *I can barely make it to the toilet.*

"I'll see you tomorrow. Love you." She carefully kissed him lightly on the lips.

Dog tired again, he was relieved Mayumi was leaving. He was also mortified he'd selfishly put her in harm's way. Letting her come to the hotel had been thoughtless and careless.

While she had been relentless in demanding they get together, he had no one to blame but himself.

He texted Mayumi: "Please don't visit the hospital again until the people who ordered the attacks are caught. I love you and would never forgive myself if something bad happened to you."

To his surprise, he received a thoughtful reply: "I very much appreciate your concern. Call anytime if you need something. I love you very much."

As he nodded off, he wondered how long he could keep his children and Kiwako from learning about the attempts on his life.

Back in the Saddle

復帰

Torn healed quickly but was still tired and weak. He texted Mamiko that he was out sick so his colleagues wouldn't worry that he was involved in the hotel attack, which was all over the news. Nevertheless, he felt vulnerable at the hospital because so many people had access to it. So, he convinced his doctor to let him go home several days early, with the promise that he'd stay home for at least a week and be careful not to tear his stitches.

Despite the perpetrators probably knowing where he lived, Torn decided the safest place for him in Tokyo was his apartment on the fortieth floor of Amaterasu Hills, named after the shrine behind it. Few people had access to his floor, which had only three apartments. In addition, an electronic key was required to access the elevator and the fortieth floor. Anyone not living there could enter the elevator and proceed to the fortieth floor only if one of the tenants on that floor buzzed them in. Finally, a separate manual key was required to open two locks on the door to his apartment, and a third lock could be closed from the inside.

Prosecutor Tsujikawa had recently suggested that Torn leave the country, but he'd refused. "I have every right to stay in Japan. As one of your colleagues pointed out when he denied me access to the US embassy, I'm a Japanese citizen." He had regretted the snarky comment as soon as the words left his mouth. "My apologies. I know you're just trying to keep me safe."

"It must be the medication," Tsujikawa had responded dryly. "I suggested you leave the country for a while in part because we can provide a police escort for only another week." *Great*, Torn thought, *the police aren't making any progress and now they're going to pull my security.*

Despite the assurances to his doctor, Torn had his driver take him directly from the hospital to a meeting with Mak. He didn't want to stay locked up in his apartment like he was under siege waiting for the barbarians to storm the gate. It was time to go on the offensive, but the only leads he had were the email and hacking attempts originating from the Russian Far East.

He met Mak at the venerable Imperial Hotel's Aqua Restaurant, where the customers were mostly rich housewives having brunch with other rich housewives. Torn had reserved a table in a quiet corner from where they could see the Imperial Palace grounds and wouldn't be overheard.

"You look like shit."

Torn managed a smile. "Tell me what you really think."

"Sorry, but shouldn't you be home resting?"

"Too much to do."

"How long will your arm be in a sling?"

"Until the stitches come out in a few days. But I already have a lot of mobility."

"Where were you stabbed?"

"Left shoulder and right chest. Ya wanna see my stitches?"

Mak laughed. "Perhaps when we shower together later."

Torn suppressed a laugh to avoid the discomfort it caused. They ordered brunch. Torn, happy to have access to caffeine and normal food, ordered a large black coffee, fresh-squeezed orange juice, scrambled eggs, chocolate chip pancakes, bacon, sausage, and ham. Mak ordered a latte and clubhouse sandwich.

Torn leaned forward in his plush upholstered chair. "So, give me the download."

"Before I forget, here's the disposable phone you requested. It doesn't have a trace on it. No one should be listening in. Use it when you're somewhere you think isn't bugged. I programmed in some numbers, including your family's. I took the liberty of texting the number to your mother."

"Thanks much, Mak."

"Let's talk about the Watanabes. According to my local guy, Tamayo was the founder's concubine and not his daughter. She was a hostess at a local club and thirty years younger. He eventually adopted her. He had no other children."

Torn chased his mouthful of pancake with coffee. "Wow. So, Tamayo's daughter Miki is her adopted father's child?"

"Yes, and that's not all. His wife died suddenly and the cause of death is unclear. Also, he had another girlfriend, but she disappeared, never to be found. And the pièce de résistance: Tamayo is the love child of a henchman for the Yamakawa Gumi, one of Japan's largest mob groups. Yes, she's a yak or at least the daughter of a yak. Her mother was also a hostess. Of course, all of this is circumstantial and it doesn't mean Tamayo committed any crimes, but there are many arrows pointing in the same direction."

Torn put his fork down. "Not just circumstantial, but ancient history. Just because she grew up poor and slept her way—and got herself adopted—to the top doesn't make her evil. Is Wakkanai doing business in Russia?"

Mak finished swallowing a bite of his clubhouse sandwich and sat back in his chair. "Yes, they were doing business there through Harden Industries, which was handling Wakkanai's sales until recently. More importantly, did you know that one of Vince's companies purchased five point one percent of Wakkanai?"

"Yes, I saw the public disclosure filing."

"Right, but here's where it gets interesting. Vince's company sent a letter to Wakkanai demanding Tom Saito be made president instead of Tamayo's daughter, Miki Watanabe, and that Tamayo, Miki, and her husband, Yoji, all resign from the board."

Torn paused mid-drink. "The plot thickens. If they publicized that letter then there's already been some private communications, and Tamayo is stiff-arming Vince. He must be lobbying for support from other shareholders. I'll bet Tamayo is hopping mad."

Mak chewed on the last of his sandwich. "And one more thing: Vince has sued Wakkanai for wrongful termination, and Harden Industries has sued Wakkanai for breach of the Distribution Agreement, claiming Wakkanai had no right to terminate it. Wakkanai probably thinks they don't need Harden Industries because they can push their international sales through Zephyrus, their newly purchased sub."

Torn sat up. "Just as he said he would. He complained Wakkanai was cutting him out of the Northern Okhotsk Project by terminating the Distribution Agreement, which means he's lost all of Wakkanai's sales globally, worth at least ten million dollars in a normal year, even without the Northern Okhotsk Project."

Torn looked out the window at the verdant grounds of the Imperial Palace, took a sip of coffee, and looked at Mak. "Where do the police keep injured suspects?"

Mak frowned. "The Metropolitan Police Hospital. Why?"

Torn leaned forward in his chair. "Is there anything you can find out about them?"

Mak considered for a moment. "Torn, that'll require some stuntman investigation services. Not strictly kosher."

"Well, I don't want to ask for anything you can't deliver." Torn knew he was poking at Mak's professional pride, but at this point he needed to pull out some stops.

Mak smiled. "OK, buddy. I'll see what I can do, but don't ask about my methods."

Torn carefully pushed his left arm out of the sling, and with both hands slowly covered first his eyes, then his ears, and finally his mouth.

Progress

進歩

After breakfast with Mak, Torn had his driver take him to Aka-saka Mitsuke, where he climbed several flights of stairs covered in a canopy of numerous orange *Torii* gates. Looking up from the bottom of the stairs, the narrow gates, planted one after the other closely together, created the illusion of a long orange tunnel. Local businesses purchased the gates in honor of a deity protecting Edo, the old name for Tokyo, enshrined in Hie Jinja at the top of the hill.

The shrine was completely deserted on this weekday except for a groundskeeper milling about and carrying a bamboo rake. Torn could no longer hear the traffic on the large street below. The only sounds were birds chirping and the breeze blowing through the trees. Using his new disposable phone, he called Hilsberry & Carter's Moscow office and asked for Larisa Anismova, the office leader.

Larisa answered, and after they exchanged pleasantries said, "As per your lawyer's request, I did some digging, but not through official channels. I didn't want to get the Russian police or prosecutor's office involved. If I do, they'll want something in return, and it also puts the firm on their radar, both of which I want to avoid."

Torn loved her accent, which reminded him of Natasha from *Rocky and Bullwinkle*, something he kept to himself. "What did you learn?"

"Well, I asked a friend to look into it. Using the Komsomolsk internet address Saki provided, he was able to determine from the ISP that the owner of the computer from which the threatening email was sent is a Russian citizen named Sergey Bogrov. He evidently runs Magadan Oil & Mining, a local company selling drilling equipment to oil and mining companies."

Torn paced in front of the shrine. "What's the best way to get information from Bogrov?"

"Well, the Russian police won't help the Japanese police unless there's something in it for them. In this case, there doesn't seem to be any upside for the Russian police. In fact, there's only downside, which is wasting time and money interrogating someone about activities, not crimes, in Russia. Why should they care? That is a rhetorical question, of course."

"Isn't there anything the Japanese police can do to convince the Russian police to help?" He sounded desperate.

"Doubtful. In these cases, sometimes people resort to self-help."

"What do you mean?"

"Well, I don't recommend contacting the police. In addition to them not caring, it's risky because you never know whose payroll they're on. But you could hire a local lawyer to investigate. They might be on the take too, but it's still less risky than going to the police. A lawyer likely would hire a private investigator whose methods might be less orthodox—but more effective—than those used by the police or private investigators in the West."

Torn stopped pacing and looked at the shrine. "Do you know a law firm that could help?"

"Yes. It's the firm that tracked down Bogrov. Their offices are in Khabarovsk. I've referred a lot of business to them over the years, which is why they did me a freebie. Perhaps they could assist further. Would you put the Japanese police in touch with them?"

"No, they likely wouldn't even contact them. For one thing, they wouldn't want to pay a Russian lawyer... or any other lawyer for that matter."

"Well then, who'll talk to them?"

"I could go talk to them or have a friend go."

Torn heard Larisa click her tongue and suck air through her teeth. "Going there could be very dangerous, Torn. It would be easier for whoever ordered the attacks to harm you in Russia. You could just disappear without anyone knowing what happened."

"I hear you. Please connect me to your contact in Khabarovsk."

"Sure. I'll introduce you by email. He's a great guy. I met him at Harvard. His father was a government official, meaning KGB. Somehow, he got his son into an exchange program in China, where he learned Chinese, and from where he eventually got into Harvard. His name is Alexei Chomkov."

"Got it."

"Torn, Russian lawyers aren't bound by the same rules of ethics as lawyers in the West. Which means they have a bit more flexibility as to how they get things done. The downside is there is no attorney-client privilege in Russia, conflicts of interest mean little to them, and Russian lawyers sometimes turn on their clients when pushed by the government or someone with more power and money.

"Alexei, however, worked at a global law firm in their Beijing office before opening his own firm in Khabarovsk. So, he knows how lawyers are supposed to behave and has always done a great job for our clients. But I don't know who his local clients are or what lines he's willing to cross. What I can do is ask him to run conflicts on Bogrov and his mining company. At least that'll give us some comfort if he confirms he has no conflict."

"That would be very helpful."

"It's the least I can do, but again, you shouldn't go. Introduce your friend and have him handle it."

After hanging up, Torn immediately called Mak, who answered, "What can I do ya for?"

"Would you be able to go to Khabarovsk to follow up on a lead for me? I found a lawyer there who can help, but someone who knows the facts needs to be there to manage the process."

"Oh boy, I'd love to help. But I'm *persona non grata* in Russia, going back to my CIA days. They'd be very suspicious if I showed up in the Russian Far East. No one goes there except to spy or fish... or both." Mak laughed at his own joke.

"Understood. What can you tell me about Khabarovsk?"

"Not much. I've never been east of the Urals, and Khabarovsk is seven time zones from Moscow. It's near the border with China and relatively close to Komsomolsk, but almost twice as big. What're you planning to do?"

Go to Russia, Torn thought. *What choice do I have?*

As if reading his mind, Mak said, "I know you're a control freak and you're probably blaming yourself for not protecting Yukie and Saya, but..."

Torn cut him off. "It's crossed my mind."

"Let me be clear. It's not your fault. Inviting Mayumi to your hotel was careless. But there's nothing you could've done about Yukie and Saya."

Torn gritted his teeth as he thought about his failure to deregister with the Sagami Ward office, but Mak knew nothing about that.

"If you're trying to make me feel better, I could've done without the Mayumi part."

"I call it like I see it."

Torn took a deep breath. "Do me a favor and see what you can dig up about Sergey Bogrov and Magadan Oil & Mining."

"Sure thing. Before I forget, since my investigation of the two thugs you danced with in your hotel room may not be strictly legal, I'm sending you another phone for communicating just with me."

While thinking it overkill to have two burner phones, Torn knew not to question Mak about security precautions.

Returning to the office, he researched flights to Khabarovsk and then made sure his clients, including Raijin Clean, were being properly served. He had been following active matters by email and text as much as possible from his hospital bed but needed to check in with the partners and associates handling his matters. He first stopped in the "war room," the conference room where his team of several patent lawyers worked on the patent filings for Raijin's technology. They brought him up to speed on their progress filing patent applications covering every patentable aspect of Saya's inventions, including those she'd initially considered protecting as trade secrets.

His original burner phone rang while he walked back to his office. He smiled. It was Sean calling on the satellite phone from Alaska.

"Hi, Sean. How're you doing?"

"We're good, Dad. I'm on speaker and Sophia's here too."

"Hi, Dad."

Torn imagined her waving at the phone. "It's wonderful to hear your voices." He was trying not to let his voice crack.

"We miss you," Sophia said sweetly.

Torn choked back tears. "I miss you too, honey. How's studying coming along?" He closed the door to his office and put the phone on speaker.

Sean answered, "They've let us attend classes online and submit our homework by email. What did you tell our teachers?"

"The truth. Your mother was murdered and you needed to spend some time with family. I haven't told anyone where you are or even what country you're in, and you shouldn't either. No posting of photos on social media!"

"We're not stupid, Dad."

Sophia started to cry. "Dad, I miss Mom so much!"

"I know, dear." Not knowing what else to say, he changed the subject. "You guys doing your practice?"

"Yes. Sean practices with me." Sophia's voice was cracking.

"I guess I'm outta shape. She can almost beat me, and I've got two years and twenty kilos on her." Sean was choking back tears.

"That's all right. Just focus on your *iaido* and help your sister with her kendo."

Sophia asked, "How much longer do we need to stay here?"

"Just a little while longer. You can't leave there until the police find those responsible."

"Does Uncle Mak know what's going on?" Sophia's voice sounded stronger.

"Why do you ask?"

"He texted Grandma this number."

"Oh right. He's helping with the investigation."

"How's he helping?" Sean asked, his voice, too, sounding steadier.

"Well, he works at a global private investigations firm and may be able to uncover evidence the police can't."

Sophia sighed. "Why's it taking so long? We're tired of being cooped up here at the cabin and it's getting cold. I don't like winter here."

Sean chuckled. "What's not to like? Ice fishing, skiing, trapping."

Torn could almost see Sophia's eyes rolling.

"The police have yet to identify a suspect, but I think they're getting close." Torn knew he was talking too much, but he felt the need to give his children hope.

Sophia persisted. "Well, can I at least go back to Seattle? I'm not even going to school in Japan."

"No," Torn responded, almost too emphatically. "You need to stay right where you are."

After saying goodbye to his children, his mother came on the line and assured him the kids were fine and everything was under control. She seemed to truly enjoy taking care of them. Torn knew his mother was tough as nails despite some health issues and could handle her grandkids. Moreover, both Sean and Sophia knew how to take care of themselves in the Alaskan wilderness.

Come to Jesus

白状

Mak, wearing blue hospital scrubs, a surgeon's cap, and rubber gloves, used a key card one of his colleagues obtained from a friend in hospital security to open a back door at the old Tokyo Metropolitan Police Hospital. It was after midnight and half the lights in the lobby were off. He took a slow, musty, and noisy service elevator to the fourth floor. When the doors opened, he turned left down the badly lit two-tone faded green and white hall. He turned right at an empty nurses' station. At the end of the hall, he found Room 401 where the two men who'd attacked Torn in the hotel were recovering.

No one else was around. Mak had cashed in a favor with one of his police friends to arrange for the officer on duty to take a break while Mak interrogated the prisoners. He also knew the schedule of the nurses, and that he had only fifteen minutes before the officer would return and a nurse would check on the two men.

Outside the room, he put on a blue neck gaiter anglers use to protect their skin from the sun when fishing. It covered his entire face, ears, and neck, with little holes at the mouth and nose for breathing and talking. Looking like a mummy, only his dark-brown eyes could be seen between the face mask and his cap. He had thought about using a surgical mask but decided on something that would cover everything down to his collarbones.

He had shaved his face clean and cut his hair short for the occasion because he was known for his beard and long hair. When he looked in the mirror that morning, he had laughed at the visage of Oddjob from the James Bond movie *Goldfinger* staring back at him.

Mak removed his loafers, walked into the room, and gently closed the door. He grabbed a box of small bandages and several syringes from a dispenser on a counter near the door.

An older man lay in a bed inclined so his torso was at forty-five degrees from the prone position. He was on a respirator, clearly unconscious. Another man, in his early forties, lay flat on his back with each wrist handcuffed to a bed railing and a restraining belt locked around his waist. From his slow shallow breathing, Mak guessed he was sleeping, perhaps even sedated.

Mak walked in his stockinged feet to the handcuffed man without making a sound. He quietly placed the syringes and the box of bandages on a tray table next to the bed. He removed the caps from three syringes, kept one syringe in his hand, and put the other two back on the tray. After the man exhaled, Mak covered the man's mouth and nose with one of Mak's catcher's-mitt-sized hands and at the same time buried the needle into the top of the sleeping man's left hand. The man's eyes flew open and he tried to scream but he couldn't draw in a breath. The handcuffs clanked against the bed rails as he tried to raise his hands.

Mak leaned over and put a finger to his lips. "Shhhh."

The man stopped struggling.

"You want to breathe, right?" Mak whispered.

The man, his eyes starting to pop out of his head with terror, nodded the best he could with Mak, using his body weight, putting downward pressure on the man's face, flattening his nose in the process.

"Promise to be quiet?"

The man nodded weakly.

"Good."

The man gasped for air when Mak removed his hand. After catching his breath, he started yanking on his handcuffs again, making a loud metallic clanking noise, and looking around frantically. Mak raised a finger to his lips. "No one can help you."

"Who the fuck're you and whaddya want?"

Mak plucked another syringe from the table and stabbed the man in the right elbow. Before he could cry out, Mak again covered the man's mouth and nose. The handcuffs clanked.

"I'll ask the questions."

The terrified man nodded yes as best he could, his bloodshot eyes wide open, tears streaming down his temples into his short, permed hair.

Mak removed his hand from the man's face.

"If you don't tell me what I want to know, I'll make sure you're worse off than your friend over there." As Mak said this, he unclipped from his belt an enormous folded knife with a long handle made of African buffalo horn, opened the forty-centimeter blade, which locked in the open position, and placed the knife on the table next to the remaining syringes. "Nod if you understand."

The man nodded vigorously.

The knife was just for show. Mak never intended to use it. He'd promised his police friend not to leave any marks.

"Who hired you?"

"Some North Korean guy." The man thought better of his answer, but it was too late.

Mak buried another needle next to the one already in the back of the man's left hand. He covered the man's mouth to stifle his cry, smashing his nose again and pushing the back of his head deep into the pillow. More clanking.

"I can play this game all day. Can you?" Mak removed his hand from the man's nose and mouth again.

Gasping, the man said in a whisper, "My boss would have me killed."

Mak put his face very close to the man's right ear. "Did I ask about your fucking boss? I want to know who ordered the hit."

The man whispered, "My boss said it was a company he'd done work for over the years. We needed to find the specifications for some new technology and kill the developers. We'd be doing a good thing because we'd save jobs."

"I want a name."

The man, almost crying, said, "I really don't know. All I know is our boss called us into his office. On the way down the hall, we passed a tanned guy in a suit with a big scar on his neck who was on his way out. He had a lady with him who would've been pretty except for her messed-up hair and bulging eyes that seemed to move in opposite directions like one a them lizards."

"A chameleon?"

"Yeah. Our boss said they were ruthless people and their boss was even more ruthless. He later told us to talk to the lady by phone because she knew the targets and where they lived and worked. Our boss said she had some weird fetish."

"What fetish?"

"She liked to follow people around, which must be true because she knew everything about them."

"Was their boss a *gaijin*?"

The man looked surprised at the question. "I don't know," he said slowly, seeming to be thinking hard. "Our clients are usually Japanese companies, but we've done work for Chinese and North Koreans too."

Mak changed the subject, slowly listing out the crimes. "Did you also attack the motorcycle, blow up the building, stab that woman to death, and ransack somebody's apartment?"

The man hesitated. Mak popped the cap off another needle.

"Yes, but we didn't mean to kill the wife and it wasn't me. It was him." The suspect nodded toward the comatose man. "The lizard lady said there might be diagrams, specs, or some other shit in the lawyer's house. The wife was just in the wrong place at the wrong time."

Mak wanted to hit the man in the face. "How'd you know there'd be two people on the motorcycle?"

"We didn't. Our orders were to take out the woman. When we saw he had a passenger, we figured it must be her because we could tell it was a woman and she never came out of that building."

Mak frowned. "How'd you know he was staying at the Andaz? Did you have tracking devices on his vehicles?"

"Easy. We put tracking devices on his giant Maybach and his motorcycles. After he removed them, we waited outside his office building and followed him to the hotel. Also, our boss was somehow able to confirm his room number."

Mak, recording the entire conversation on the smartphone hidden in his jacket pocket, was so angry he wanted to kill both men right then and there. Instead, he said, "I want to know the name of your boss, and I don't care if he fuckin' kills you."

Heart of Darkness

闇の奥

Torn looked out the window of the lime-green Boeing 737-800. He was on an S7 Airlines flight to Khabarovsk, the capital of the Russian Far Eastern Federal District. From his maroon first-class seat, he could see below the endless deciduous forests, braided rivers like giant mating snakes, and numerous small lakes like giant potholes. In a few more minutes, he'd be able to see Khabarovsk on the banks of the Amur River, so big it looked like a lake when viewed from the city. He felt small and alone and was reconsidering the wisdom of his hasty decision to travel to Russia. No one from the "outside" could help if he got into trouble.

That morning, Torn had considered sending Detective Taniguchi an email outlining his itinerary and flight information for his trip to Russia. It was a condition of the return of his passports, and he wanted someone to know where he was going. But with his paranoia in the red zone, he decided not to take any chances that someone might leak his travel plans to Bogrov.

On his way to the airport, Detective Taniguchi called and Torn was afraid the police might have found out about his trip. But Taniguchi said he'd called to tell Torn that residue found at the bomb site was consistent with ammonium nitrate fuel oil, or ANFO, more commonly used as an explosive in mining than to raze buildings.

Taniguchi explained, "For a building like Raijin's, which was made of steel girders and reinforced concrete, the explosive of choice is something called cyclotrimethylenetrinitramine, or RDX, which allows for a more surgical demolition instead of the massive explosion that brought down their building."

Combined with what he already knew, this information pointed the finger in only one direction.

After the plane landed, a bus took the passengers to the terminal, where Torn lined up for Russian immigration. When it was almost his turn, he queued with the tips of his shoes on a red line on the floor in front of a small cubicle. Two lights were attached to a beam hanging from the ceiling.

When the lights changed from red to green, he stepped into a small space and faced a large bulletproof glass window with a small opening at the bottom. He passed his passport and Russian entry form through the opening and said hello to a beautiful alabaster-skinned woman with dark hair wearing an insanely formal navy-blue uniform and hat.

The immigration officer ignored his greeting. Her expressionless face looked like it was chiseled from marble. Torn wondered if she ever smiled.

She spent an inordinate amount of time looking sternly at his passport, his Russian visa, her computer screen, and back at him. At one point, she made a telephone call and spoke to someone in clipped Russian while looking at the passport page with his visa as if it were some vile creature. He worried about being arrested—had someone figured out his intentions? Finally, she hung up, stamped his passport, and returned it to him.

He collected his bag and cleared customs. A driver took him to a restaurant where the maître d' led him to a table next to windows overlooking a beautiful white Orthodox Russian church with golden domes and the wide Amur River beyond. Alexei Chomkov and his young wife were already seated.

Standing and extending his hand, Alexei said in excellent English, "Ah, Mr. Sagara, welcome to Khabarovsk, or as I like to call it, a taste of Europe in the Far East. I hope you had a good flight. This is my wife, Natalia."

Natalia stood and put her napkin on her chair.

Torn introduced himself. "It's very nice to meet you both."

He focused on looking Natalia in the eyes but couldn't help taking the rest of her in too. She was a tall, thin, strikingly beautiful brunette with somewhat northeast Asian features and large breasts he suspected were manmade. Dressed to the nines, she wore a long white dress, matching scarf, and white high heels. Momentarily spellbound, thoughts of kissing and placing his hands all over her briefly flooded Torn's mind.

"You look Asian," she said in heavily accented English. He couldn't place her accent.

"My father was Japanese and my mother was Caucasian American."

She smiled. "Interesting. My father was Chinese and my mother was white Russian."

Well, that combination worked well, thought Torn. He realized biracial people of Chinese and Russian heritage probably weren't that rare in Khabarovsk, given its proximity to China, right across the river, which they would soon be admiring during dinner.

Still standing, Alexei, a man in his forties of medium height with a shaved head and tired deep-set eyes with dark circles, said, "Allow me to present my credentials." He handed Torn a Russian bar license card in a little red book containing Alexei's photo, printed Cyrillic letters, a manual signature, and an impressive-looking gold seal. It looked to Torn like what he thought a KGB ID might look like.

Handing back the tiny book, Torn asked them to be seated. "Thank you for agreeing to meet with me today. Larisa told me a lot about you, and it was all good."

"It's our pleasure. I don't get enough opportunities to take Natalia to dinner. Larisa's being generous. The feeling's mutual. We were in the same study group at Harvard, and she assisted me a great deal with my studies. We remained good friends after we started practicing at our respective international law firms. Later, when I opened my own shop here, she began referring clients. She has really helped me build our practice. We're a full-service firm, practicing labor law, handling incorporations and collections, assisting with real estate transactions, and helping with criminal defense matters."

Torn smiled. "Larisa tells me you've developed a good practice here and also understand how international firms work."

"Indeed. What Larisa probably didn't tell you is that I grew up in Yekaterinburg, which is east of the Urals. I met Natalia when I was visiting Vladivostok on business. Natalia is from Harbin, the closest thing to a melting pot in China. Chinese is her first language, but she also speaks fluent Russian and some English."

That's why Torn couldn't recognize her accent. It had both Chinese and Russian characteristics.

To Torn, Alexei looked threatening. But during their conversation, Torn warmed to Alexei's frank and open manner and his sense of humor. Alexei treated Natalia with respect and consideration, which comforted Torn. He seemed to love her very much, with his feelings reciprocated. Torn was relieved to have someone like Alexei representing him and believed he might be a bargain at $350 an hour.

Still, Torn remained apprehensive about traveling the next day. He didn't know if he would succeed in finding information that would lead to the perpetrators. He did know, however, that he'd put himself in danger by coming to the Russian Far East, and he questioned again the wisdom of coming alone. He recalled Larisa's words: "You could just disappear."

They discussed the need to extract as much information from Sergey Bogrov as possible, including who had him send the email to Torn, whether Bogrov was involved in the hacking attempts on Raijin's and Hilsberry's servers, and if so, at whose direction. Alexei said, "We first need to determine if he's actually the one who sent it."

Torn asked, "You think someone might've engaged in identity theft?"

"Exactly. It happens all the time. Someone could've stolen his computer or hacked it."

"I guess the only way to find out is to ask him. What's our plan?"

"Well, Bogrov's in Brakian this week, working near one of Magadan's mining sites. Brakian is a little town about three hundred kilometers north of Komsomolsk where we'll stop first to pick up some colleagues. I'll meet you tomorrow morning at the hotel at eight o'clock. Wear warm clothes and boots and pray for good weather so we can fly. It's been raining for three days."

The next morning, Alexei arrived at Torn's hotel in a large black Mercedes GLS 450 SUV with tinted windows. Alexei was sitting in the back, where he asked Torn to join him. The driver was a tall, fit, handsome young man with short dark hair wearing a black turtleneck sweater, black jacket, black jeans, and black tennis shoes resembling dress shoes. He had a shoulder holster holding a large pistol Torn couldn't identify, leaving Torn unsure whether to feel comforted or concerned.

They drove to a heliport on the other side of town where two fat Mil Mi-8 helicopters sat heavily on the grass. To call it an airfield would have been charitable. There was a giant lawn of dying grass with a concrete slab in the middle and an air sock off to one side, a run-down mobile home with a rusty, red fuel truck parked in front, and a boneyard of old helicopter parts in the back. An outhouse, located strangely close to the mobile home, leaned to one side. He assumed its proximity to the mobile home had something to do with frigid winter temperatures.

Torn wasn't keen on riding in a Russian helicopter. He'd heard about bad accidents involving aging Russian aircraft. The alternative, however, was a 690-kilometer, fourteen-hour drive to Brakian on bad roads, at least half of which were dirt, and he didn't have the patience for that. Besides, Alexei had said they'd be safer flying because anyone with ill intent was more likely to ambush them on the road than in the sky. He suspected Alexei also didn't want to drive for fourteen hours and agreed flying probably was safer than driving.

They "checked in" by telling the man in the creaky mobile home they'd arrived. He didn't ask for identification. Alexei had sent copies of their passports in advance and told the helicopter company Torn was an American investor in raw materials.

On the wall behind the man hung a large yellow sign with photographs of forbidden carry-on luggage: machine guns, shotguns, pistols, machetes, large knives, grenades, dynamite, chainsaws, and other assorted dangerous things. Alexei noticed Torn looking at the sign, smiled, and slapped Torn on the shoulder. "Don't worry, Torn. It's OK to take any of that stuff as long as you put it in your check-in luggage."

While waiting for the helicopter, Torn texted Mak from his disposable phone: "Any updates?"

His phone showed Mak was typing, followed by Mak's reply: "Wakkanai responded to Vince's letter with an angry screed. It's all over the news. They said Vince was a disgruntled former employee who'd been scheming to take over the company and who wanted to fire all the employees and sell off the assets. It's a strange response to a letter demanding only that Tom Saito be appointed president instead of Miki Watanabe. I'll text you a copy of the article."

Torn typed back: "Wakkanai's response doesn't surprise me. A Japanese company challenged by activist foreign shareholders always claims the barbarians are going to fire all the Japanese employees and sell off the assets. Anything else?"

"Vince's company purchased more Wakkanai shares. He must still believe the stock's undervalued. The stock price jumped quite a bit after Vince published his letter. It dropped a little after Wakkanai responded. One analyst opined that Wakkanai's excessive reaction indicates Vince may be on to something, which is why the price has remained relatively high."

"Thanks, Mak."

"Where are you? I've been trying to call you all day but haven't been able to get through."

Torn hadn't told Mak or his family his destination because he knew they'd try to stop him, and he didn't want them to worry. But he was about to fly into what was feeling more and more like Joseph Conrad's *Heart of Darkness*, and decided he'd better let someone else know, just in case.

"I'm in Khabarovsk, about to fly to Komsomolsk and then on to Brakian. If you don't hear from me by Monday, call in the cavalry, or at least Saki and Taniguchi. Sorry to spring this on you, but if I'd told you before I left, I know you would've tried to talk me out of it. Cheers." Then he turned off his phone.

While texting, Torn had heard the sound of a chopper in the distance. He looked and saw the hulking bird approaching. *Looks like a giant bumblebee*, he thought. As it came closer, he saw a newer-looking version of the two helicopters on the ground. The chopper landed heavily on the concrete slab in the middle of the giant yellowing lawn.

After the two-person ground crew refueled the aircraft using the old, red fuel truck, Alexei's driver drove Torn and

Alexei to the chopper on a little gravel track that cut through the lawn. One of the two pilots checked their identification, including Torn's US passport, while another man loaded their minimal luggage. Then Alexei and Torn boarded the giant airship, followed by the pilots.

Torn watched the pilots review their preflight checklist. Once they started the engine and the main rotor began turning, the third man closed the cockpit door, which the pilots locked from the inside. Torn could hear the engines getting louder and the rotors picking up speed through his noise-canceling headphones. Slowly, the giant bird defied gravity and rose from the ground.

They flew northeast. Their low altitude surprised Torn. They couldn't have been more than 150 meters off the ground. He could see through large round windows the Amur River below. It had several tributaries and islands and was braided in numerous locations. Gradually, it grew larger as they moved downstream and its tributaries fed it more and more water. The surrounding countryside was mostly treeless, except along the rivers and lakes that pockmarked the terrain. Torn turned his phone back on only to discover that they had lost mobile service.

About ninety minutes later, when they neared a cell tower in Komsomolsk, Torn's phone vibrated and he saw a message from Mak. He wasn't his usual carefree self: "You're damn right I would've talked you out of it. If things go sideways there, you're screwed! What am I supposed to tell your kids?"

"Is that really you, Mak? Oh my gracious! The language!" He added a smiley face. "Tell them I was looking for their mother's killer. They'll understand."

"It's no joke. I'm really pissed at how thoughtless you are. Your kids won't understand why they had to lose another parent!"

"It's the only way to get to the bottom of this. Alexei Chomkov, the lawyer I told you about, is helping me collect information."

"No, it's not. I got more information last night. Let's talk live."

"I'll call you from Komsomolsk or Brakian. We're approaching Komsomolsk now."

"Make sure you do."

"I love you too, Mak."

"Fuck you, Torn. Just call me."

A text from Sean appeared: "Dad, where are you? I can't get through to your phone. I tried your office too, and Mamiko-san said she didn't know where you were. Please confirm you're OK. We're all very worried."

Torn tried to respond but the connection was lost.

The Mi-8 approached the city of Komsomolsk-on-Amur, passing over several residential areas consisting of row upon row of blocky, drab, beige apartment buildings before slowing down and descending into an industrial area. He could see a filthy stream with rubbish strewn along the banks. Seeing people fishing, Torn wondered, *What in God's name could they be catching in that sewer?*

The chopper banked over a high fence into an abandoned industrial park with an empty courtyard that could hold two football fields. It landed on its giant tires next to a four-story, 300-meter-long gray building riddled with broken windows. It looked like it hadn't been used in years.

After the helicopter powered down, everyone piled out to relieve themselves. Two fit young men, each carrying a large black duffle bag, approached and shook Alexei's hand. Alexei introduced them to Torn as Misha and Oleg. They wore flannel shirts, camouflage pants with matching jackets, and new heavy boots. Misha was average height with a bulging neck, huge arms, and thick legs. He had short, dark hair and a neatly trimmed beard and mustache.

Oleg was at least two meters tall with a large, shaved head and extremely broad shoulders. He looked like he should be carrying a giant hammer. They each wore shoulder holsters cradling large pistols. The pilots didn't seem to care that Oleg and Misha were packing.

Misha and Oleg each charged $1,000 per day plus expenses. Torn hoped they wouldn't cost him even more.

Alexei said, "They're partners in an investigation firm based here in Komsomolsk, and they work all over the Russian Far East. They were born and raised here and served in the Spetsnaz GRU, the Russian Special Forces, before returning to start their own company. They're the ones who figured out that the email you received came from Bogrov's computer. They also determined he's in Brakian."

"So, what will we do when we get there?"

"Find Bogrov and ask him some questions."

"How will we find him?"

"It shouldn't be too hard. We know where his office is, and Brakian is a very small village."

They reboarded the chopper, joined by Misha, Oleg, and their gear.

As the helicopter lifted off, Torn received a text from Kiwako: "Torn, I saw the news. I'm glad you're safe, but we need to talk."

The Wild Wild East

ワイルド ワイルド イースト

They headed almost due north, away from the Amur River. Soon after takeoff, Torn lost mobile reception and realized he hadn't checked in with Mak. He wasn't concerned, however, because he thought he could text Mak from Brakian, where he expected there to be a cell tower. He was more concerned about Sean worrying about him. And Kiwako now knew someone had tried to kill him. It was only a matter of time before his children found out. Also, Kiwako likely knew that Mayumi had been in his hotel room.

As they moved further north, the empty plains gradually turned to boreal forest.

An hour into the flight, the helicopter circled a cluster of ramshackle buildings. A dirt road entered the tiny village from the south and went no further. There were no other roads in or out of Brakian. The only way to go north, east, or west was by chopper.

To Torn's surprise, he still had no reception. Checking in with Mak would have to wait until Torn's return to Komsomolsk.

The helicopter landed on a small concrete slab in a clearing surrounded by tall, drab leafless trees looking like massive scarecrows being held at gunpoint with their hands up. Another helicopter sat on a landing pad on the other side of the clearing next to a limp windsock. A small, dilapidated office and a fuel truck were perched precariously halfway up a bare hillside, the top of which was covered with more naked trees.

They deplaned and zipped up their coats against the cold, damp air. Torn was surprised when he heard no birds and saw no signs of life, not even a stray dog.

"When do the zombies attack?" asked Torn.

Alexei grinned. "Don't worry. I told the pilot to keep the engine running."

A black diesel Land Cruiser with a raised air intake snorkel rising up along the edge of the windshield next to the passenger side door waited nearby. Alexei and Torn put their gear in the car and climbed into the back.

Oleg drove with Misha sitting in the passenger seat, their duffle bags lying on the floor at their feet. They ascended the slope from the helicopter pad on a long gravel driveway into the bare trees and onto the main road. It was muddy from all the rain. A few gray, wooden houses on both sides and one old, tired store lined the road. Two dark, mangy stray dogs, shivering in the damp cold, wandered the street and a few crows sat in the dead trees, waiting for who knew what. No sign of people. Appearing here and there were mounds of dirty, melting snow cleared from the road before the rains came.

Torn had been expecting a quaint little town in the woods. Not this shithole.

They drove a few minutes to the edge of town where a rusty dark-brown freight car sat on an elevated wooden deck. A sign hung on a door facing the street. The shades were drawn on a small window on the side of the freight car around the corner from the door. Steps led up to the deck in front of the door. More steps led from the deck outside the window down to a small outhouse. Oleg stopped the SUV about twenty meters away. He said something to Alexei, who told Torn they'd wait in the truck while Oleg and Misha went to question Sergey Bogrov.

Oleg and Misha exited the Land Cruiser and pulled on black leather gloves and ski masks. Torn started to sweat despite

246 | BOTTLED LIGHTNING

the chill in the air. His injured shoulder and chest ached, and he took slow, deep breaths to calm himself.

Oleg and Misha climbed the steps and knocked on the door. They waited a moment before opening the door and rushing in. Two seconds later, a man's body came flying out of the window, spraying glass everywhere.

Crashing on the deck, the man jumped up and started running down the steps toward the outhouse as Oleg dove out of the window, landing on his feet. Torn was surprised that Oleg's giant body fit through the window without touching its frame. Oleg jumped off the deck and tackled the man in front of the outhouse as Misha exited the front door.

"That must be Bogrov," Alexei said as he put on a black ski mask. Laughing, he tossed one to Torn. "Don't worry, it's clean. Let me do the talking. This is how we take depositions in the Wild Wild East!"

Torn put on the ski mask. They hurried over to where Oleg had the man pinned against the outhouse. The stench was overwhelming. Oleg pressed the man's face into the wooden planks of the outhouse wall with one of his beefy forearms while using his other hand to pin one of the man's arms behind his back. Using one of his giant feet, Oleg forced the man to spread his legs while Misha patted him down.

Alexei asked something in Russian, and the man replied with barely a whisper because Oleg was crushing the man's neck against the wall. Evidently the wrong response, Misha kicked the man in the groin. He groaned and went limp, but Oleg continued to hold Bogrov up against the wall.

Alexei asked him something again.

"Da."

Alexei said in English, "Now we're getting somewhere. This is indeed Mr. Bogrov."

Alexei pulled a piece of paper from one of his jacket pockets, showed it to Bogrov, and asked him something. Bogrov responded weakly, and Oleg threw him hard onto the wooden planks of the outhouse deck and dragged him through the propped-open outhouse door. Over the hole lay two filthy wooden slats for squatting, but there had been so much rain over the past few days that feces-filled water almost touched the undersides of the boards. Oleg started to push Bogrov's face into the sewer water when he yelled something. Alexei motioned for Oleg to stop.

Alexei said to Torn, "Well, he sent the email."

Alexei again asked Bogrov something.

He hesitated and Oleg pushed Bogrov's face into the cold, dark sewer water. They could hear Bogrov's muffled screams emanating together with bubbles from the filth. When Oleg pulled Bogrov's head out of the water he said, "Wakkanai," and then spit several times to clear remnants of the nasty liquid from his mouth.

Alexei looked at Torn and raised an eyebrow.

"He means Wakkanai Drilling, a Japanese company. Ask him who at Wakkanai."

When Alexei asked in Russian, Bogrov, water and specks of feces dripping off his face and snot running down his nose, again hesitated. Misha, who by now had his giant pistol out, cocked the gun, the sound of which was unmistakable, and pointed the barrel between Bogrov's eyes.

He froze for a moment as he contemplated the inside of the barrel. Then paragraphs started flooding out of his mouth. Alexei interpreted and Torn recorded it all on the phone in his pocket.

For many years, Bogrov's company, Magadan Oil & Mining, had been purchasing drilling and other equipment from Wakkanai through an American company, Harden Enterprises. Vince Harden usually worked with a Tom Saito, General Manager,

Strategic Planning, at Wakkanai. A month ago, Tom sent Bogrov a Snapchat message asking for help scaring an American lawyer to stop him from representing a start-up called Raijin Clean, because Raijin's technology would kill the oil and gas industry… and Wakkanai and Bogrov's company along with it. Tom Saito said Wakkanai would pay Bogrov for his troubles. Tom convinced Bogrov to send the email to Torn and to hire someone to try and hack into Raijin's and Hilsberry's servers. Wakkanai paid Bogrov $10,000.

Alexei then demanded the passwords to Bogrov's phone and laptop. Bogrov complied and Alexei wrote them down.

Oleg dragged Bogrov by his collar from the outhouse and tied his hands behind his back and his legs together with plastic handcuffs. While Misha kept his gun trained on Bogrov, Oleg grabbed Bogrov's laptop. Alexei took Bogrov's phone and immediately changed the password so Bogrov couldn't erase it remotely after they'd left. Torn worried the Snapchats with Tom Saito would be gone, but Alexei had assured Torn that Misha and Oleg knew how to recover them.

When Alexei and Torn turned toward the car, Bogrov said in thickly accented English, "They're going to kill you." Misha hit Bogrov in the face with the butt of his pistol, opening a gash in his cheek.

As they drove away at top speed, Alexei said, "I don't know why Americans say waterboarding's ineffective. Perhaps they're just using the wrong water." He laughed and slapped Torn on the back. Torn laughed nervously but was too tense to feel any mirth. He could smell his nervous sweat through the layers of warm clothing he wore and resisted the urge to put his head in his hands. *What the hell am I doing here? I'm not a spook. I'm just a lawyer*, he thought to himself.

They arrived at the airstrip to find the crew sitting and drinking coffee on the porch of the tiny office. The chopper was powered down and hadn't been refueled. Alexei tried to light a fire under them with no success. They seemed to be intentionally dragging their feet to make the point that they were in control. Pilots in the Russian Far East were masters of their domain and didn't like being pushed or rushed. They held all the power because everyone needed them to go places and move things around. No one goes or transports anything anywhere without them.

Oleg and Misha loaded their gear and the spoils from their interrogation of Bogrov and their search of his freight car into the helicopter as Alexei approached Torn.

"Torn," Alexei said with a mischievous smile, "as you Americans say, 'It's time to get the hell out of Dodge.' Someone's going to find Bogrov. He could show up here with his friends at any moment, but the pilots don't care. It's not their fight, and they know no one will harm them. The bigger problem is their insistence that they can't refuel until the one-person ground crew returns from a late lunch, which could be another hour from now." Alexei cocked an eyebrow. "Any ideas?"

Torn started to panic. His hands were shaking inside his gloves and it wasn't from the cold. He wanted to grab Alexei and scream, "What the fuck do you want me to do? I don't even know where I am! You need to convince these motherfuckers we gotta go now!" Instead, he paused, took a deep breath, and said calmly but forcefully, "Tell them I'll pay a ten-thousand-dollar tip in cash when we arrive in Khabarovsk if we can leave in ten minutes."

Alexei turned on his heels without saying a word and trotted over to the pilot. No sooner had Alexei said something than the pilot started barking at his crew. One of them threw down his cigarette and ran up the hill to the fuel truck. The copilot started inspecting the outside of the helicopter while the pilot boarded the copter and started going through the preflight checklist.

As they were boarding, Alexei, holding two AK-12s he'd received from Misha, asked, "Can you shoot?"

"Yes, I grew up hunting."

"Good." He handed Torn one of the guns. "Just in case. Here's the safety."

Twelve minutes later the big bird was lifting off when a Mitsubishi Pajero came flying out of the trees and down the slope at them, throwing mud and gravel as it sped down the driveway. It screeched to a halt in front of the landing pad. Three armed men, including Bogrov, his hair still wet and the gash on his cheek clearly visible, jumped out almost before the Pajero had come to a complete stop.

They started shooting their semi-automatic rifles at the chopper. Bullets plinked into the fuselage and some of them penetrated the cabin. Visions of Yukie's dead body and burned bones flashed through Torn's mind.

"Aim for the truck!" he heard Alexei say.

Oleg and Misha had prepared for this by sitting on the side of the helicopter facing the hill and opening four portal-shaped windows. They put down suppression fire with their fully automatic AK-12s. The three shooters dove to the ground as a hail of bullets rained down around them and on their car. Alexei and Torn focused their attention on the Pajero. They rendered it inoperable by shooting out three tires and shooting up the gas tank and engine compartment.

Shooting the AK-12 gave Torn a feeling of control. He no longer felt like a helpless bystander. He held onto the gun like a blanket for the rest of the flight.

Alexei yelled over the din of the helicopter rotor and engine. "Oleg and Misha intentionally refrained from killing those idiots because that would just create problems with the authorities."

Then he laughed. "Unfortunately, you'll have to pay for the bullet holes in the chopper!"

The copilot came out of the cockpit and said something to Torn. Alexei interpreted. "He apologizes for not lifting off in ten minutes."

"Don't worry, I'll still pay them in cash upon arrival if they take me directly to Khabarovsk International Airport, but the bullet holes are on them. I don't want to stop in Komsomolsk or stay overnight in Khabarovsk. I want to leave on a plane tonight. I can pay Oleg and Misha an extra per diem and for bus tickets to Komsomolsk. And I'll tip them two thousand each, but they must go straight to Khabarovsk with us."

"That's wise. Let me see what I can do." Alexei spoke in Russian to the copilot, who nodded affirmatively, but then he and Alexei engaged in a relatively lengthy discussion. When they stopped talking, Alexei turned to Torn. "He says they can't land at Khabarovsk International because the authorities will question them. When they see that the helicopter's been shot up, they'll ask even more questions and they might hold you overnight. I suggest we fly back to the helicopter field and drive from there. I'll have my car waiting. It's only fifteen minutes from the airport, and between Oleg, Misha, and my driver we'll have plenty of firepower to protect you."

"Understood. Just get me to the international airport as soon as you can."

Alexei then spoke to Oleg and Misha, who both nodded affirmatively and gave Torn a thumbs-up.

Getting reception when they flew over Komsomolsk, Torn checked flight availability. The only plane departing that day was the 7:00 p.m. S7 flight to Incheon International Airport near Seoul. He would need to lay over for several hours before changing planes to get to Tokyo, but he gladly booked it. Anything to get the hell out of Russia.

They made it to the heliport a little after 5:00 p.m. and Alexei delivered Torn to Khabarovsk International around 5:20. He had another long wait while the stern uniformed male immigration agent examined Torn's passport, Russian visa, and the computer screen, and looked at Torn's face several times.

Torn, dripping in sweat, hoped he didn't look as nervous as he felt. If they pulled him aside, he'd be finished.

They let him through.

He thought with a smile, *I guess what happens in Brakian stays in Brakian.*

In the excitement, he forgot to respond to Sean.

Koi

鯉

"You're even more of a marked man than before. Now they know you're on to them. They've already tried to kill you twice. They'll be bolder now," said Mak.

Sitting in a large, comfortable chair in a corner of his airline's First Class Lounge at Incheon Airport, Torn responded into the phone, "Or maybe they'll decide it's too risky to come after me again."

"Wishful thinking. Dead men don't tell tales."

"Always so upbeat. Anyway, at least now I have enough information for the police to act."

"I already had enough information before you went on your little expedition. I recorded everything the guy told me," Mak replied.

"Did you get a name?"

"I got the name of the goon's boss, Hiroki Okaguchi. He's the head of the Yamakawa Gumi. The police can lean on him for more info."

"And now we also know who sent the threatening email and who paid him to do it. I told Alexei to have copies of Bogrov's Snapchats, emails, and texts sent directly to you, without copying me."

Mak said, "And I found more proof linking Vince and Magadan. Russian law requires partnering with a local subcontractor to bid on the Northern Okhotsk Project. Vince picked Magadan as the local partner for Wakkanai's proposal."

"Great. Even the Japanese police won't be able to sit on their hands any longer. They'll have to open an investigation into Vince and Tom Saito. Once you've received the info from Alexei, you should have someone hand deliver to the police all of the evidence we've collected. To be safe, send a copy to both Taniguchi and Tsujikawa. I don't want it sitting on someone's desk if one of them is out of the office for some reason."

"I'll take care of it. As for the confessions, I can send them just the relevant excerpts. They don't need to hear the sausage making."

"Make sure the English interpreting and my voice are deleted from Bogrov's interrogation. The police will want to get their own translation anyway. Send everything as soon as you can, anonymously, and don't contact me again unless you run into a problem."

"Sounds like a plan. There's one more thing," Mak said.

"What's that?"

"Vince's activism against Wakkanai."

"Oh, I almost forgot. What's going on?" Torn raised a bottle of water to his lips.

"Wakkanai is calling an Extraordinary General Shareholders Meeting to get shareholder approval to increase the number of authorized shares."

Torn almost spit the water out. "Seriously? They must be planning to issue shares to a white knight to prevent Vince from garnering enough shareholder votes to remove the Watanabes from the board. He'll probably mount a proxy fight to have the Watanabes kicked out and Tom Saito appointed shacho."

"I'll send you a link to Wakkanai's public disclosure, which they posted today. It contains a copy of the notice of the shareholders meeting, which is scheduled for October 10."

Torn sat back in his chair. "Wow. That's only a week from now. I'll bet Vince didn't see that coming. He probably thought he had until next year's Annual General Shareholders Meeting to drum up support from the other shareholders to remove the Watanabes."

"Also, Wakkanai has counterclaimed against Vince for embezzlement because he allegedly took kickbacks from Twain, for breach of his fiduciary duties as director, and for insider trading and securities fraud because he purchased shares in Wakkanai shortly after being fired as Vice Chairman."

Torn couldn't help but smile. "Send me the counterclaim docs and let me know when Vince files his proxy solicitation materials."

"Will do."

Torn took another drink of water. "He's really in for a rude awakening after you drop that evidence on the police. You should let the police know what's going on with him and Wakkanai."

"I'll include the information about the shareholders meeting and lawsuit in our data dump."

Torn smiled. "I'd like to be at that shareholders meeting. Should be a lot of fireworks."

"Yeah, but don't go. Too dangerous."

Torn laughed. "OK, Mom."

"I'm not joking," Mak said sternly.

Torn's plane landed at Haneda International Airport just before 9:00 a.m. Unable to get on a flight the night before, he had checked into the transit hotel for a few hours before jumping on a 7:00 a.m. flight. He hadn't slept well, but it beat sitting in the lounge all night.

Arriving in Japan, he had a knot in his stomach. Having trouble breathing, he could move only by force of will. Russia had been frightening, but now he was back where people he didn't know had attempted to murder him twice, blown up Saya, and murdered Yukie. He had felt safest during his layover at Incheon.

He was trying to pull himself together, but the realization that his life was in shambles came crashing down. Someone still wanted him dead. His wife had been murdered. His client, for whom he cared deeply, lay in a coma. His children were in exile. Kiwako likely knew he'd been cheating on her—*That's on me. I'm such an idiot*, he told himself. He'd violated his agreement with the police. He was an officer of the court involved in illegal activity in two countries. The police still had an open investigation against him but hadn't aggressively pursued those responsible for Yukie's murder and the attempts on his and Saya's lives. He'd probably be fired if he wasn't cleared soon. And he would always be looking over his shoulder until the perpetrators were behind bars.

To continue to execute effectively on his plan, he needed relief from the emotional paralysis he felt.

He took the monorail, which had just yesterday started running again following the repair of earthquake damage, from Haneda to Hamamatsucho Station, and then the five-minute taxi ride to his apartment at Amaterasu Hills. He found himself furtively keeping an eye out in all directions and trying to be inconspicuous, no mean feat for someone 190 centimeters tall in Japan. He decided against taking a taxi from the airport because he didn't want someone trying to run him off the road again. He felt safer surrounded by people.

Once home, he showered and prepared to go to the office. His hands shook as he buttoned his shirt. As he was about to get into a car, he recalled his relaxing walk with Saya at Meiji Shrine. Against his better judgment, he climbed the eighty-six-steep "Stone Steps to Success" to Amaterasu Shrine behind his apartment building. He hadn't been outside to relax for so long that he decided to spend a few minutes at the tiny oasis atop the highest land point in central Tokyo.

Stopping briefly at the giant stone *Torii* gate at the top of the steps, he put his hands together, closed his eyes, and bowed. Having shown appropriate respect to the deities within, he walked along the side of the trail to the shrine, avoiding the middle, where "God travels the path." Before going into the sacred area of the shrine itself, he stopped to purify his hands at a small cement water trough filled with cold well water flowing from the bronze head of a dragon. Several bamboo ladles lay across long pieces of bamboo suspended over the trough. He picked up a ladle by its long handle and used it to wash his hands and rinse his mouth.

Having purified himself, he walked through a small red, wood gate to the shrine and dropped *go-en* (a five-yen coin), the Japanese word that also means good luck, into the wooden collection box in front of the shrine. He grabbed the thick red-and-white rope of the shrine bell hanging nearby and shook it once to call the gods to hear his plea. He bowed twice at the waist to show his reverence, closed his eyes, and clapped his hands twice.

With his eyes closed and hands together, he prayed. He prayed for the safety of his children, for Kiwako, and for Mayumi. He prayed for Saya's recovery. He prayed for peace for Yukie. He prayed for the nightmare to end soon. And he prayed for justice. As an atheist who hadn't prayed in decades, it felt awkward to surrender himself to something whose existence he doubted, but as he went through the process, he felt a weight lifting from his shoulders. When finished, he bowed once more, thanking the gods for listening.

He purchased several small paper bags of fish pellets from a priest at the shrine. He then walked to the edge of the koi pond with its brightly speckled *nishikigoi* (decorative carp), a gurgling waterfall, a small red Shinto gate in the water on one side, and a little wooden dock and boat that looked like they had been made for leprechauns on the other. So many trees and bushes surrounded the pond that no buildings in the sprawling city around him could be seen. He heard no traffic and saw no people. The only sound was that of the waterfall and birds chirping in the trees.

Torn took slow, deep breaths as he looked at the fat "swimming jewels" in the pond: some black, some white, some orange, some brown, some yellow, and many mottled. Many fish started swimming in his direction and gathering at his feet, opening and closing their mouths at the surface in anticipation. He began throwing food pellets to them: first one, then two, then three, and eventually handfuls.

The koi swarmed the bank, drowning out the music of the waterfall with their slurping, slapping, and splashing. They crowded in so tightly that some were pushed onto the backs of others before slithering back into the water. Some were even briefly pushed up onto the bank, only to flop back into the pond. Torn laughed as he watched the fat fish constantly opening and closing their round whiskered mouths whether a pellet was anywhere near or not.

In the midst of this feeding frenzy, Torn got down on his hands and knees and stuck into the water the tips of his fingers, which immediately the carp tried to devour. He laughed out loud at the pressure and sound from their slimy sucking. Even after he had run out of food, koi lingered at the pond's edge, opening and closing their mouths until they realized the well had run dry.

He watched the fish drift away and disperse throughout the small pond. The gurgling of the waterfall and chirping of the birds returned. By now, completely relaxed, his fear was gone.

Closing In

迫る終焉

"You violated the terms of your parole. You were specifically required to notify us in advance of any travel abroad." Tsujikawa sat with Torn's passports laid out in front of him on the conference room table.

"You're right. I apologize. I had to make a quick business trip to Khabarovsk. In the rush, I forgot to report to Detective Taniguchi."

That morning, the police had raided his office with a warrant and started rifling through his files and emails. They confiscated his regular phone and the first burner phone Mak had given him. He had used that phone to communicate with Taniguchi and Tsujikawa. Luckily, they didn't know about the second one. Detective Taniguchi had demanded Torn hand over his US and Japan passports.

When Torn inquired what this was all about, Taniguchi asked him if he'd traveled abroad recently. Knowing the police would eventually figure out he'd been to Russia, Torn came clean and provided his flight information. Three hours later, he and Saki sat in a conference room at Hilsberry & Carter with the two lawmen. Saki had managed to convince Tsujikawa to hold the meeting outside of the police station in light of the recent tragedies in Torn's life. It was an easy sale, in part because prosecutors and the police liked to get out of their dreary, crowded offices whenever they could.

259

Tsujikawa slapped the table. "What do you know about this info dump we received?"

Knowing this was a trap, Torn shrugged his shoulders and looked at Saki. "Do you know what he's talking about?"

Caught off guard, she stiffened and responded emphatically, "No, this is the first I'm hearing it."

Torn hadn't told Saki anything about his evidence collection efforts. The less she knew, the easier it would be for him to feign ignorance.

Tsujikawa, red-faced, slapped the table again and pointed a bony finger at Torn. "Don't play dumb with me! You know exactly what I'm talking about."

"Actually, I don't. I was in Russia on business. Local counsel there, Alexei Chomkov, will confirm."

"Who's the client?"

"That's confidential. I can tell you that it was an energy-related matter. Russia is rich in oil and gas." Torn knew he was playing a dangerous game, because the rules governing attorney-client privilege in Japan were murky.

Tsujikawa looked like smoke was about to stream from his ears. "If you don't want to go back to jail, you'll tell us who the client is."

Technically, Torn had met with "local counsel" and he didn't know that the police had received new evidence, because he hadn't heard from Mak that he'd actually made the drop. At this point, not afraid of going back to jail, and angry he'd been forced to do their job for them, he decided to go on the offensive. "So, who's responsible for the attacks?"

"Don't change the subject!"

Saki, regaining her footing, jumped in. "What's the real issue here? My client made a mistake, which he acknowledged and for which he has apologized. And he returned to Japan. It's not like he left the country never to return. If you want our help, we need to know what you know."

Torn appreciated the "we." Saki hadn't made a distinction between lawyer and client, which would resonate with Tsujikawa.

Tsujikawa sat up straight, took a deep breath, and put his hands on the table. "Those are fair points, and of course we need Sagara-sensei's cooperation. Detective Taniguchi, please fill them in."

Taniguchi proceeded to explain that Sergey Bogrov likely sent the threatening email to Torn, and he'd implicated Vince Harden and Tom Saito, a senior executive at Wakkanai. He said that the police believed one or both of them may have ordered the attacks. He added that someone else implicated a man with a scar and a woman with "'messed-up hair and bulging eyes that seemed to move in opposite directions like one a them lizards.' Ring a bell?"

This was the first Torn had heard of a man with a scar and a strange woman. In his haste, he hadn't compared notes with Mak, who had mentioned only that the guy he had interrogated disclosed his boss's name.

Saki looked at Torn, who was organizing his thoughts. "That's all news to me. Does Tom Saito have a scar?"

The lawmen looked at each other. Then Taniguchi asked, "You don't know him?"

"No. I worked closely with Vince on the Project Ibis transaction for Wakkanai, but Saito-san had been taken off the deal to work on something else before Wakkanai hired us."

Taniguchi looked at Torn. "What do you know about Harden-san's termination?"

"Just what's in the pleadings." Torn explained Vince's claim against Wakkanai for wrongful termination as Vice Chairman—and Wakkanai's counterclaims against him for embezzlement, breach of his fiduciary duties as director, insider trading, and securities fraud—and Harden Industries' claim for breach of its Distribution Agreement with Wakkanai. He also explained Vince's proxy fight to have Tamayo, Miki, and Yoji Watanabe removed from Wakkanai's board and Tom Saito installed as president.

"We're aware of the lawsuit and the upcoming shareholders meeting," Tsujikawa said matter-of-factly.

Torn asked excitedly, "So you're going? It would be a great time to arrest Vince and Tom Saito."

Saki gave Torn a sharp look. Knowing he needed to cool it, Torn pursed his lips and looked down at the table.

Taniguchi looked at Tsujikawa and back at Torn. "We don't have enough evidence to arrest anyone." He paused before adding, "And your illegal involvement in the collection of the evidence taints what we do have."

Torn broke into a cold sweat but held Taniguchi's gaze. "I'm not following you."

Saki, still trying to process what she was hearing, didn't say a word.

Tsujikawa tapped a pen on his notepad. "Was your client in Russia with you?"

"That's confidential information and not relevant to this discussion," Torn replied as calmly as possible.

"Well, it's quite a coincidence that we received all this information just a day after your return to Japan from a trip that violated the terms of your bail."

Torn, regaining his composure, smiled. "You should be talking to Bogrov, Vince, and Tom Saito, not me. Have you looked into whether Vince's company, Harden Industries, sells ANFO, or whatever the hell explosive material was used to destroy Raijin Clean's office building?"

Tsujikawa pulled on the lapels of his jacket. "We'll get to Mr. Harden and Saito-san if and when we have enough evidence. We're looking into the ANFO issue. Now tell me again what you were doing in Russia."

Saki looked at the two men. "Tsujikawa-sensei, asked and answered on the bail issue. And you have no jurisdiction over what my client does outside of Japan."

Tsujikawa frowned. "True, unless he violated Japanese law. The evidence we received includes what sounds like a forced confession from one of the hospitalized suspects. He said he was tortured. And he had several needle marks covered by Band-Aids in places where nurses don't administer shots."

Torn asked, "When was this alleged attack?"

"While you were en route to Russia. We've confirmed you were on a flight to Khabarovsk at the time. However, another recording is of what sounds like the tortured confession in Russian of Mr. Bogrov, but we don't know who recorded it or where or when. We suspect it was recorded in Russia, and it's highly irregular for us to receive an anonymous recording of an interrogation overseas in a foreign language."

Saki chimed in. "Since Sagara-sensei has an alibi for the alleged attack on the suspect in Japan, and you admittedly don't know when *or even where* the alleged interrogation of Mr. Bogrov occurred, you have no evidence of Sagara-sensei's involvement in either."

Tsujikawa said, "We wish to know his involvement in collecting such evidence and who he worked with to get it."

Saki, hitting her stride, sat up straight and said forcefully, "Sagara-sensei has already denied any knowledge of the information you received or how it was collected. He's been extremely cooperative and has kept his word at all times. There's no justification whatsoever for harassing him in this way. Moreover, aren't you going to cut a plea deal with the two hospitalized suspects anyway?"

She knew the police would use the recording of the interrogation of the Japanese thug as ammunition to elicit confessions from both Japanese suspects. "By now, you should have more than enough information to go after the people who are responsible for Yukie-san's murder and the multiple attempts on the lives of Brooks-san and Sagara-sensei."

Torn put his hand out in front of Saki. "It's all right. I'm happy to cooperate to the extent I can."

It was Saki's turn to slap the table, except she did it with far more force than Tsujikawa had a few moments prior. "No, Sagara-sensei, it's not all right! As a former prosecutor, I'm embarrassed by how this investigation's been handled and how you, a victim several times over, are being treated by my former colleagues! You're being victimized yet again."

The two lawmen looked like someone had been screaming at them through a bullhorn. They glanced at each other briefly and looked down at their hands.

Taniguchi looked up first. "Katayama-sensei, please know we're in no way trying to harass Sagara-sensei, who as you say is a victim in this matter. We're just following up on all loose ends, including his admitted violation of the terms of his bail."

Tsujikawa furrowed his brow and pointed his finger at Torn again. "And if there are any more infractions, you'll be in jail. Do you understand me?"

Torn nodded.

Taniguchi added, "The good news is we have enough evidence to prosecute the two suspects who allegedly attacked Sagara-sensei and Ino-san. And we received the DNA results, which put one of them at the scene of Yukie-san's murder."

Torn wanted to say, "Well, if you weren't such lazy idiots, I wouldn't have to do your job for you," but he suppressed his anger. He took a deep breath and said quietly, "Detective Taniguchi, Tsujikawa-sensei, I understand you're just doing your job and I appreciate the progress you've made. I really hope you find the people who ordered these heinous crimes so I can wake from this nightmare and bring my children home."

Taniguchi sat up straight. "We'll do our best, Sagara-sensei. I think we have enough from you for now."

Tsujikawa added quickly, "One more thing. Stay away from Wakkanai's shareholder meeting."

"Why?"

"As you have alluded to, the people who want you dead may be in attendance."

Torn paused and then replied, "Understood. Thank you for your concern."

Tsujikawa bowed his head slightly. Taniguchi put his hands on the table, bowed his head, and said, "And thank you for your cooperation and patience, Sagara-sensei and Katayama-sensei."

With that, the playacting was over. Saki and Torn saw the lawmen to the elevators and bowed deferentially while Taniguchi and Tsujikawa stood facing them with their heads bowed as the elevator doors closed.

After returning to the conference room, Torn smiled broadly. "Saki, that was brilliant."

"They deserved it, although it certainly is curious that they received such information anonymously out of the blue. Oh, and since you never mentioned anything before, I assume you really don't know anything about it. And before you say anything, let's just leave it there." With that, she grabbed her bag and walked calmly out of the conference room.

———

Early the next morning, unable to sleep, Torn called his children. Following his return to Japan, he'd texted that he was fine but had yet to speak with them.

Sean answered, sounding somewhat panicky. "Dad, is that you?"

"Yes, Son. It's great to hear your voice."

"Thank God. I was afraid this might be another bad news call. Why're you up? It's 2:00 a.m. there."

"Lots of work to do. Where's your sister?"

"She went snowshoeing with Grandma. What's up?"

"It's been quite hectic and I had to go to Russia, but I'm back in Japan now." He was oversharing again.

"Russia? Why Russia?!"

"Work." *Just not "legal" work*, he thought with chagrin.

"Seriously? You've never gone to Russia before."

He didn't respond and wondered what his kids would think if they knew their father was having people tortured. But by now he was willing to do almost anything to find the perpetrators.

"You should've told us. What if something had happened to you there? Who would know?"

"Don't worry. Mak always knows where I am."

"Yeah, yeah. Have the police found anything yet?"

"They seem to be getting close." *Don't ask me how I know that.*

"That's good news! Sophia and I want to get out of here. We're getting cabin fever and probably driving Grandma nuts."

"Hang in there for just a little longer."

"Can't we come and stay with you?"

"As I said, just a little longer."

Sean sighed. "Sophia and I talked, and if we're gonna die, we'd rather be with you. Plus, we could protect each other."

Torn, unable to speak for a moment, finally said, his voice cracking ever so slightly, "No one else is going to die. Just give me a few more days."

Nothing Is More Times Opened by Mistake

綸言汗の如し

Three days before the shareholders meeting, Torn noticed a missed call from Mak on his disposable phone at 1:47 in the morning, immediately followed by a text urgently requesting a callback. Working his way through another sleepless night, Torn had been in the other room making tea. He immediately hit Mak's number.

"Hi, Mak. What are you doing up?"

"Torn, I fucked up."

"What do you mean?"

"I told Sean you'd been attacked at the hotel. I didn't think it was fair to treat him like a mushroom anymore."

"What?"

"Keep him in the dark and feed him shit."

Exasperated, Torn said, "I know what it means. Let's back up. Why'd he call you?"

"He said he was worried about you and that you'd been acting weird and seemed to be hiding something. I told him you'd been under tremendous stress since the attacks and he asked, 'What attacks?' Then I knew I'd screwed up, but I felt he deserved to know. So, I told him about the attack at the hotel."

Torn put his hand on his forehead. "How'd he respond?"

"'Those people need to die.' Then he asked if the cops had figured out who'd done it. I said two guys were under arrest,

267

and the police were investigating Vince Harden and Tom Saito at Wakkanai. I told him about the evidence we'd found."

"Anything else?"

Silence.

"Mak?"

"He wanted to know their whereabouts. I said I didn't know where they lived and if I did, I wouldn't tell him."

Silence.

"Mak, what am I missing?"

"He asked if I had any idea when the police might move against Vince and Tom."

Again, silence.

"And?"

Mak sighed. "And before I thought it through, I said they hadn't decided whether to move against Vince and Tom yet. Look, Torn, I know I messed up."

"What'd he say?"

"'Thank you very much, Mr. Karahashi, for helping my father and my family.' Then he hung up. Maybe it's nothing, but he sounded very formal and distant all of a sudden when he said that last part, like he wasn't all there."

Torn took a deep breath. "When did you speak with him?"

"Yesterday around 9:00 p.m. I didn't tell you earlier because I didn't want to worry you. And I figured he'd call you. But the more I thought about it, the more I thought you should know."

Torn rubbed his temples. "He was bound to find out at some point. You did the right thing calling me."

"Let me know if there's anything I can do. Torn, I'm sorry."

"Let's talk later." Torn frantically tried Sean's sat phone. *Please answer the phone.* But no one did.

Heart racing, slightly dizzy, and palms sweaty, he texted Sean, Sophia, and his mom. None of his texts went through.

He tried to think as he paced, and every thought was negative.

The police were less than worthless and gave him a hard time about him doing their job and finding evidence when they would have nothing without his efforts. They hadn't even cleared him of charges related to the expressway attacks. He couldn't reach his family. And the bad guys now had even more reason to have him killed.

His phone buzzed with a text: "Hi Torn."

He could hardly believe his eyes. He texted back: "Saya! You're awake! How are you?"

"Hanging in there. I've been up for two days but too tired to reach out to anyone until today. Still can't talk much because my throat is sore from the breathing tube. And I feel exhausted all the time. So, I decided to text to let you know I'm alive. I wasn't expecting you to be up. Why are you awake?"

"Just catching up on some things."

"Mom told me what you did for me. Always the savior. How are you?"

"I'm fine." He decided not to burden her about Yukie's murder or the attack at the Andaz.

"Have the police found the people who attacked us?"

"They may arrest someone soon." He hoped that was true.

"Torn, what I said in the video..."

He squinted as he typed: "Yes, that was very sweet and I'll never forget it, but let's discuss it later. You need to rest."

"It's best we talk face-to-face anyway. I hope to be in Japan in a few weeks."

"So soon?"

"Yes. The brain swelling is down and I'm healing nicely. I found a good place in Tokyo for rehab."

"Don't overdo it."

"Thank you. I need to get back to work. Let's chat live when I can talk so you can update me about Raijin."

"Sure. Any time. Take care."

He sat on his bed thinking about Saya until his phone rang at 3:00 a.m. It was Kiwako. *When it rains, it pours.*

She sounded frantic and angry. "Oh, thank God you're up! Torn, what's going on? You didn't tell me someone tried to murder you. Why did I have to hear about it on the news?! Are you all right? You never responded to my text. A friend sent me a link to news about the attack at the Andaz on you and Mayumi-san."

Torn's blood ran cold.

"And then I get a frantic call from your mom. You've been through a lot I know, but you've been sleeping with Mayumi-san. How could you cheat on me?!"

"Sweetheart, there's a lot to explain. First, tell me what happened."

Kiwako choked back tears. "Your mom said Sean left. I asked her if she'd called you, and she said not yet because it was the middle of the night there. She didn't want to disturb you. She sounded desperate and not very lucid.

"I asked her where Sean went. She said he'd found out you'd been attacked at the hotel and went crazy, demanding they fly back to Anchorage immediately. Sophia and your mom are now at her place in Anchorage. But Sean left without telling them. I told her she needed to call you and the police right away. She said she'd call the police but wait until your morning to call you. I wish there was more I could do to help her."

"Kiwako, you've already done so much. Thank you. I'm sorry to have been incommunicado. It'll all be over in a few days. Then I'll explain everything. I didn't tell you about the attack because I didn't want you to worry. Let me call my mom."

She paused and said without emotion, "Torn, I told you to stay away from Mayumi-san. You've disrespected and humiliated me. All my friends and family, including my kids, know. It's bad enough that you were still married. How long has this been going on?"

"Sweetheart, can we please talk about this later?"

"Torn, there's not going to be a later." The line went dead.

He paused for a moment, his addled mind thinking perhaps it was for the best. Only later would the enormity of the loss and the guilt sink in. He was comforted he still had Mayumi and a lead on Saya. Realizing that was a strangely inappropriate feeling to have at any time, let alone a time like this, he thought, *So not only do I have someone else to turn to, but I've got one in reserve? God, I am seriously fucked up.*

—

Torn had no time for introspection. He called his mom and got the story from her. She sounded frazzled and beside herself with worry. She said Sean disappeared after they'd returned to Anchorage at his insistence. She had reported Sean missing to the police, but they wouldn't act for twenty-four hours. Torn suspected he knew Sean's destination.

"Mom, as I've told you before, feel free to call me any time of the day or night if you need to reach me. You can also text and email me."

"Of course, I'm sorry. I'm not thinking straight."

"I understand. Would you put Sophia on, please?"

Sophia came on the line. "We're all very worried about you, and Grandma's blood pressure has skyrocketed. You know how that can make her a bit loopy, particularly after she takes her medication."

"I'm doing the best I can. I need you to stay with your grandma until this is all over. It's not safe here."

"Well, Sean may be headed your way."

"What did he tell you?"

"He said you'd been attacked at the hotel and the police were closing in on someone named Vince Harden."

"Vince is just a suspect. Nothing concrete yet," he lied. "I need to know right away if you hear from Sean."

Sophia raised her voice. "Our mother's dead, we're in hiding, our father's been attacked—twice—but won't communicate with us, and now Sean's disappeared. What's going on? You need to tell me now!"

"It'll be over soon. Just be patient."

"Dad!" she shrieked.

Torn said with all the control he could muster, "Please take care of your grandma. She needs you right now. And I need you to be safe. It's bad enough that Sean is missing. I don't want you running off halfcocked too."

"Well, I could help you with shopping and cleaning and stuff. And I want to find whoever killed Mom just as much as you and Sean do. Let me come and stay with you." She had calmed down almost as quickly as she'd become enraged. Now she was almost begging.

Her hot and cold approach tore at his heartstrings. He knew she must be scared, worried, and lonely. Her family was splitting apart at the seams.

"You can help me most by staying there. Once this is over you can come to Japan. I love you both more than anything, and there is nothing I want more in the world than to see you both... *except* to keep you both safe."

"OK, Dad," she said, and the phone clicked off.

He looked at his phone for a moment, surprised she'd hung up on him. He tried to call Sean on his Japan mobile phone but only heard an out-of-area message. His texts didn't go through either. He sent an email asking Sean to call him right away. Then he had an idea.

He texted Mak: "See if you can trace Sean's phone."

Wild Card

鬼札

"I'm so sorry to bother you, honey. I know you're busy, and I don't want to cause you any more worry." His mom's voice trembled and she sounded like she'd been crying. It was 2:30 in the morning on the day of Wakkanai Drilling's Extraordinary General Shareholders Meeting, scheduled to start at 9:00 a.m.

"Mom, it's no bother. I'm never too busy to talk to you. Please take a deep breath and tell me what's going on."

"Honey, it's Sophia. She's gone."

Torn leaned against the wall, closed his eyes tightly, and cupped his mouth with his left hand.

"Are you there, Son?"

"Yes, Mom. Please go on."

"Yesterday, after she talked to you—and it's not your fault—she said she was tired of being cooped up in the house and was going to a movie. I offered to go with her, but she said she wanted to be alone. She never came home. But I didn't notice she was gone until this morning. I'm so sorry! I wasn't feeling well because my blood pressure has been spiking. So, I took some medication and went to bed early. I should've gone with her or at least stayed up until she got back."

"Mom, it's not your fault. I'll let you know as soon as I find them. Please call the Anchorage police and let them know Sophia is missing too."

"I'll call them right now. I'm so sorry."

"Stop saying that. Now I need you to do something else."

"Sure. Anything, honey."

"I need you to take care of yourself. You've done all you can. Just please stay safe, try not to worry, and get some rest. I love you, Mom."

"I love you too, Son," she said, her voice trembling again.

After hanging up, he almost threw his phone against the wall. *Why doesn't anyone in this goddamn family listen to me?* But then a thought occurred to him: *What if they haven't gone rogue? What if Vince's henchmen found them?*

His heart pounded and he wanted to puke. He sat for a moment with his face buried in his hands. Just as quickly, he had another thought: *But they'd kidnap them only as leverage. They'd gain nothing by just killing them. And if they'd kidnapped them, they would've contacted me.* This line of thinking calmed him down somewhat, but an uneasy feeling remained.

He texted Mak to search for Sophia's phone too. The only other thing he could do was contact the Japanese police later in the morning, which he realized he should've done when he first learned about Sean's disappearance. Clearly, he wasn't thinking straight.

At a loss as to what to do next, he leaned against the wall in his bedroom. Closing his eyes, he slowly let his legs buckle and his back slide down the wall until he sat on the floor with his head between his knees. So tired yet unable to sleep. *Would the police ever make an arrest?* They seemed so close to cracking the case wide open. *So why haven't they?*

He wished he could read the transcript of Mak's interrogation of the goon in the hospital. But he knew if he'd had possession of a hard or soft copy when the police raided his office, they would've found it.

His head was foggy as he slowly went over the list of suspects in his head: Vince, Tom Saito, Bogrov, the two thugs in the hospital, their boss, the guy with the scar—*Tom Saito?*—

and the woman with the bulging eyes—*who the hell was that?* He remembered what Mak had said about Tamayo's daughter and her husband. Using his phone, he looked up the biographies of Tom Saito, Yoji Watanabe, and his wife, Miki, on Wakkanai's website. Their photos were grainy black and whites. Old school. Nothing of interest.

Perhaps I should go to the shareholders meeting to see who's on Vince's team. He was grasping at straws, *but what do I have to lose at this point?* On the other hand, both Mak and the police had warned him to stay away. *But it's gotta be safer than driving on the expressway, being in Russia, or being home alone. No one's going to do anything in a crowded hotel conference room,* he reasoned.

Torn texted Asahi Susono to ask for permission to join the meeting as an observer. Susono responded a few hours later: "It would be an honor to have you, Sagara-sensei. You can sit with the Wakkanai employees. I'll have a name badge for you at reception."

Torn texted his driver too.

⁓

On his way to Wakkanai's shareholders meeting, Torn called Taniguchi from his car about Sean and Sophia. Taniguchi said they'd try to track his children's phones and would check flight manifests, but it would take time. Torn didn't disclose his plan to attend the shareholders meeting.

Reception for the Wakkanai Extraordinary General Shareholders Meeting opened at 8:00 a.m. in front of a cavernous conference room on the second floor of a 1980s-era hotel in Shinjuku. Inside the conference room, giant, gaudy chandeliers hung from impossibly high ceilings. Pleated floor-to-ceiling drapes spaced ten meters apart clung to walls decorated with faux gilded chrysanthemums and flying cranes sprinkled liberally on pearl-white wallpaper.

Torn, wearing a dark suit and red tie, arrived at the hotel a few minutes early and took an escalator to the meeting's reception. He signed in at a long table where what he assumed were Wakkanai employees dressed in dark suits stood behind a desk waiting to receive attendees. They were not the typical fresh-faced junior corporate employees Torn usually saw staffing such reception desks. Susono was among them.

"Sagara-sensei, good morning. How nice of you to come. I'm sure Watanabe-shacho will be delighted to see you. Here's your badge. Please take a seat in the third row on the left side."

"Good morning, Susono-san. Thank you. Do you know where Tomohiro Saito-san will be sitting?"

"Front row of the employee seating area. He has a reserved seat second from the aisle."

Torn attached his badge to his jacket pocket using the clip on the back and entered the conference room through one of three sets of floor-to-ceiling double doors with one-meter-long vertical brass handles. A hotel employee wearing a black uniform and white gloves opened one of the doors for him. Inside he could see three similar double doors, including one near the dais, along each side of the room. He took his seat.

At 8:30 a.m., Vince Harden and his entourage entered and took over the first and second rows of the tables on the right side of the room. Torn recognized one of the lawyers from a Japanese law firm Vince had hired to handle the proxy fight. There were at least twenty rows of tables behind Vince's team. They were filling up fast.

Between Torn and Vince's team was a wider column of tables in the middle of the conference room separated from the left and right columns of seats by spacious aisles. Like the column on the right side of the room, it was reserved for shareholders and almost every seat was taken.

On the dais at the front of the room were two long tables arranged end to end, angled toward the audience like swept wings. Each table had several chairs and name tents for the board members. In the middle of the dais in front of the tables stood a podium adorned with Wakkanai's drill bit corporate seal.

After sitting down, Vince, always wanting to know who was present, looked around and saw Torn. He immediately stood up and sauntered over, extending his hand.

Torn stood. His skin crawled when he shook Vince's hand.

Vince smiled. "Long time, no see. You don't look so good. Are you getting enough sleep?"

Torn remained standing and looked Vince in the eye. "Evidently not."

"So, you're working for Wakkanai on this?"

"No. Wakkanai has separate counsel for their corporate governance matters. I'm just an observer. Susono-san said I could sit with the employees."

"You should've represented me. When I said I was going to sue them and take them over, I wasn't kidding."

"I see that. But you wouldn't want me to represent Harden Industries on some big matter and then turn around and sue them for someone else."

"I suppose not. You should sit with us. Wakkanai doesn't care about you."

Torn winced. "And you do?"

Vince sighed. "Ya know, Torn, I don't know why you're so antagonistic toward me. I've been nothing but a great client to you. I may be tough, but I'm fair. I feel bad for you and your family, but I had nothing to do with any of the attacks."

I'm sure, thought Torn, but he didn't respond.

"Suit yourself." Vince turned on his heels and walked over to Tom Saito, who had just sat down.

Torn watched as Saito stood and shook hands with Vince. He could see Saito's face clearly.

Torn received a text from Mak: "I found Sean's phone. It's near Yukie's house. He, or at least his phone, is in Tokyo. No sign of Sophia, though."

As he read Mak's text, the board members took their seats. At 9:00 a.m. sharp, Tamayo Watanabe, wearing a bright-blue, long-sleeve business jacket, matching skirt, and white bowtie-neck blouse, stepped to the podium to convene the meeting. She started with some opening remarks about the history of Wakkanai. Torn looked at the dais and saw Miki's name tent in front of a fidgety woman with bulging eyes who needed to comb her hair. Then he saw Yoji Watanabe's name tent in front of a tanned man with a prominent scar on his neck. Torn didn't know that the scar was from an injury suffered during an explosion on an oil rig. Torn's eyes widened and suddenly he had trouble breathing. His palms started to sweat. He looked at Miki and then back at Yoji.

Tom Saito wasn't the mysterious man with the scar, and Miki looked like the woman Taniguchi had described. Torn struggled to understand the roles of each of Vince, Tom Saito, Yoji, and Miki in the conspiracy to destroy Saya and her light-ning technology. He looked at Tamayo and wondered whether she had a role in all of this as well.

As Tamayo started to announce that the number of proxy votes Vince had obtained was insufficient to remove her, Miki, and Yoji from the board and replace her with Tom Saito, Torn heard a commotion behind him. Turning his head quickly, he saw Sophia bursting through two of the large doors to the conference room.

She was barefoot, wearing her dark blue kendo uniform without the usual armor and helmet. Her hair was pulled back in a thick ponytail. In her left hand, she held a short katana by its black and blue sheath. Torn recognized the katana as part of the Ishikawa family set of ancient swords.

Looking around for a moment as she stood in the right-hand aisle, Sophia grabbed the handle of the sword with her right hand, pulled out the shiny blade, and dropped the sheath. As she lifted the sword with both hands, her right hand up near the *tsuba*, the guard separating the handle from the sword, and her left down near the bottom of the handle, the blade flashed like in many *jidaigeki* (samurai movies) Torn had seen over the years. He half expected to hear the iconic "*sha-kin*" sound made in the movies when a sword flashes.

When she had the sword over her head with the curved blade pointing downward slightly behind her left shoulder, Sophia started sprinting down the right aisle in long loping strides toward Vince. He was easy to spot, standing out like a sore thumb in a sea of Japanese faces. There was no mistaking Sophia's intent. Everyone in the room, including Vince, froze.

Torn felt like everything, including himself, was moving in slow motion. He stood, jumped on the table closest to him in the center aisle, and started running across the top toward the right aisle. Out of the corner of his right eye, he saw Sean, holding the unsheathed long Ishikawa katana, burst through the door and start running down the left-hand aisle.

Torn ignored him for the moment and kept his eyes on Sophia as he ran, trampling phones, notebooks, laptops, and coffee cups along the way. But she was moving so fast he wasn't sure he could reach her in time, part of him hoping she would win the race.

When he was halfway across the center column of tables, Torn saw Yoji rise with a gun in his hand. *No one has a gun in Japan except yaks*, he thought once again.

Shortly before Sophia reached Vince's table, Torn launched himself into the air to tackle her.

As he launched himself to grab Sophia, Torn saw the muzzle of Yoji's gun flash twice and heard two pops, followed by several people screaming. But he couldn't see Yoji's target.

Sophia would've flown by Torn if he hadn't grabbed her long ponytail with one hand, yanking her down as he crashed into Vince's table. People, laptops, phones, papers, pens, coffee cups, and water bottles scattered everywhere.

Vince stood back, looking on, mouth agape.

After landing in a heap, Torn bear-hugged Sophia from behind to keep her from getting up.

"What're you doing, Dad?! Let me go!" she screamed in English.

"I won't let them destroy your life too!"

"But he tried to have you killed! He almost took everything away from us! He's caused so much pain. He needs to pay!"

Torn hugged her tighter with one arm and held down the arm holding the katana with the other. Speaking more softly he said, "Your mother wouldn't want you to throw your life away. And she wouldn't forgive me if I let you."

Torn felt someone tugging on his shoulder. He looked up to see Tsujikawa leaning over him. *Oh shit*, he thought. A police officer stood behind Tsujikawa. And then he saw Mak standing behind the officer.

"Sagara-sensei, I don't know who this young woman is or the purpose of her presence here, but I suggest you let this officer take her and her, um, accessory outside right now. You should go to your son."

Torn's blood ran cold.

He looked around and saw police flooding into the room. Three of them had Yoji on the ground already. He looked at Tsujikawa, who read his mind and said, "Harden-san's not involved."

"See, honey. There will be justice. Let the police take care of it. You have a long life to live."

Sophia let the sword roll out of her hand.

Last Supper

最後の晩餐

For the next several days, Torn spent most of his time at home with Sean and Sophia. Tsujikawa called frequently, saying he wanted to meet right away, but Torn kept pushing him off. Still angry with the police, he wouldn't even speak to Tsujikawa over the phone, relying instead on Saki to wrap up the legal issues.

Saya remained in the US longer than she had expected as her doctors recommended against her taking a long-haul flight until she was stronger. Several times Torn and Saya spoke by telephone, but they talked only business. He could tell she wasn't ready to discuss what she'd said in her video. At first, he wasn't either. But gradually the numbness from recent events, including at the shareholders meeting, began to thaw, and he started thinking about moving on with his life.

The firm said he could take as much time off as he needed, but he decided to keep working because he wanted to help Raijin Clean get back on its feet as soon as possible. Torn checked in with the office every day. The Raijin IP team continued working on the patenting process. He and his litigation group filed several lawsuits against Wakkanai and the Watanabes seeking damages for the destruction of Raijin Clean's building, assault and battery on Saya and Torn, and the wrongful death of Yukie.

He spoke with Mayumi but pushed her off when she asked to meet, claiming he needed to focus on his children. And while it was true that he wanted to be there for them, he also wanted to see how things would go with Saya. From her tone, he could tell Mayumi was mustering all her willpower to be patient, but he knew she was too smart not to be suspicious of his motives. At times, he thought he should be honest with her and let her go, but he wasn't strong enough to do that.

He tried to call Kiwako a couple of times and was relieved when she didn't answer or return his calls. She finally texted that although she was "glad" he and his children were safe, she couldn't trust him anymore. Not surprised by her reaction, he felt relieved that he wouldn't have to juggle his relationships with Kiwako and Mayumi any longer, but also sad that the relationship was over and guilty about the pain he had caused Kiwako.

He also spoke with Mak. When asked why he went to the shareholders meeting, Mak replied, "You led me to believe you wouldn't go to Russia. Why would I believe you when you said you weren't going to the shareholders meeting? So, I wanted to be there to help to the extent I could. And even if you didn't go, I thought I might be able to identify Scarface and Chameleon Eyes as people signed in, but I wasn't able to get into the meeting until after Sophia and Sean had stampeded their way in."

Saya eventually returned to Japan and invited Torn to dinner. Wanting to put the entire nightmare behind him and move on with his life, Torn finally decided to meet with Tsujikawa. They agreed to meet at the offices of Hilsberry & Carter in the afternoon before Torn's dinner with Saya.

—

"We leaned on Hiroki Okaguchi, the boss of the goon whose confession someone poked out of him—I'm sure that someone was just a good Samaritan having nothing to do with you." Tsujikawa smiled ever so slightly. "Anyway, we told Okaguchi too many *katagi*—you know, civilians—have been hurt, and if he didn't give us names, we were going to send him away forever, shut down his entire operation, and confiscate all of his assets. You see, Okaguchi has several legitimate businesses—mostly *pachinko* parlors and liquor stores—he wants to leave to his eldest son. So, he gave up Tamayo Watanabe, her daughter, Miki, and Miki's husband, Yoji. Okaguchi said it was common knowledge among the yakuza that Tamayo had her future husband's wife offed and another girlfriend disappeared. We would've arrested the Watanabes earlier, but we weren't able to drag this information out of him until the day before the shareholders meeting."

Torn sat next to Saki in a conference room listening to Tsujikawa. It was getting late, and Torn wanted to get to the heart of the matter.

"What about the Snapchats to Bogrov from Tom Saito?" asked Torn. He knew they were dancing around the real issue, but also wanted to know how the police had put the pieces together.

Tsujikawa smiled a bit broader. "Yoji created a mirror of Saito-san's company phone and sent Snapchats to Bogrov as if they were coming from Saito-san. We have Yoji's confession."

"What about Vince Harden?"

"Neither Harden-san nor Saito-san had anything to do with the crimes. By the way, Harden Industries doesn't sell ANFO for Wakkanai. Wakkanai sells it directly."

Vince is just a hard-ass businessperson. No crime in that. I guess I owe him an apology. Ugghh, thought Torn.

"Why didn't you arrest the Watanabes when they first arrived at the shareholders meeting?"

Tsujikawa pushed his glasses up higher on his nose. "It was a long shot, but we wanted to see who else attended in case there were other persons of interest and see if we could collect more evidence. That's why we had undercover officers staffing the reception desk and cameras monitoring the stairs, escalators, and elevators to the second floor. Toward the end, we recruited Susono-san, who knew we were conducting an investigation but didn't know why or whom we were investigating. We swore him to secrecy."

Tsujikawa paused to sip some tea. "In addition, we wanted to see if any of the Watanabes would make any incriminating statements. So, we were recording the proceedings from cameras hidden in the chandeliers.

"On the cameras we saw Sean and Sophia coming up the escalator. Our undercover officers tried to stop them, but they couldn't reach Sophia before she ran into the conference room. One of them tackled Sean by the legs but he was able to kick his way free, which is why he entered the conference room a few moments after Sophia."

"So why did the Watanabes do this?" But Torn knew the answer.

Tsujikawa leaned back in his chair. "They wanted to bury Brooks-san's lightning generation and energy storage inventions. After Harden-san suggested Wakkanai invest in Raijin Clean, Yoji and Miki saw an early demonstration. They told Tamayo the technology could dominate the global energy market. And once the Japanese and Chinese governments discovered it, they might not finance any large new oil and gas projects. Tamayo didn't want to give the Japanese government or the Chinese government any reason to stop supporting the Northern Okhotsk Project. Wakkanai needed the money from that project to repay the acquisition loan for the Project Ibis purchase. And they wanted you dead because Harden-san told her you knew the technology as well as Brooks-san and were working on the patents."

"Why did Tamayo ask me to represent Wakkanai for its investment in Raijin Clean?"

"Okaguchi said Tamayo knew Project Ibis would close soon, and when they failed to kill you the first time, she wanted to keep tabs on you after the closing until they had another chance. As in 'Keep your friends close and your enemies closer.' She also wanted to throw you off the scent; you would be less suspicious of her if she expressed an interest in continuing to work with you. It was all an act."

Tsujikawa paused, then added, "At any rate, you're now completely in the clear. Oh, except for one thing."

Torn tried his best not to fidget as he thought, *Now what?* "What's that?"

"Can you confirm you know nothing about the evidence from Russia or the hospital interrogation?"

Torn thought, *It's you who owes me an explanation, not the other way around.*

Saki jumped in. "He's answered that question numerous times."

Tsujikawa paused and then responded, "Quite right. So, we'll just need Sagara-sensei's cooperation at the trials."

Torn smiled broadly. "Of course. Delighted to help."

Tsujikawa asked, "Do you mind if I ask why your children decided to kill Vince?"

Torn looked at Saki, who said, "Don't worry. Tsujikawa-sensei has assured me that in exchange for your continuing cooperation, no charges will be filed against you or anyone in your family. This is strictly off the record." Then she looked at Tsujikawa, who nodded affirmatively.

Torn thought about Sophia reluctantly giving up her weapon. He had tried to hand her off to Mak instead of the officer Tsujikawa had suggested. She would have none of it. Together they ran over to a staggering Sean, shirt stained with blood, his eyes trained downward, the long sword lying on a desk.

Several cops hovered around someone on the floor. It was Taniguchi. Sean later told Torn that Taniguchi burst through the side door as Sean neared the end of the aisle. He thought Taniguchi was going to try to stop him but when Taniguchi got close, he turned around, held up his hands, and faced the dais. A moment later shots rang out hitting Taniguchi in the chest. The force of the second shot spun him around, and he collapsed in Sean's arms.

As Torn approached, Taniguchi, coughing up blood, weakly waved Torn over with a bloody hand. His shirt and jacket were stained red. Torn knelt next to Taniguchi.

"Sagara-sensei, this is all my fault. I'm so sorry," he said in a raspy voice. His breathing was shallow and labored.

Before he could continue, the emergency medical technicians whisked him away to the hospital.

"Before I go into that, tell me about Taniguchi," Torn asked.

Tsujikawa sighed and sat on the edge of his chair. "To be blunt, he was on the take. He used to be an exemplary officer, but he needed money to pay for the rebuilding of his parents' home after it was destroyed in the Fukushima tsunami. So, he took money from the Yamakawa Gumi once in exchange for information about a planned police raid against one of their smuggling operations. One thing led to another and he stayed on their payroll to pay for his kids' college tuition, taking bribes from time to time in exchange for information.

"Internal affairs had started investigating him by the time you were arrested, but we didn't have enough evidence to arrest him. Although Taniguchi died at the hospital before we could question him, Okaguchi confirmed that he had asked Taniguchi to recommend to me that you be released on your own recognizance. The Watanabes believed it would be easier to have you killed if you were out of jail. But according to Okaguchi, he never told Taniguchi why they wanted you out of jail. My suspicions about Taniguchi grew stronger by the day, which is why I stepped in and approved Brooks-san's Life Flight to the US."

Torn leaned forward. "So, Taniguchi is the one who told Okaguchi where I was staying at the Andaz?"

Tsujikawa paused and scratched his sparsely covered pate. "Okaguchi's goons, together with Miki Watanabe, had followed you there, and Taniguchi confirmed the number of your hotel room. Again, Okaguchi didn't tell Taniguchi why they were asking, but Taniguchi must've known.

"I believe Taniguchi knew about the internal affairs investigation and suspected we had tapped his phone. That's probably why he asked to speak to you outside the crematorium. It's highly unusual for a police officer to contact a family member on the day of a victim's funeral, let alone show up at the crematorium. But Okaguchi said Taniguchi was trying to find out for the Watanabes if you could rebuild the prototype. After talking to you, Taniguchi evidently suspected you were lying about your access to all of the technology. Detectives are trained to spot lying, you know."

"Why did Yoji shoot him?"

"He wasn't shooting at Detective Taniguchi. He was shooting at your son. Yoji said he thought Sean and Sophia were coming to kill the Watanabe family. Taniguchi saved your son. I'm not sure why. My guess is that he did it out of guilt or to atone for his sins." Tsujikawa raised an eyebrow. "Any other questions?"

Torn gritted his teeth. "Not now." He had numerous questions, but first he wanted to consult with Saki about possible claims against the police for the way they had handled the matter. But now wasn't the time to be making accusations.

"Now, do you mind telling me how your children ended up at the shareholders meeting?" asked Tsujikawa.

"Sean arrived two days before the shareholders meeting after learning from Karahashi-san that Harden-san and Saito-san were suspects. He found out about the shareholders meeting by Googling Vince Harden and Wakkanai and reading the articles about the proxy fight. Staying at his mother's place, Sean had planned to go to the shareholders meeting and confront Vince. He didn't contact me because he knew I'd stop him. Sophia arrived the next day and tried to talk him out of it. She succeeded, at first. And they agreed to come and see me the next day.

"But that night she couldn't sleep. She wandered around the house looking at the blood stains, getting angrier and angrier about her mother's murder and the attempts on my life. And quite frankly, she despaired that the police hadn't done anything about it and likely wouldn't—I mean no offense."

Torn didn't tell Tsujikawa that Sean had told Sophia about the evidence Torn and Mak had collected.

The prosecutor looked away and coughed into his fist.

"Eventually, she decided to take matters into her own hands and do more than just confront Vince, whom she thought was the culprit. She told Sean her decision, and they decided to do it together."

Tsujikawa smiled. "Where are your children now?"

"They're both staying with me. Sophia has decided to transfer to a university in Japan. Why?"

Tsujikawa straightened his tie and pulled on the bottom of his suit vest. "Well, there is something you need to know but your children don't."

Torn frowned, looked at Saki and then back at Tsujikawa. "Your failure to deregister with the Sagami Ward office didn't lead Okaguchi's henchmen to your wife's house."

Torn sat up straight and leaned forward. "What?"

Tsujikawa took a deep breath. "Miki Watanabe followed

your son home from school one day. She was evidently very good at digging up information about you. Thanks to her, they knew your office address, about your apartment at Amaterasu Hills, what bar association in Tokyo you belong to, where your children attend school, where you own rental properties, and where your friend, Mayumi Ino-san, lives.

"Even if they hadn't followed your son home and even if you had deregistered with the Sagami Ward office, your name is on the deed of Yukie-san's house and on all of the utility bills because you were still paying them. One way or another, they would've found her house. As I said, there is no need for your children to know any of this. But I thought you should."

Torn said, "Thank you for that."

He saw Saki and Tsujikawa off and then rushed to meet Saya face-to-face for the first time since the night of the earthquake. He had a good feeling about his dinner with Saya. Recent events had reminded Torn how fragile and short life can be, and he wanted to get on with his.

He had come to a decision. The situation with Taniguchi demonstrated the importance of being with people you can trust. Torn's relationship with Mayumi wasn't going to work. It was too volatile, she wanted nothing to do with his children, and he didn't trust himself to stay faithful. With Saya, however, he felt confident that he could be true to her. His relationship with Kiwako also wouldn't have worked out, he reasoned, even without his infidelity, given the long distance and how infrequently they could spend time together. Saya, on the other hand, spent most of her time in Tokyo. They would be able to build a life together.

After ordering dinner and discussing the reconstruction of Raijin's offices and lab, the rebuilding of the large and small prototypes, and the status of the patenting process, Torn took one of Saya's hands in his and looked into those piercing green eyes. She squeezed his hand. "Saya, I feel so stupid. I should've told you this before, but since you're a client I hesitated and initially buried my feelings for you. Then all this craziness intervened before I had the chance to tell you how I feel. But I care for you very much, and I want our relationship to be more than professional."

Saya and Torn were dining at the Oak Door, the high-end steak joint at the Grand Hyatt Hotel in Roppongi Hills. An open bottle of red wine sat on the table between them. Saya's crutches leaned against a chair. She would be off them in a few weeks but would require extensive rehabilitation for several months.

Saya smiled a sad smile and pulled her hand away. "Are you still dating those other women?"

Torn held her gaze. "I'm only seeing one of them, and I'll break it off."

"Did one of them break up with you when she found out Mayumi-san was at your hotel? Her name was all over the Japanese news."

Torn looked down and didn't say anything. He was tired of lying.

"Torn, your wife was just murdered."

He cleared his throat. "She wasn't really my wife anymore. As you know we'd been separated for a long time."

Saya smoothed her napkin and looked up at Torn. "But you were still legally married, and you were cheating on her since before you moved out."

His mouth felt dry. He was usually in control of these situations, and now he wasn't. "Yes, but we were sexless and living separate lives."

Saya reached out, took his hand, and looked him in the eyes. She bit her lower lip. "Torn, I had a lot of time to think during my recovery, and you are the best and most trustworthy lawyer and the smartest, toughest, and sexiest man I know." She smiled as she said the last part. "Besides, you saved my life and my company. You were also honest with me. I appreciate and respect that very much. But you're looking for absolution I can't give. Right now, your priority should be your children, who need their father more than ever."

She released his hand. "Also, and I don't mean to be harsh, but you didn't even have the guts to break up with Mayumi-san before asking me to have a relationship with you. You're hedging your bets and that's not fair to her. Or me. I can't be with someone who might treat me the way my father treated my mother. Even before all this, you were confused, unhappy, and unfulfilled despite everything you've accomplished and having what most would consider an idyllic life."

Torn took a deep breath. "You're right, of course. But I never lied to you about my relationships. People change and grow..."

Saya cut him off. "But you've clearly been lying to other people. What's to stop you from lying to me?"

He blanched at her comment and started to say something, but she cut him off again.

"Besides, it wouldn't go well. A relationship with me now would be a rebound from both Yukie-san's death, which you're still processing, whether you know it or not, and your breakups with your girlfriends. You need to deal with yourself before you can commit to anyone, and as much as I care for you, I can't fix you. Right now, I don't even know if I can fix myself."

Torn looked down. Her stinging words devastated him, both because of her rejection and because she was right. Saya stood, put her arms around him, kissed his cheek, and whispered, "I'll always love you." He put his arms around her and held her tightly, trying not to cry, but his subconscious was again in full defense mode: *At least I have someone to return to.*

Just then, Mayumi walked in with a man from work. She frequently dined out with male colleagues and acquaintances but she never cheated on Torn, who filled her heart. As the maître d' showed them to a table, she froze when she saw Saya hug and kiss Torn, and Torn, eyes closed, hug her back.

Torn opened his eyes to see Mayumi staring at him. She grabbed her date's hand, looked up at him with her big dark eyes, and pressed a perfect breast into his arm. "Do you mind if we eat at the sushi place next door?"

Bemused, he responded, "Ah, of course not. I like sushi better anyway."

Torn felt nauseous. Given Mayumi's history, he knew she would sleep with her date that night because of this latest betrayal. And he could hardly blame her.

He released Saya, who looked at him. "Are you all right? You look pale."

He sipped some water. "I'll be fine. This is not exactly what I had in mind for tonight." His heart raced, he felt tightness in his chest, and he had trouble breathing. Saya's rejection and Mayumi's discovery of his relationship with Saya had pitched him out of the illusory emotional fortress he'd built in his mind to protect himself from the surrounding void of loneliness, and he was free-falling through its darkness.

"I'm sorry it's not what you expected to hear. You're the last person I want to hurt."

She kissed him on the forehead and turned toward the door.

He watched her hobble away on crutches. Like looking at someone through the wrong end of a telescope, she seemed small, far away, and no longer part of his world. He closed his eyes and continued tumbling through space, wanting to scream. He took a deep breath, held it for several seconds, opened his eyes, and motioned to the waiter for the check.

THE END

Acknowledgments

It takes a village, or at least this book did. Having written my first novel, I now understand the importance of acknowledgments. I'm sure I'm inadvertently leaving deserving people out, and for that I apologize, but I wish to thank, in no particular order:

Those authors who have been so generous with their time and advice, including Ronald Barak, Natalie Baszile, Susan Breen, Phillip Kim, Margit Liesche, Leza Lowitz, Tucker Malarkey, Andrew Savage, Roy Tomizawa, Laurie Weeks, and Ellen White. Hearing their stories of struggle, perseverance, and success helped me to continue pushing forward.

My editors, including Will Fortna, Henry Easton Koehler, and Jeff Wexler, who spent countless hours to help me polish the manuscript to improve both the story and the writing. With each iteration, words, sentences, paragraphs, and sometimes characters and entire chapters were slashed and burned, each cut feeling like a knife through my soul. But in the process, those murderous deletions turned a writer of legalese for more than thirty years into an author of fiction. And each new draft was proof that you could make a story both shorter and better.

The publishing team, including Marla Markman, Jaye Rochon, Tamara Dever, Marika Flatt, Doug Flatt, and everyone at South Fork Publishers, who worked tirelessly to turn my manuscript into a real novel, available to everyone with access to a virtual or brick and mortar bookstore. They made the finished product look far better than I had dreamed it could. And they helped me put in place the communications tools and mechanisms for getting the word out about *Bottled Lightning*.

The official and unofficial beta (and in a few cases, "sensitivity") readers, including Kate Afanasyeva, Larisa Afanasyeva, Marc Christensen, Craig Anderson, Tony Andriotis, Dixie Blome, Robert Blome, Alex Chachkes, Rob Day, Victoria Day, Paul Dixon, Steve Dyer, Allan Finkelman, David Halperin, Ted Johnson, Kei Komuro, Karen Lacey, Kilian Lafay, Jamie Larkin, Henry Lipschutz, David Lopina, John MacKerron, Joe Malkin, Kelvin Ng, Joseph Perkins, Scott Peterman, Steve Pollock, Jon Santemma, Mikhail Skopets, Chuan Tay, Jonathon Uejio, Greg Watkins, Stephen A. Weeks, Steven R. Weeks, Susan Weeks, Noreen Weiss, Chuck Wilson, Tony Wolf, Christine Wong, Mariusz Wroblewski, Asahi Yamashita, and Kumiko Yoshii. They took this project seriously and provided professional levels of service and advice, albeit on a pro bono basis.

Many of them went above and beyond the call of duty, reviewing more than one draft of the manuscript and providing chapter-by-chapter and sometimes page-by-page written feedback. One such beta reader was my eighty-nine-year-old stepfather, Robert Blome, who read two drafts of the manuscript despite being in the throes of a losing, but valiant, battle with pancreatic cancer. He had very insightful comments about *Bottled Lightning*, as he did about most things. As an aside, he was a big Torn fan and was disappointed by the book's ending. He believed that Torn had not been treated fairly in light of his good works but understood well the concept of karma.

This book would not have been possible without a relationship with Japan that started in 1978 when I became a high school exchange student and includes living in Japan for more than half of my adult life. If it weren't for being sent to Yamada High School in Aomori, which is considered the boonies in Japan, without access to any English media (this was long before the internet), during my junior year in high school, then studying at International Christian University in Tokyo in the early 1980s, my Japanese would be nowhere near the level it is today, and I would not have had the wonderful career I have been blessed to experience.

The main people who made my first trip to Japan possible are Odette Lobo, a beautiful college exchange student from Kolkata, India, and my parents, Dick and Dixie Weeks. Odette stayed with us for several months while studying at Northwest Nazarene College in Idaho. She recommended I broaden my horizons by studying abroad as an exchange student. And since in my view she walked on water, I dutifully looked into it. To my delight, my parents agreed. I can't thank them enough for setting me on the adventure that has been my life.

Nor would *Bottled Lightning* have been possible without practicing law at two great US law firms, Hughes, Hubbard & Reed LLP and Orrick, Herrington & Sutcliffe LLP, and a great Japanese law firm, Nakamura & Partners. At Hughes Hubbard, I worked in the Japan and technology practices of their New York office, eventually becoming a partner. While a junior associate at Hughes Hubbard, they seconded me to practice in Japan for a year and a half at Nakamura, where I honed my business Japanese and my Japanese client relationship skills. I joined Orrick as a lateral partner in their New York office in 2001. In 2004, I transferred to Orrick's Tokyo office, where I served for ten years as its Managing Partner, stepping down only to pursue another passion, fly fishing for tarpon. But that's another story.

While at Hughes Hubbard, I was trained and mentored by many, including Yas Okamoto and Bruce Aronson, the co-heads of the Japan Practice, and Ron Abramson, the head of the Technology Practice. At Orrick, the firm and its management, including two successive Chairmen, Ralph Baxter and Mitch Zuklie, supported me from the beginning, enabling me to develop a wonderful cross-border practice that kept me busy all over the world, including Japan, China, Singapore, Russia, Europe, Australia, India, Latin America, and Africa. I could not have asked for a more exciting and interesting practice as an international lawyer.

My desire to become a lawyer started when my father pulled me out of ninth grade to watch him defend an indigent elderly man with a tracheotomy who had been charged with the murder of his young Native American roommate. The trial, which my father won on self-defense grounds, was better than any TV lawyer show I had ever seen and set me on a path to law school. While I was in Japan as a high school exchange student, my host father told me about an "international lawyer" he worked with who spoke both Japanese and English, was admitted to practice law in both Japan and the US, and advised Japanese and American companies on cross-border transactions. I had no idea what advice this lawyer was giving, or even what he really did for a living, but it sounded very cool. Thus, at the age of sixteen, I decided that was what I wanted to be.

I want to also thank the people of mixed race who shared with me their experiences living in and out of Japan, including my son, Brendan Weeks, who lives and works in Japan, Kilian Lafay, Kristoffer Mack, and Mai Mack.

Finally, I want to thank the love of my life, Kumiko Mack, who has supported me throughout the life of this project.

About the Author

L. M. ("Mark") Weeks is uniquely qualified to write this international legal thriller. Like Torn, Mark was born in Alaska and for many years has practiced law in Tokyo, representing technology companies from all over the world in connection with their fundraising, intellectual property matters, cross-border mergers and acquisitions, and related disputes. For more than 10 years, Mark was the Managing Partner of the Tokyo office of the global law firm Orrick, Herrington & Sutcliffe LLP. He speaks, reads, and writes fluent Japanese, was an International Rotary Club scholar to Japan during high school, and graduated from International Christian University, a Japanese liberal arts college. Mark attended Fordham University School of Law in New York City, where he practiced law for almost sixteen years before relocating to Orrick's Tokyo office in 2004. During his formative years in Japan, Mark earned a black belt in aikido. Also like Torn, he is an avid motorcyclist, and his adult son is biracial and bilingual and lives in Tokyo. In addition to riding motorcycles and writing, Mark's other passion is saltwater fly fishing.

For more about Mark and his books, visit

LMWeeks.com

⁓

To connect with Mark on social media, visit

Linktr.ee/LMWeeks

⁓

To book a speaking engagement
with Mark, please contact

info@southforkpublishers.com